Ordo Seclorum

A.J. Curry

Crossroads of Crosstime

Volume III

RCD Press
Portland, Oregon
rosecity.digital

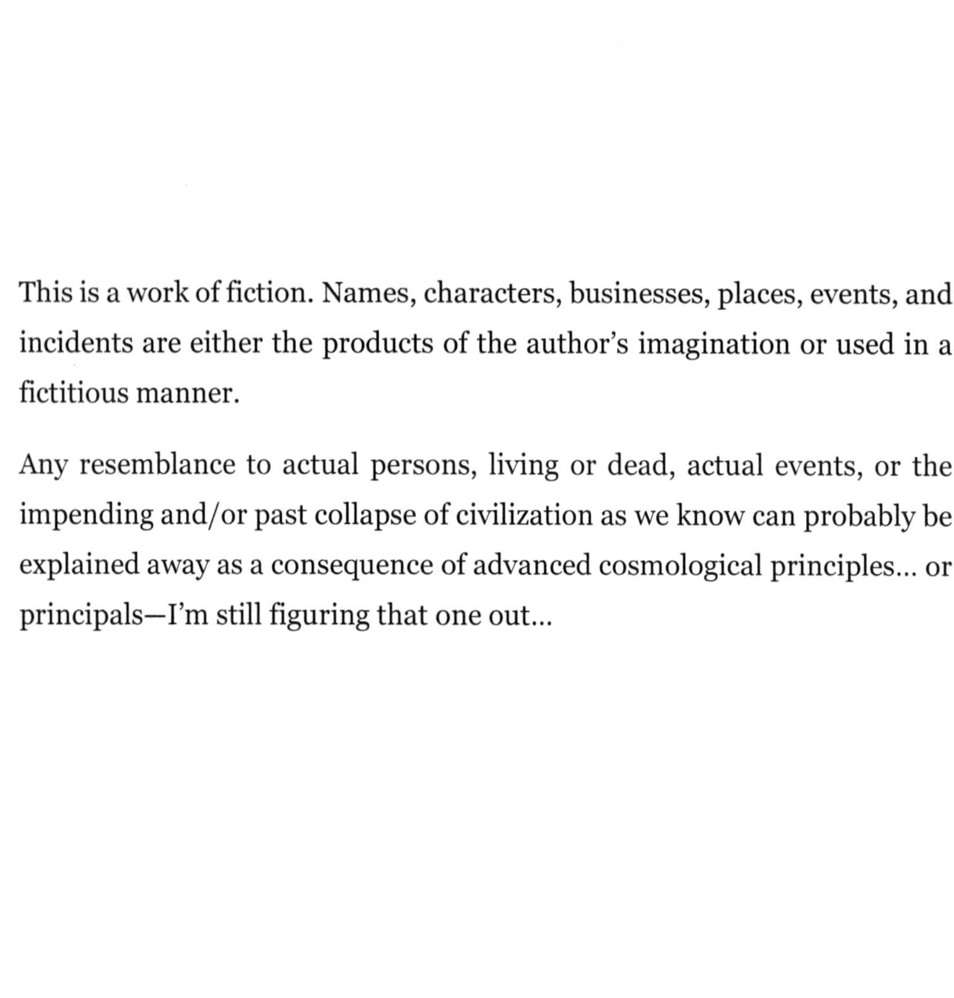

This is a work of fiction. Names, characters, businesses, places, events, and incidents are either the products of the author's imagination or used in a fictitious manner.

Any resemblance to actual persons, living or dead, actual events, or the impending and/or past collapse of civilization as we know can probably be explained away as a consequence of advanced cosmological principles... or principals—I'm still figuring that one out...

Table of Contents

Prologue

London: 1560

Dee had always loved to look at the stars, even before he had reason to believe they might be looking back... or had ever aspired to learn Heaven's language. Even after hard-won knowledge and unflagging ambition had won him other pursuits and other entertainments, it was still this he loved best: To sit alone without lights and gaze into the complex wonder of the firmament.

Given the proclivities of his current patrons and clients, a nocturnal and solitary nature had other uses as well—and in particular suited the regal patroness he served above all others.

Thus it was he found himself of a late winter's eve, his thoughts lost among the stars, when there came a gentle rapping at his chamber door.

His secretary... and nothing more.

"Aye, Will?"

The heavy door creaked open slightly. "The Captain has arrived, Master. I told him you were awaited at Court. But he was insistent."

"I daresay he was. 'Tis no matter—his business shan't keep me long. Show Captain Murgenstaarn in—then do you retire, Will. I've no further need of thee 'til 'morrow."

The secretary nodded and withdrew. Will Blakely was a God-fearing man, for all that he took wage from one many called a sorcerer. There were things he preferred *not* to know, things he preferred *not* to see... his master's dealings with the Flemish sea captain who styled himself 'Lucius

Murgenstaarn' not least among them. He would *happily* remain in his chamber until light of day.

Then the door opened wide.

Dee had it on good authority that there had been no *true* giants at creation's dawn... regardless scripture's thoughts on the matter. But the living source of that authority gave him cause to retain doubts of his own.

Lucius Murgenstaarn towered over any other man Dee had ever seen. His alabaster skin and silver-blond hair seemed more in the dimness like a massive statue brought to life than the likeness of a man. Entering, he swept the plumed Spanish bonnet from his head and bowed. "Hail, Johannes. How fare thee?"

"Well enough." Dee drew the woolen shawl over his black gown closer around his shoulders. What little heat had been in the chamber had fled through the door Murgenstaarn had flung wide and left open. "And thee?"

The giant shrugged. "'Tis a day. It differs little from any other. But perhaps a good one for you, sir." As always, the massive sea captain was dressed to within a half penny of violating the sumptuary laws–this time in a doublet of finest gray velvet, adorned with gold lace and fine pearls, trunk hose to match, tall black boots, and a black woolen cloak. He strode near to the casement where Dee had warmed himself by a brazier while watching the stars. There was a fire as well in the fireplace, but it was burning low.

Murgenstaarn found and helped himself to a chair, unclasping his cloak to drape over it. "Shall I bring them in?" he asked.

"As you please," Dee replied. "I am sure that Will has adjourned to his chamber... and his nightly prayers."

"He has," Murgenstaarn replied with his usual certainty, turning and beckoning to something in the outer hall.

Although the dutchman claimed it was a 'trick of the mind' and not the work of invisible devils, Dee–again–had doubts. Tricks of mind could be learned, and he had learned many, offered much to learn *this* one. But whether on the backs of unseen devils or by the force of Murgenstaarn's mind, two brass-bound sea chests now floated into Dee's chamber, settling as lightly as feathers next to the hearth. Noiseless, the chamber door closed behind them.

"The one chest holds the original codexes you gave me," the Dutchman said. "Guard it well; they are more rare than you knew. The other contains my corrected translations. Guard them even *closer*. Your church—*any* of Europe's current churches—will regard what is written there as blackest heresy."

"I thank thee, both for the service and the advice," said Dee. "Which I shall certainly heed. Are you so very sure there is no payment I may offer?"

"We've *had* this conversation, Johannes," Murgenstaarn replied. "There is nothing in your world I may not have as I please; what I *truly* wish is not yours to offer." Staring into the fire, there was a brief–*very* brief–moment when all animation left him... more statue-like than ever.

Then the moment passed, and he turned to John Dee with the perfect semblance of a smile. "It *entertains* me to do these things," he said. "The days in which I do them differ at least slightly from the many that have preceded them. That is payment enow, my friend. But it would please me to share a glass of your wine, Johannes—for you stock a more than adequate cellar."

"In this–if perhaps little else–you are predictable, my good captain. The bottle was fetched earlier. Bide a moment, and I shall pour. But do be advised: A certain personage has requested my advice upon their stars before this night is done. A glass, perhaps two, then I must yield to my other commitments."

"Understood, *magister*," Murgenstaarn replied, accepting the offered glass. "Your commitments are either well-known or widely suspected... and assuredly no secret to *me*." The giant then fell into a revery, seemingly lost in contemplation of the many shades of red that firelight revealed in a glass of wine... seeming, in his revery, even more like a thing made of marble in the fire's glow.

For not the first time, Johannes Dee wondered just who or what Murgenstaarn truly was. He no longer thought the seeming chance of their first meeting anything of the sort. At the very least, Murgenstaarn was the *true* wizard Dee had led others to believe himself to be–once he had cultivated his reputation.

The truth was probably as complex as the color of wine by firelight.

The melancholy giant was as good as his word, departing after a single glass. "I leave you now to your commitments," he said. "For I have a few of my own. Do take care, Johannes. You have a keen and inquiring mind, as well as the wit to appreciate how little men truly care for these things. I should hate to see you burned at some village hangman's stake. Luckily, you have patrons–or perhaps I should say a *patroness*–wishing this even less than do I."

Donning his cloak and his beplumed Spanish bonnet, Murgenstaarn was then gone. Dee did not trouble to see him out, was unsurprised to see the chamber door swing shut behind him. He knew the servants would find the house door no less locked come morning than it had been when they retired.

And another appointment was soon at hand as well.

At the appointed time, the casement where Dee had earlier contemplated Heaven opened of its own accord, what seemed like moonlight streaming through it on a moonless night.

Dee had told his secretary he was due at court… but he had not specified *which* court that might be.

An abomination, a Thing like unto an animated church gargoyle bound down the beam as though it were a staircase, followed by one less abominable… but no less strange.

As tall as Murgenstaarn, inhumanly regal, her deep red hair was bound back by a tiara. Her oblique blue eyes were as cool and unflinching as the stars themselves, her bare feet beneath the simple silk gown as inhumanly long and graceful as the hand she held forth for Dee to kiss as he bowed before her. The abomination took station before the chamber door, eyes reflecting the moonlike light.

"Hail to thee, queen of night," Dee said. "What bid thee, Titania?"

"That you do arise and follow," she replied, glancing back at the moonlight bridge. "I've new tasks for you and your Order… we've *much* to do."

Part 1: Exposition

one: evangeia

"Come to torture me some more?" the thing asked in a husky voice.

"That is not why I am here," I said. "But it can be arranged. I have questions."

The creature chuckled, then the chuckle veered into a high-pitched titter the human part of me found unsettling. I take no pleasure in what had been done to this thing. But what was done had been done for a reason. "Perhaps I have answers," the creature said. "Ask away..." It twisted then, in the web of force suspending it, the better to look at me with its eyes.

I held the thing's gaze until it looked away. I had no desire to remind it that its continued existence, with or without pain, was entirely at my sufferance. But I would, if needed... and it knew that. We call ourselves The Obligate. We have taken on an obligation to defend the greater cosmos from the things that had made this thing.

I do what my obligation requires.

This thing and I are both hybrids, living stealth weapons in a shadow war spanning millennia... although the process of my own creation had been significantly simpler–and my own mother at least a *willing* participant in that process. The end result, cosmetic issues aside, was perhaps not greatly different.

Save for one thing: I had always known what *I* was.

Not so the creature that had once called itself 'Colvin Case'. For most of its short life, it had believed itself entirely human–had, unlike myself, lived unremarked and unremarkable among my mother's people. I envied it that.

Had its makers not awakened it to hidden purpose, it could possibly have remained undetected among my mother's people to this day. Possible... but not *likely*.

The Selenites, the alien others that created Case, are so little like humankind that only their alien sciences could bring such a 'hybrid' into existence at all. In contrast, my father's folk count humankind as primitive cousins. I had dwelt for centuries in the shadows of my mother's world, on the strength of nothing more than my father's Fortuned DNA.

But even million year-old Selenite science has its limits. Case had already begun to fail, perhaps by design, by the time we took him. Perhaps a decade at best would have remained before his true nature was misdiagnosed in some autopsy report as a 'degenerative disease'.

What I had caused done to this thing had extended its life–but I expect no thanks for that extension. We had needed a tool with certain abilities, we had made Colvin Case into that tool. But the process had... side effects.

We had needed a tool with certain sensory capabilities. To create that tool, we had made this thing more like its makers... but only *somewhat*. There is a basic bilateral symmetry to Selenites, a symmetry one could call 'humanoid'–for all that Selenites are far closer to insects than to any primate.

There was very little symmetry left to the thing before me.

Some of what the Case hybrid calls 'torture' is simple necessity. We could not merely nullify gravity in the place of its containment; humans have spent too little time away from their homeworld to tolerate weightlessness, and–regardless its appearance–Case was still, genetically, more human than not. So we lowered gravity as much as we could in the hybrid's containment, used a web of force to suspend the creature as best we could.

It was unfortunate that the genetic regression therapy resulted in a thing too misshapen to support itself, even more unfortunate that every one of its major organic systems now required cybernetic augmentation to keep it alive. Had its nervous system been more like a human's, we could have suppressed the pain caused by those augments–but had its nervous system remained *human*, this experiment would have been terminated already... as an exercise in futility.

If what I suspected was true, it was perhaps futile anyway.

The place of Case's confinement is a forgotten corner of my mother's world, a remnant of a struggle of empires–even as my mother's world is itself a forsaken corner of a greater cosmos, a token in a larger struggle. My father's folk have made use of many such forgotten places, few as forsaken as this. In such places, my kind are free to do as we will.

Rumors of such places fill the folklore of my mother's people. Once they told tales of fairy rings, now they are tales of secret bases. The truth *behind* the tales has hardly changed at all.

This particular fairy ring was a geodesic dome next to an assortment of rotting quonset huts and the remnants of an airstrip. A sign by the airstrip declared it the property of 'Ordo Seclorum Enterprises', declared it off-limits, and advised that those guarding it were authorized to employ deadly force–all of which was true... just not in ways known outside the *ordo*.

Inside the dome, a smaller dome–the hyperbaric chamber in which I now stood.

Half the space was taken by life-support equipment and a force-web projector. On the other side: the airlock I had used to enter, and an array of screens displaying Case's biometrics and other data. A large screen in the center of the array was multi-purpose; occasionally we permit Case the luxury of using it to 'watch television'.

Not all of the technology used to keep Colvin Case alive is of my father's folk. My mother's people are *quite* inventive. Much of what they've contrived in the last century rivals the technology of older races. It is now often cheaper to use what they have made than to import better tools from elsewhere.

It is also *safer*. There are already too many inexplicable artifacts in too many of this world's museums. There may yet come a day when it is no longer necessary to conceal from my mother's people that they are not alone in the multiverse... but that day has not yet arrived.

Inventive as they are, my mother's people remain brutal and violent children, easily provoked into fear and atrocity. Only a select few are permitted the truth of their place in the greater cosmos, even among the very few with which we share any truth at all.

Case had further deteriorated since my last visit to this place. His skin was now as gray as those who'd made him; his head grown as large, even though wisps of blond hair still clung to the ashen skin. Although his eyes had grown large, they remained blue, not the black of his creators. Regardless of the shape or color of his eyes, Case could now *see* in much the same way as those creators... into other worlds.

A mass of silver cables ran from the creature's skull to other machines. What he saw... we saw as well.

Activating my own augmentations, I looked through Case's eyes.

Only for a moment can I bear to do this, for I am also partly human. The vision that overlaid my senses had too many dimensions, the objects within that vision had too many colors, and changed constantly from infinitesimal to infinite. I knew that I beheld the naked Greater Cosmos of probability space–or at least that part most close to my mother's world.

In the changing flux of higher dimensions, I knew that some of what I saw were other worlds–parallel universes, more of them accessible daily… as the stable cosmic order in which my father's folk had built an empire continues to collapse into chaos.

I could bear no more. I turned it off.

Case chuckled. "Quite a sight… isn't it?"

"The connection into your brain is *not* bidirectional," I said. "You should have no idea what I am looking at."

The creature attempted a shrug. "Maybe I'm guessing. Or maybe I'm not as locked down as you fucking space elves *think* I am."

"As it happens," I told it, "That possibility is *precisely* why I am here."

I walked to the large screen in the center of the dome, attached a data tablet to it. As the screen lit, I turned again toward Case.

"What I am going to show you," I told him, "is in no language or display format you would be expected to understand. I can have it translated as needed. But I suspect that will *not* be necessary."

On the screen, a moving complex shape began to form. "This is a time-compressed graphic of the telemetry feed between Foothold Base and the survey craft that dispatched your former friend Mr. Murphy on his mission. I remind you: success of that mission ranks *highly* among the reasons you still live."

"You remind me all the time," Case said, with a cold dry chuckle. "One of these days... try reminding me why I even *care*."

I ignored it. "The recording starts with the survey craft's departure from Earth's Moon, documents the trip into the Oort Cloud, ends on arrival at the interdimensional rift, resumes on the survey craft's return.

"Upon the craft's return to this universe, we noticed a minor fluctuation, seemingly random at first, in some of the telemetry data checksums. Further analysis made it clear that the data encryption had been compromised by an exploited flaw–a flaw that should *not* have been there. *Something* had accessed the encrypted data feed during Murphy's insertion.

"We then conducted a detailed review of the telemetry records–including a crossreference to the data feed between *this* facility and the uplink transmitter at Foothold Base." I touched a control surface on the data tablet. On the screen, a second complex shape now overlaid the first. I touched the tablet again, and the image began to zoom into part of the overlay.

"I think you already know what we are going to see: the flaw that was exploited is one *you put there*. It was well done: had it not been for the additional tampering that occurred during Murphy's insertion, we would have suspected *nothing*.

"I need to know *exactly* what you did while Murphy was in transit to the rift. I need to know who or what could have been in a position to take advantage of that tampering on an 'Earth' where the most advanced computers have less power and capacity than this tablet. Mostly, I need to know if you have done *anything*, intentionally or otherwise, that might have compromised this mission.

"You think you have been 'tortured' in the past? You may soon have a new definition of that word... if you do not tell me *exactly* what I wish to know."

two: murphy

A bit at a time, the world returned. At least parts of it.

Instincts I didn't use to have kept me still as I came around. I had no idea if I was still in the cave where I'd taken shelter from a storm. A faint smell I recalled, like the den of some predatory animal, was now stronger. Opening my eyes to slits showed only darkness. Around me, I heard rustling sounds in the dark. I opened the slits of my eyes slightly wider. Were those... *eyes* I saw in the dark?

I saw something else, eyes open or shut. According to the heads-up display inside my head, 'Social interface' was still active on my implants.

"*You there...?*" I asked, in the barest of subvocal mutters.

"Yeah, I'm here, old buddy... I'm just not real sure where 'here' is."

"*Talk later...*" I wondered whether or not Case was manifesting a visual avatar. I didn't see one, which either meant he wasn't or that my optic nerve had been damaged–possible, given what I remembered of a near-miss lightning strike. The red eyes I seemed to see in the darkness meant nothing. If they were what I thought... I'd see them whether I had actual sight or not.

A slight flexing of ankles and wrists told me I hadn't been bound while I was out. Good.

I hadn't bothered until recently to confirm that what I like to call 'magic' was as much a part of this world as the one where I'd once learned to use it. It *should* have been–after all, all the folklore was pretty much the same. But you never know.

The folklore was pretty specific about my present situation. I probably had an advantage, having recovered more quickly than they'd expected from past dealings with more standard-issue humans. Again, good. I heard a chittering sound in the dark amid the rustling. I should use that advantage... and quickly.

I snapped my eyes open wide, leapt to a crouch. Throwing a spread hand before me, I shouted a few choice words in an extremely old language. Blue arcs leapt from my fingers, forming a glowing lattice. With my other hand, I tore free the moon dagger from my boot scabbard.

Some of the chittering came from behind me. I lashed back with the moon dagger. The chittering became an unearthly howl. A quick glance past my shoulder revealed a Thing writhing on the cave floor, leaking phosphorescently, a cave wall immediately behind it. There were no others between me and the wall.

I turned my attention to the other things before me.

In different parts of North America, they had been called 'Jersey Devils' and 'Mothmen'; elsewhere, they were Yakshas, sometimes Rakshasas. Locally, the term 'Chupacabra' was more common. I had stumbled across an entire nest of them.

In the witchlight I'd summoned, they were easy to see–far easier than their normal semi-invisibility. The red eyes were beady, set in a pig-like face ending in a lamprey-like snout ringed with teeth. The wings would not have lofted anything their size composed of ordinary matter. To a one, their absurdly clawed 'hands' were held before the beady red eyes. These were things best suited for darkness and stealth.

In the same language I'd shouted earlier, I picked a few other and less ceremonial words, holding the moon dagger before me. It, too, blazed with light. "You are not immune to this blade... or *me*. Stand aside, if you care to hunt another day."

There was more chittering, but not much argument. Sucking a goat or bleeding a lone traveler was one thing. Taking on someone able to tell them to fuck off in Old High Lemurian and show that he meant it was something else. They gave way. A dimness of starlight past where they stood confirmed what I'd guessed. The cave I'd sheltered in concealed an entrance to their nest.

Out of the nest, I could see that the driving rain had put out my fire. In the witch light, I could see a blasted tree mere yards from the cave mouth where the lightning had struck.

Using the moon dagger, I drew a line across the nest entrance in the packed earth. I then drew a circle around the place I planned to sleep. My bedroll was where I'd left it, still dry. I rummaged a bottle from my rucksack and drained what was left of my Oregon peach brandy.

As I was polishing the bottle off, a ghost flickered into existence–but not the supernatural kind. Think of it as a self-aware computer virus. A gift, of sorts, from an old friend. "Holy blistering *fuck*," said the data ghost of Colvin Case. "What was *that*?"

"We can compare notes in the morning," I told him, reaching for the control stud behind my ear. "No offense, but social interface *off*."

three: kayce

"Agreed, then," Admiral Díaz said. "Not a word more until we know more. Not even to the rest of your crew, Captain Howard. Details of this flight are to be treated as both 'top secret' and 'need to know'–that need to be determined by myself alone."

Captain Howard nodded. When the head of Bureau of Strategic Intelligence says 'Don't talk about that'... you don't talk about that.

The clouds had parted, and we could see below us the lights of Dayton, Ohio. It was a rainy night, flashes of lightning in the distance. A flashing beacon to the northeast of the city was our destination: Patterson Aerodrome, home to the U.S. contingent of the Multilateral American Joint Exotic Science and Technology Investigation Commission–more commonly referred to by those who knew of it by the acronym: 'Majestic'. To the back of the aerodrome, an old and heavily guarded airship hangar held the reason Majestic even existed: the warehoused remains of a device that had once fallen from the sky into Texas.

It was the most closely guarded secret in North America... at least that I know of, and I know a few. But even a Gold-Alpha security clearance carries with it the 'need to know'. I decided a long time ago I didn't need to know one damned thing more than my job required. I get tired of lying to my wife.

Next to me sat Saul Ellsberg, gripping the armrests of his seat as though that grip were the only thing keeping us aloft... which might even be true, for all I knew. In the seats before me, Admiral Hiram Díaz–my *jefe*–and Doctor Helene Abenard. In front of them, the flight crew of Republic of California Airship *Morrison,* going about the business of a standard landing... a standard landing that should *not* be happening. Beneath the studied professionalism, they were pale and shaken. I probably looked the same way.

As clouds fell away before us, so did clouds in my mind. There was a hole in my mind and my memory, but around that hole, everything else was still the same. I was still Kayce Cullen-Figueroa, wife to Esmerelda, daughter to Elliot; still a commander in the California Navy, still a professor of history.

I was also a spy, of sorts... or at least I was one now.

The *Morrison* dropped smoothly and quickly. In mere minutes, we had reached our designated berth at Patterson's airship moorings, the turbo impellers holding station while Patterson's ground crew secured the lines. Then the engines cut. The *Morrison* surged up tight against the moorings.

We'd arrived.

The gangway at the back of the flight deck lowered to the ground. With the admiral leading, we disembarked. I like to fly, but this was one time I was more than happy to be back on the ground. Saul heaved an enormous deep breath once he set foot on the tarmac, as color came back into his face. Helene's paper on 'Ellsberg's syndrome' might need some last-minute edits before delivery–that is, if we planned to tell the Yanquis *everything*.

For the duration of our visit to Patterson, our team would be staying at a nearby hotel, while *Morrison's* crew was housed in guest airman quarters at the aerodrome. A century ago, none of this would have been remotely as friendly, and a lot of Estaditos still had grudges against California–not least their current *presidente*.

But after a couple of military defeats, the U.S. had learned the value of cooperation. Majestic wasn't the only joint operation between U.S. and California military... just the most important. We had worked together for decades to defend North America, no matter how unhinged U.S. politics occasionally became. At this point, the tradition of military cooperation was well established.

It still bothered me to be in *Los Estados*, though–it always does.

A security officer met us at the Aerodrome gate, where a local cab waited to take us to our hotel. Our luggage would eventually catch up with us, no doubt thoroughly searched. It didn't matter. Anything remotely sensitive was in our personal possession and enjoyed the same diplomatic status as ourselves.

The security officer was a tall, sallow man in a long coat over a black uniform. Not U.S. Air Force, Federal Domestic Security. He snapped a salute as we approached the gate. "I am Chief Inspector Monroe, FDS. Welcome to the United States, Admiral Díaz–good to have you with us again."

The admiral turned to me. "The Inspector has been my security liaison on past visits. He is very efficient, very good at his job–which is essentially to record and analyze every single word we say."

The inspector smiled thinly. "I promise that you are under no greater amount of scrutiny than any other visitor to this freedom-loving country of ours. You are a guest, Admiral, and a very well-respected one–Director Stone sends his regards. As much as anything, my job is to see to your own security. It would be much easier if you accepted on-base housing for your stay, rather than insist upon a hotel."

"Kind of you, Inspector, but my own state department dictates the protocols of these visits–and *they* prefer that I travel under a diplomatic passport, and use accommodations they have secured on my behalf. Other than verifying our passports, is there anything else you require?"

"Nothing at this time," Monroe said. He turned to me. "You would be Commander Cullen. Welcome to America. Papers, please?"

* * *

The FDS officer had been quick and efficient. He confirmed our passports and gave us the badges that would get us back onto the base and into the secured sections of Patterson. The cab was a smelly and ancient contraption–a petrol burner, the likes of which had been banned in California for decades. The driver was a burner of another variety–a pale man with a constant cough. A tobacco addict.

Welcome to *Los Estados Unidos de América...* the United States.

'America', they like to call it, as though their nation were not merely one among many, as though grandiose past notions of *Los Estados* owning all of North America had ever come close to being true.

The part of 'America' Grandpa had emigrated from was cleaner and prettier than this, but had all the same problems: out-of-control corporate capitalism, an out-of-control government effectively owned by corporations, a rigidly controlled population owned by it all–who somehow managed to still believe themselves 'free'.

It was a country steeped in racism, religion, and intolerance. It was a country that exploited natural resources as cheaply as possible, manufactured resources into goods as cheaply as possible, and distributed the resulting shoddy products as cheaply as possible to anyone in the world who might want them. Dayton isn't even a big city–but it stank worse than every city in California combined into one. By the time we got to the hotel, I felt physically ill.

It had not always been so. Those of us who study history know that *los Estados Unidos de América* was once a beacon of hope and a citadel of liberty. Republics, California among them, had formed in its image.

But then things changed.

The fallout from a failed insurrection and two failed wars in pursuit of an imaginary 'manifest destiny' had left *Los Estados* in economic ruin and political turmoil, easy prey for charlatans promising to return a 'greatness' that had never really existed... charlatans like their current *presidente*.

The economy was eventually rebuilt by handing wholesale control of it to even worse charlatans–even as ordinary 'Americans' found themselves in greater poverty and greater risk. But even though I know *how* it happened... I will never understand *why*.

At the hotel, our passports were checked again, as well as our U.S. Air Force-issued security badges; only then were we given the keys to our rooms and access to the lift. At least the guard when we got off the lift was one of ours: a BSI operative on assignment to the Diplomatic Service. There was no nonsense of asking for 'papers'; she knew damned well who we were.

An entire floor of the hotel had been reserved for our stay, including a well-furnished common lounge–far more than we needed, but it was secure. I collapsed onto the sofa, looking out into the rain and smog. Even though this was one of the better hotels in the entire city, it was still located directly next to what the Estaditos liked to call an 'expressway'. The stench of burned petrol was inescapable.

Thank god no one does such things in California.

"Now we may talk," the admiral said. "Our own people have swept this place for listening devices. It is clean. Consider yourself off duty,

Commander, and free to have a drink. Whatever else I might say about Yanquis, at least the ones that run this hotel know how to stock a bar."

"Perhaps later, sir," I said.

"As you like." The great man took his own advice and poured a whiskey for himself. He was now sitting on the sofa across from me, taking up most of it. Hiram Díaz is a great brick of a man–broad, tall, and broad shouldered, with wavy gray hair and olive skin. He also has more secrets than anyone else I have ever known.

Saul and Helene were huddled into chairs facing us both, as pale as shock victims, just as silent. Helene Abenard is a tiny woman with dark hair and enormous dark eyes, a registered psychist who gave up private practice to work for BSI. Saul Ellsberg is a middle-aged writer I'd once arrested so the admiral could offer him a job–at least that's what he *used* to be.

Saul had secrets of his own, secret even from himself. Under Helene's therapy, those secrets were beginning to unfold. Outwardly, he wasn't much different from the day I'd arrested him. He had the same thinning hair, the same ostentatious tinted glasses. But the eyes behind those glasses gave away nothing. He'd at least learned that much from working for BSI.

"It is important that we compare our memories of what just occurred," the admiral continued. "If it is what I *think* it is, those memories may differ in significant ways. They may also... change. I would have liked to have included *Morrison's* flight crew in this discussion, but I see no way to have done so without raising FDS suspicion. Kayce, I should like you to go first."

Suddenly, a drink seemed like a good idea after all. I helped myself to a scotch on the rocks. The admiral was right: the Yanquis running the hotel knew their liquor. I returned to my seat.

"I remember we'd lifted out of 'Frisco and were coming up on the Sierra Nevadas. The sun had just come up, and..."

"And?" asked the admiral.

"And *nothing*, sir. The next thing I can remember is Captain Howard announcing we were minutes away from Patterson. In between, there's... nothing."

"Yes," said Admiral Díaz. "*Nothing*. Yet here we are, arrived on schedule, exactly when expected. But when we arrived, my own watch showed us not more than two hours from San Francisco–*not* the twenty actually required. I checked *Morrison's* master chronometer before leaving the flight deck. It did *not* match my watch–yet I have no more recollection of that journey than you do.

"I have experienced such things before, so have others. The term for it in popular literature is 'missing time'. This missing time sometimes accompanies a 'displacement event'–but I do not know of anyone ever having been displaced so far."

He turned to face Helene and Saul. "Dr. Abenard, Sr. Ellsberg, I need your recollections as well. But I also must ask you both: were we... *taken*?"

"I don't think so," Helene said. "I perhaps remember more than you do." She turned to Saul. "Saul," she asked, speaking softly. "Was this *your* doing?"

Saul Ellsberg was looking out the same broad window I was, but what he actually saw I couldn't imagine. "We would've died..." he finally said. "I think they *wanted* us to."

"They?" I asked. "Do I even want to know who *they* are?"

"No, Kayce. You really, really *don't*."

four: evangeia

Once a *true* immortal had wandered the Earth.

This was not true of *all* Earths. Nowhere else in the Greater Cosmos had an 'Earth' been visited by an 'angel.' It was a distinction unique to my mother's world. On this one planet, a remnant of creation had seen fit to alight and remain, eventually losing the ability to leave–until its attempted abduction by alien Others backfired and set it free.

Set free, the being that called itself 'Morningstar' had returned to the outer void–far from *any* Earth, far beyond any reach of those who had attempted its abduction.

It entertains my mother's people to imagine that travel between stars could be as simple as their current ability to traverse their own planet. My father's folk found it otherwise, so have others. Only angels travel at will between stars. We lesser beings must settle for traversing universes.

The limitation may work both ways. In all the millenia that Morningstar knew visitors from elsewhere walked his world. Never once did he show the slightest interest in them, or the alternate worlds from which they came.

At least until some among those visitors expressed an interest in *him*.

We may never know why Selenites twice attempted the abduction of an archangel. Once could have been an accident–a mistaken attempt at doing unto a disguised immortal as they do at will unto humans. *Twice*... argues a purpose.

Three times could *not* be permitted. Morningstar claimed to have once been a shaper of galaxies. Whatever power it, or any like it, truly retained could not be permitted in the hands of Selenites. And in a changing Greater Cosmos, that third attempt became frighteningly possible.

For millions of years, it had remained the same: a double score of timelines spread across millions of years of probability space, connected by natural rifts. Divergences could be as slight as the mere million or so years that separated my mother's people from my father's folk, or as great as the chasm separating hominids from sentient saurians or quasi-insectoid hive minds. Closer connections had never happened... until now.

For reasons unknown, that double score of linked timelines is now over a hundred, with new rifts opening across mere millenia of probability–in some cases, far less. The once-stable order of the Greater Cosmos now approaches the unbridled and unmanageable chaos of the *true* multiverse. In that chaos, *anything* was possible... even another fallen archangel.

So I was charged by my masters with searching these new worlds for 'Dawn Matter', the fearfully powerful stuff of angels. For whatever reasons Selenites desire such stuff, they may not be permitted to have it. And when Case's altered senses found evidence of Dawn Matter in a world mere centuries distant from my mother's world, we sent another tool–another living weapon–to secure what Case had found.

Only now... there were complications.

"I take it you confirmed this... tale?" Aelestaire asked.

“What the Case hybrid confessed to have done conforms to the data we have,” I said. “Is there other confirmation you require?”

“The thing has lied to us before. You should have made certain before making your report.”

Although my superior could require me to report in person, this was not such an occasion. We inhabited a shared virtual space painted by our sensory implants. Because we were separated by the three second transmission gap separating Earth and Moon, the simulation was not smooth. But we had slowed and synchronized our time senses so it would not matter.

Like myself, Aelestaire d’Aigremont is both Fortuned *and* Obligate, and has for many centuries been obligated to the defense and oversight of my mother’s world. *Unlike* myself, he has discharged his duties from outside that world–from the relative comfort of the lunar colony my father’s folk began their war by taking from the Selenites.

The illusion we shared was of Aelestaire’s choosing: a balcony on a slim tower that disappeared downward into the clouds of a blue planet thousands of miles below and rose upward to join a ring encircling that planet. Below us: Tir na’nog–the ‘Earth’ of my father’s fortuned people, once the one closest in probability space to my mother’s world. To my knowledge, Aelestaire had not returned in centuries.

Possibly he was homesick, for all that my father’s folk claim to be beyond such things. But my father’s folk claim *many* things. They call themselves ‘The Fortuned’. They claim as right, privilege, and obligation the patronage and protection of every sentient species in the known multiverse not enslaved or consumed by Selenites. Not all accept that patronage or even know they are under it. To my mother’s people, my father's folk are mere myth and folklore... we go to some lengths to *keep* it that way.

In the illusion we shared, Aelestaire appeared in his true form: pale, spectrally tall and thin by human standards, with rose-tinted silver hair spilling down upon elegantly slim shoulders, clad in a black robe shot with scarlet and silver. I chose as well my own native appearance: tall by human standards, though a dwarf among the Fortuned, humans have found me both inhumanly beautiful and inhumanly strange. When I look upon my reflection, I see eyes the same blue I recall of my mother, but set in a face like my father's, framed with my father's dark red hair. Unlike Aelestaire, I chose to dress my avatar *formally*... in the black tunic of the Obligate.

I joined Aelestaire at the illusion of a balcony overlooking a world seen from space. In the illusory blackness before us, many lights that were clearly *not* stars moved before lights that clearly were. Millenia before, my father's folk had found the paths between universes searching for a road to the stars. No other 'Earth' in all the known multiverse conducted as much commerce with other worlds... or other Earths. I discount the homeworld of the Selenites; those who venture there do not return. It is unknown and unknowable.

I looked down at the illusion of my father's homeworld, thought of my one visit there in reality. I had found it overwhelming, knew that the world beneath those clouds could never be my home. The usefulness of my mother's world to my father's folk is drawing to a close. I will soon have a choice between my Obligation... and my home.

Perhaps as soon as the end of this mission.

"Your pardon, Elder," I said. "I lack your knowledge and subtlety. Confirming through torture the confession of a thing I have *already* tormented on your orders over decades, confirming that what I have tortured out of it is *not* merely a lie told to end pain–*particularly* when this tortured thing *freely* admits it acted to *escape* torment... I am sorry, it is beyond me. I threatened it, although I stopped short of 'showing the instruments.' I believed the threat sufficient. I find the torture *pointless*."

Aelestaire shrugged. "I yield to your experience in this matter. But the purpose of what the hybrid has confessed eludes me."

"Myself as well," I replied. "But we are not this... *thing* we have mutated into a tool and a weapon. Our senses do not see into other worlds; we are not trapped in flesh that is no longer our own. Given what we have done to Case, it is asking much to understand what Case has done. It may not fully understand its own purpose–but I believe it speaks the truth."

"Is this merely an unforeseen complication? Or does this compromise the mission?" The expression Aelestaire chose to share was no less inscrutable than he would have shown in flesh, but I knew the danger in those words–and that my own words must be chosen with extreme care.

"A digital clone of Case's mind is well within the storage capacity of Murphy's implants–however much or little Murphy may appreciate having it there. We *know* Murphy still lives–or at least that the psychic link between Murphy and Case still functions. The Dawn Matter source Murphy was sent to obtain remains where Case found it."

"And remains a risk," Aelestaire said. "A risk *you* were charged with mitigating. Has this risk now grown greater?"

"The *specific* risk I was charged with 'mitigating' was preventing Selenite acquisition of Dawn Matter. There remains no sign of Selenite incursion on the world Case found. The survey ship found no evidence of any current rift activity not our own."

"Nevertheless," Aelestaire said, "*something* tracked our survey vessel back to the rift–back to this very universe, for all we know. Nothing on that Earth should have any such capacity. Could it be the Dawn Matter entity itself?"

"We do not know that the Dawn Matter Case found even *is* an 'entity', Elder. If so–if it is a being like unto Morningstar–it should have sufficient ability to compromise our systems and leave no trace."

"Then either the primitives of that world are more advanced than we thought–or others than ourselves have found that world as well."

"Or perhaps others found it first," I said. "Even though the rift granting *us* access is recent, rifts to universes not ours could have preceded it. Or perhaps what has found this world is not a crosstime species at all, but unknowns native to that universe."

"*That* seems unlikely."

"Pardon again, Elder, but we no longer enjoy the luxury of assuming what is and is not 'likely.' The Greater Cosmos *has changed*–it is no longer what we have known, grows ever closer to the chaotic totality of the *true* Multiverse. Unknown star travelers may be the least of unlikely things we now face. Completing Murphy's mission is now more important than ever."

"These unknowns, whatever they are, may or may not permit that," Aelestaire said. "But it was never 'Murphy's mission', Evangeia–he was merely your chosen tool for this. I recall you promising to find others."

"I did. I have yet to do so."

Before we imprisoned him, Case had once taken control of Murphy's mind. It had left a residual psychic link we could use to send data through a subatomic wormhole between worlds. But it was limited, unreliable, and unique. Attempting to replicate this link had not gone well.

"The hybrid claims it can no longer infect minds. As it weakens in other ways, I believe this also to be true. And duplicating Selenite mind control through either technology or sorcery remains beyond our means.

"Because he is part human, we can force Case's mutation. But what he is mutating into we understand little better than we do the Selenites themselves. We may yet build something that replicates Case's abilities– but not, I fear, in time. And not before this mission becomes more urgent."

"And just how constrained by time are we?" Aelestaire asked.

"Very," I replied. "We can *physically* keep Case alive for as long as we please. But for all practical purposes... the hybrid is dying."

five: murphy

"So... what *did* you see?"

Once again, I was talking to myself. My other self. The data ghost in my head.

I was sitting by the campfire I'd restored when I woke up. I'd taken the tarp off the Armstrong and stood the old motorcycle up to dry. Then I packed the tarp and most of my other supplies into the sidecar I'd shortly be hooking back up for departure. I was drinking a cup of 'cowboy coffee' and thinking wistful thoughts of the real thing. One among several reasons to look forward to my arrival in Greater Galveston.

Case was 'leaning' against the opposite wall of the cave from where I was sitting. For reasons of his own, he was an illusion of himself as he'd been when he was originally recruited by the people we used to both work for, long before he'd become my boss, *long* before being outed as an alien hybrid. He looked like a big corn-fed blond kid from the Midwest trying to be one of the cool kids. Having run out of other entertaining costumes for his digital avatar, he'd decided to mimic me–boots, dungarees, white t-shirt and black leather jacket.

It looks better on me.

"I saw lightning strike a tree," he said. "It knocked you out. Anytime you're unconscious, so am I–well, not *really*, but I got no idea what's going on."

"I get it."

"Then you came to... and shit got weird. You jumped to your feet and started slashing the air with that crazy knife I'm not supposed to know about, shouting gibberish. Then you walked back up to the front of the cave, drew lines in the dirt and switched off 'social'. Until you switched back on a few minutes ago, I got nothing."

"So... you didn't see *anything* but me after I regained consciousness?"

"Nada, old buddy. Not a damned thing."

It effectively confirmed the theory I'd been forming. It would've been nice if I could've confirmed it via wood nymphs or something along those lines, but this was *Texas*, after all–Chupacabra would just have to do. "Apparently we are even, then. You see the things I see but don't notice. I see the things you *can't*."

"Such as?"

"Such as images on the faces of cards from an enchanted Tarot deck. Or a pack of bloodthirsty Chupacabra. Or apparently witchlight, for that matter. I can't say I'm surprised."

"Even when I was alive, I didn't believe in magic, old buddy."

"And *that's* why you never saw any–and now you can't. The things that attacked me exist in our world as well. But in both worlds, they aren't exactly real. You *can't* see them. You're a reasonably good digital copy of the mind of a man who used to be my friend, but you're not him, and you're not exactly alive–no offense. Only a *living* mind can see the things that lurk on the edge of probability. But living minds and living bodies can be touched by the things you can't see."

Case's avatar froze. *Literally* froze, like someone had hit 'pause' on the playback. Nothing like this had ever happened. It reminded me a little of when Morningstar would become so focused on using his angelic powers he would forget he was pretending to be human. What it meant in this situation, I had no idea. It didn't last very long, whatever it was. Maybe he just really had to 'think' about what I was saying. He unfroze, as though nothing had happened, and replied to me.

"No offense taken," he chuckled. "Let's say I believe *any* of this," he said. "What does it mean, old buddy?"

That was a good question.

My full name, not often used anymore, is Miguel Estefan Alejandro Murphy. There have been other names and aliases along the way. I usually just go by 'Murphy'. Once upon a time, I was the plausible anomaly of a small-time drug dealer in a southern U.S. city who had cleaned up his act and turned native hacking skills into a career–a career doing high-level data-mining and IT consulting, mostly for a generically named company based somewhere in the suburbs of Washington D.C. Occasionally, the work required disappearing for weeks at a time doing 'onsite consulting,'

An extremely small number of people knew that the generically named 'company' was actually *The* Company... and that the 'consulting work' involved a lot more than just fixing computers. But even the people who knew *that* had no idea that I had been a double agent almost the entire time... or that the people I *really* worked for were an occult Order of agelessly beautiful and highly advanced saucer people from a parallel universe.

After a particularly interesting and profitable piece of 'onsite consulting'–for a client who turned out to be Lucifer Himself–I'd retired from it all... that is, until the agelessly beautiful saucer people restored my own youth, with a few added enhancements, in exchange for accepting an *extremely* long-term 'onsite' gig. This time, in another universe. One apparently very recently diverged from my own.

The current gig was, in principle, fairly simple: I'd been given a package to deliver, the means to find where to take it, tools to ensure that I could make up on the fly whatever I needed to get there–as well as tools to ensure that anyone who stood in my way wouldn't be doing so for very long. I'd also been given a way to call for a ride home if I wanted one, but was told as well that ride might be a long time coming–and that I was free to live out what remained of my life as a resident of this version of Earth... if that's what I wanted.

I was still trying to figure that part out. Being made young again had involved some DNA from the agelessly beautiful saucer people. Not only was I faster, stronger, and prettier than I'd ever been when I was *really* young, there was an outside chance I'd gotten some extra-human longevity as part of the mix. The 'rest of my life' might wind up being a pretty long stretch.

There was also a side-hustle of sorts: collect data on when and how this universe had diverged from mine. According to the people who'd sent me here, this place–this whole universe–wasn't actually supposed to be here.

Along the way, I'd found out I had a sidekick: a self-aware piece of viral code had been stowed away in the data chip I now had in my head–the 'ghost' of my old friend and former boss, who'd also been a double agent for aliens (not the same ones as me). He'd also telepathically mindfucked me in a way that could be considered 'torture', which was why I was even here. But he'd also been dealing with some mindfuckery of his own. I'd decided to give him a pass on that one.

He was a major annoyance, but the original Case–now mutating into a sort of Seth Brundle with psychic powers, floating in a tank back in my original universe–had rigged it so I was sort of stuck with him.

At least I could switch him off if he got too annoying. And he'd proven useful along the way.

"What it means," I said. "Is that some of the tricks of one of my former trades just got useful again."

"If you were practicing magic back in the old days," Case said, "it doesn't seem to have done you a lot of good–unless maybe you *like* being miserable."

"It's just something I had a knack for," I replied. "I didn't say I was particularly *good* at it. I got it from my mom, she got it from hers. I learned a few things from both of them."

I had finished packing, would soon be on the road again–first due east for more supplies, then south... to finish this thing, one way or another. I planned on leaving 'social' switched off for a while. If this conversation was going to happen, it needed to happen now. The last thing I did was to carefully obliterate the barrier and charmed circle I'd drawn with the Moon Knife. I had no wish to either keep pent a nest of soul suckers... or leave traces of my passing.

Case watched, with what seemed to be amusement. "What, your grannie was an old witch?"

"Not the kind you're thinking about," I said. "But she knew things. She lived with us when I was a boy. She was a good teacher. Later, I had others."

"The Order?"

"Actually, I was pretty deep into this stuff before they got around to initiating me... and that's part of the reason they did. But, yeah–I didn't really know *what* Evangeia was when I met her, still don't really know how many of the other initiates were completely human–but The Order taught me a lot.

"They taught me to see 'magic' and 'science' as two sides of the same coin, even though the techniques and philosophies are completely different. They also confirmed what I learned at my *abuela's* knee... that the world don't just sort out into discrete piles of what's real and what ain't.

"You *think* you know what's real, Case, but you aren't even real yourself–even though, from a certain perspective, you're just as real as me or that rock you're pretending to sit on. There are not-quite-real things that only a living mind can see."

"Which makes me kind of shit outta luck."

"You were probably 'kinda shit outta luck' even when you were really alive. The 'real' Colvin Case is more or less half human and half something else."

"I know what I am," he scowled. "The Greys don't qualify as 'living minds'?"

"Not the way humans do," I told him. "Some of this I've known for a while, some of it I was taught for this mission. The Greys are really, really, *old*. They haven't been a natural organic species since before the dinosaurs got wiped out. Long ago, they did to themselves what humanity is currently doing to itself back on our world: becoming so integrated into their own information systems that they can't see the world without them.

"The Greys move between universes with their minds, Case–which sounds one helluva lot like magic, even if it isn't–but when they get there, they see exactly what they saw in the universe they left: data and raw material for their own constructed reality, nothing more. If they ever had chupacabras, djinn, or gods of their own, they can no more see them now than you can post a photo of a sasquatch on Snapchat."

"You have some *serious* hate for social media, dude."

I laughed. "Yeah, maybe."

Case 'walked' to the edge of the clearing in front of the cave and looked eastward across the Texas hills. As always in the aftermath of a thunderstorm, the air smelled fresh and the hills were green and vibrant, where they weren't covered with wildflowers. I wondered once again what he *really* saw... and if he could see that it was beautiful.

After a long pause, he spoke. "Put it in operational, tactical terms. Tell me what it means in terms I can understand."

"It means magic is real here–and whether you can see it or not, *I* can... and I can use it. Those card images you couldn't see were just a little too metaphorically accurate, and the person casting the cards knew I wasn't from around here. None of this may matter at all. But if I need some allies to finish this thing up... I may have a pretty good idea where to find them."

six: ellsberg

This is how it works when you dream impossible things–impossible things that wind up being true.

What you see and experience doesn't exist in the waking world. While you're experiencing these things, they are as 'real' as anything else you've ever known. In the dream, sometimes you're yourself–but just as often someone or *something* very, very different. Then you wake up, wondering if you really *are* awake... or simply in yet another dream.

Then one day you wake up to someone telling you that you are, *yourself*, the reason these things happen.

And everything changes.

My name is Saul Ellsberg–at least this much of what I *thought* I knew about myself is true. Almost everything else isn't. Helene, my therapist, calls them 'screen memories' and says everyone has them... they just don't have as much to screen out. Everyone has dreams, too... just not the way *I* have dreams. I still don't have all the details, but the dreams come from somewhere else–and maybe so do I. Something was done to me years ago, something I still can't remember, done by something I still can't make myself think about.

Things got better after I figured out how to turn the dreams into sellable fiction, then got worse when the stuff in my fiction started turning up in the newspapers as well. Then the stuff I'd been writing to try to cope with it all got noticed by some very interesting people... with some very interesting secrets..

And now I work for them.

One thing led to another, and I wound up on the flight deck of an airship, watching it drift helplessly into rising foothills, watching the flight crew brace for an impact none of them expected to survive.

I didn't expect to, either.

For a solid week, I had dreamed it–variations of the same scenario, each dream slightly different... but all of them ending in disaster.

Then a thing happened... a thing that had never once been in *any* of my dreams.

In a bright flash of light, a swarm of unknown objects had killed every one of RCN *Morrison's* control systems, then vanished. Unlike the 'ghost airships' and 'mystery disks' I had written about for years, these were *truly* unknown... even though they *felt* familiar.

But there was *nothing* familiar about what happened next.

I can't really describe it, and even though it *feels* like it's something I did... it also *doesn't*. But I can see it in my mind. It's like pages in a book. On this page, the airship has been disabled and it's about to crash. On this page, the airship had never been disabled by 'impossible things' in the first place and it's about to land. All you need to do is skip from one page to the other.

So I did... and took my friends with me.

I knew Helene *sort of* knew what I'd done–and didn't want to talk about it for about the same reasons I didn't. I knew Admiral Díaz only suspected what had happened–and even though he had names for what had happened, those names didn't really mean what he *thought* they meant. I knew Kayce knew least of any of us, didn't really understand any of it, and just wanted to go home to her wife. I had a sneaking suspicion that wasn't going to happen as soon as she wanted... but there wasn't anything I could do about that.

And now all eyes were on me. I had to say something.

"They?" Kayce asked. "Do I even want to know who *they* are?"

I shuddered. "No, Kayce. You really, really *don't.*"

Not all of the things in my dreams are human–and sometimes, in my dreams, neither am I. I *know* there's an intelligence that guides these things, I sense it in my sleep. But in the waking world, it's an unknown... and a nightmare.

I turned to Díaz. "No, Admiral, we weren't 'taken'. But we were almost killed."

"And... *you* are why we were not?"

"I'm having a hard time with this, Admiral. The things you've already forgotten are also getting harder for me to think about. There's something behind it all that I can't make myself think about *at all.* Maybe it's some ability I never knew I had. Maybe it's something... I don't know, something acting through me. I just know it's why we're here."

It had been a long day. If everyone else was getting a drink, I wanted one as well. As I walked over to the bar, I continued. "You brought me here because you think you're being lied to and you think I'll see through it.

You might be right. But what's going on with me isn't just about *seeing* things anymore–something's changed. I don't know how it works, but it feels like I'm also making things happen."

"You mean," Kayce said, "like magic?"

The first time I ever met Kayce Cullen, she had turned up on my doorstep with an arrest warrant and a few hundred kilos of armed marines. I later found out the marines were mostly for show. When she isn't working for BSI, she teaches both history and unarmed combat at the RCN academy. Even though her head barely comes up to my chin, I've seen her throw Hiram Díaz halfway across the dojo in a sparring match. Basically, one of the smartest, bravest, most capable people I've ever met in my life.

Who was now clearly frightened–at least clear to anyone who knew her.

"I *hate* that word," I told her. "Sci-Rom writers only use it when they've written themselves into a corner and they've used up better options. But, yes, Kayce–if not 'magic,' something a lot like it."

* * *

The next day was Day One of the Majestic Conference, as well as Day One of the 'Dayton Aeronautics Exposition and Air Show'–which I expected to be a lot like a Sci-Rom Con, just with more expensive merchandise. The badges we'd been given were actually for the expo, but had hidden features that also granted access to the Majestic Conference. Anyone who tried to do the same thing in reverse would get to spend the rest of their life regretting it in a maximum security U.S. military prison–not that it would be a particularly *long* life: Estadito prisons made Californiano prisons look like hotels.

In my room, when I finally retired, I found a hospitality kit apparently identical to the ones issued at the Dayton Expo. To the world at large, I was a onetime writer of what even I admitted were mediocre scientific romances–a writer who had somehow gotten onto a long-term contract assignment with California Navy's Bureau of Strategic Intelligence. My presence at the Expo would make complete sense to the world at large. "I usually attend the last day of the Exposition to maintain my cover," the admiral had told us. "Also... that is when the defense contractors host the good parties."

I suspected this would be the one year Admiral Díaz skipped the parties.

Sitting next to the hospitality kit, I found a single typed page with the agenda of the conference I was *really* attending. Even though it was carefully devoid of actual dates or any mention of the location–its title was simply 'Agenda'–the anonymous publisher of *Mystery Disks Revealed* and *Aethernauts Among Us?* would have loved it. The conspiracy theorists on the fringe end of the Sci-Rom community had speculated on things like this for years. Now that I was on the inside of the conspiracy, I knew just how much of that speculation had been spoon-fed to them as calculated misdirection. In my current assignment, I was doing more than a little spoon-feeding of my own.

Luckily for me, anyone else who had access to this agenda was just as likely to do time over its release as I was. Mysterious fan-pubs containing classified information might've gotten me a pretty nice job, but that could change in a heartbeat... if they kept showing up.

Once upon a time, I had what some people might've called a 'drinking problem'. I eventually found other ways to cope, but I still recall what the aftermath of a week-long bender feels like. Whatever had happened on the flight to Dayton left me feeling as drained as the worst hangover I'd ever had. I collapsed into a black hole of unconsciousness, not troubled by dreams or much of anything else... until the next day.

When I woke up, I tried once again to remember what had really happened the day before, and found it increasingly difficult to remember *anything* other than the normal flight from San Francisco that was supposed to have happened.... Even though I *knew* that's not what happened.

This too, is part of what happens when the impossible shifts from dream to reality. It's happened to me before, maybe more times than I can remember. But this time, other people had experienced the impossible with me... and remembered.

I wondered if they still would. Even if I hadn't been under orders not to say anything about what happened, part of me refused to anyway. Another screen memory was forming in my mind.

Only this time, I could feel it happening.

I bathed and dressed. The amenities in the baño were scarcely better than what I remembered from my one U.S. book tour. Hopefully, whoever had stocked the suite's bar had also picked out the coffee. I needed it badly, shuddered to remember the 'coffee' I'd had to settle for on my book tour.

I was in luck. Whether it had been provided by the hotel or the BSI advance team that had secured the suite, I found a cafetière and a canister of good dark roast in the suite's lounge.

Admiral Díaz had awakened already and brewed his own. He was sitting in the lounge in the Navy blue sweats he favored when not in uniform, peering through his antique gold-rimmed glasses at the morning edition of a local newspaper.

"Hola, Saul," he said, gesturing toward the canister. "Enjoy your morning cup. It is far better than we can expect at the conference."

"I'm fairly low on expectations, Admiral."

* * *

Not long after, Helene joined us as well. I've had a difficult history with pychistic therapy. None of my previous therapists had been particularly helpful, probably because they all routinely assumed I was delusional. Helene knew otherwise, which might be why she was the first therapist who helped me any more than I was already helping myself with booze and writing. I still wasn't crazy about having someone meddle with my mind while I was in a deep mesmeric trance state–but given the results, I had to at least admit she knew what she was doing.

Helene seemed as restored from the previous day as I was beginning to feel. She had dressed for the conference in a gray tweed blazer and skirt, with a dark blouse that matched well with her eyes. Like myself, a laminated card was pinned to her lapel identifying her as an attendee of the Dayton Aeronautics Exposition. Small print at the bottom of the badge read 'all access'. A chip embedded in it made sure that access included the *real* conference.

She made herself a cup of tea, joined us at the newspaper-strewn table where the admiral had been finishing breakfast around the time I'd awakened. Kayce, apparently, would be joining us shortly.

"Good morning to you both," Díaz said. "I am giving Commander Cullen the privilege of the additional sleep I wish I could have enjoyed myself. We shall both be joining you at the conference, once I have had an opportunity to visit the aerodrome."

"I wish I was going with you," Helene said. "We should find out what *Morrison's* crew remembers... while they still can."

"Regrettably," Díaz said, "we must assume any conversations taking place at the Aerodrome are susceptible to FDS monitoring. I do *not* wish to bring these matters to the attention of 'Homeland Security'–certainly not before our own investigations have occurred, preferably not at all.

"I prefer that we return to California, then investigate the... anomalies, let us say. Investigate the anomalies of our trip to this place with every tool at our disposal. This will include your services as a memerist, Helene."

"I defer to your judgment, Hiram–of course," Helene said. "But are you so very sure we *will* return to California? How can we be sure that what happened to us yesterday won't just happen again?" She turned to me. "Saul, my memory of yesterday is not clear, but I know that you were at least partly responsible for whatever saved us. Is this something we can count on, if we are attacked again?"

"I'm having memory problems of my own," I said. "Something in my mind *really* wants to believe nothing happened. I don't think that's a question I can really answer."

"I am less certain of this than either of you," the admiral said. "And experiencing issues of my own. But if what I suspect is true, there is no safety for any of us, not anywhere on this world. We have no choice but to learn as much as we can here, return home as soon as possible, and learn whatever further we can from what has happened."

* * *

The admiral's plan was simple. "We shall work in teams and cover as much of the conference and its near vicinity as possible. Luckily, everything even remotely connected to Majestic is in the near vicinity of the conference, all of it accessible to your badges."

He turned to me. "Helene has attended this thing before, can answer any questions you might have. Except as dictated by the conference schedule, I suggest you *not* separate without good reason. Remember that you are under constant surveillance from the time you leave this hotel suite."

On that happy note, we took the lift to the lobby, where our FDS-supplied driver was waiting for us. It was the same man who had driven us from the aerodrome the night before. Except for the fact that he was smoking in a hotel lobby–one of the cheap mass-produced cigarillos favored by American smokers–he could've been any cab driver I'd ever met in San Francisco.

Once upon a time... he could've been *me*.

He saw us, stubbed out his cigarillo in one of the many ashtrays, and led us to the sedan that would take us to the conference. The entire lobby smelled like an ashtray, one of the other things I remembered from my book tour. In California, tobacco is as regulated as opium; in *los Estados*, they smoke it like cannabis–and send people to prison for *that*. In California, private vehicles in urban areas are a heavily taxed luxury; in *los Estados*, they are *everywhere*–and public transportation is virtually unheard of.

I'd had to adjust to a lot of things when I toured this country trying to sell books, starting with the fact that the endorsement on my passport had to specify both my 'race' and my 'religion'–not to mention the Estadito customs officer wanting to see proof of both. I had considered asking him if my circumcision would work... but only briefly.

At least no one had asked to see my damned birth certificate when I arrived *this* time–there's a lot to be said for traveling on a diplomatic passport. Even so, I was remembering all the reasons I had all but kissed the ground once I'd returned from that book tour. The places my mind goes in my dreams are strange and sometimes frightening.

But hardly any of the dream realities my mind visits are as wrong or disturbing as the waking reality of the United States of America.

* * *

It had been odd, seeing my name on the agenda as a presenter–almost as odd as *not* seeing it in the summary of Helene's presentation.

Helene Abenard knew more about what had been done to me than perhaps any other human on this planet–with the possible exception of Hiram Díaz who, I was beginning to realize, knew far more than he admitted, and had from the very beginning. Helene's official reason for being here was to present a paper on 'Dream Communications and Interventions by Non-Local Biological Entities'–sometimes also called 'Ellsberg Syndrome' within our team, even though I am merely named in the paper as 'Patient Alpha'.

Kayce would be presenting a paper of her own–'Historic Analysis of Unexplained Aerial and Related Phenomena'–with strong implications that *none* of this was anything new. Díaz would be presenting as well, to a small and private audience, his own assessment of what he still seemed to regard as a military threat and a possible invasion–despite the clear and growing evidence that what was happening was greater and stranger than any such thing.

My own presentation was entitled 'Disinformation Techniques and Media Management'–even though most of the techniques my clever little crew of writers had come up with would be of little use to the U.S. Majestic contingent. We were in *California*, after all, trying to redirect attention in one of the most literate countries on the planet, in an open media market.

None of what we were doing was even *remotely* necessary in the 'United States.'

Even though the free press protections in the California Republic's *Artículos de Inicio* had been copied directly from the U.S. Constitution, those protections had become all but meaningless in *los Estados*–after the U.S. Supreme Court extended them to corporations.

Between the corporate monopoly on media and the generally abysmal state of U.S. education, 'Americans' had a tendency to uncritically believe whatever they were told–particularly if it reinforced a religious or racial bias they were fond of, or reinforced the peculiar notion of 'American Exceptionalism.' As far as 'literacy' is concerned? Let's face it: a significant percentage of Estaditos sincerely believe the world is *flat*.

It didn't really matter, though; the presentation was just a cover–a plausible reason to have me here. The admiral believed the Estaditos were hiding something. He thought that whatever was happening to me would let me see through the subterfuge.

He might even be right.

Even though we'd been ordered to stick together, I decided to convince Helene to let me mingle on my own once we'd checked in. "You've been to this thing before," I pointed out. "Have you ever felt unsafe?"

"I have not," she admitted. "There is probably no safer place in all of the United States to be a Californiano traveling on diplomatic passport. But nothing like our trip here has ever happened. Hiram is concerned–and so am I."

We were standing in front of the small auditorium our driver had taken us to, next to the Aerodrome's administrative offices. Perhaps a mile distant, I could see the airship berths and *Morrison*. A similar distance in the opposite direction stood a single, very old, airship hangar. I had been told that this was where they had housed 'the Device' after stealing it from the Texicans.

But I'd already known that before I was told.

We were standing in line, waiting to be checked into the conference. To me, it felt just like being at a Sci-Rom Con. Maybe that's why I felt confident enough to tackle it on my own.

"We have our phones," I persisted, "and as long as you stick to text or audio, the local network works well enough. I'm certainly not going to leave the base or the conference center."

"This is very much not like you, Saul." The look of concern was no different from the one she'd had when we were leaving San Francisco on an airship I'd had vivid visions of being destroyed.

I lowered my voice and leaned toward her. "You know better than anyone that the 'Patient Alpha' in your paper is who and what I *had* to be to cope with what I'd been through. I don't think either one of us knows what I'm 'really like' anymore.

"Maybe this is who I'm *supposed* to be, Helene. I just know that I have a–I don't know, call it a hunch or an intuition. I'm going to work the room a little on my own."

She smiled. "I'm your therapist, Saul, not your keeper. If Hiram did not trust your intuitions, you would not be here. I trust them as well. I also trust that the... abilities you are growing into are certainly equal to anything you're likely to encounter here.

"Do as you think best... but still, be careful."

* * *

I'd known Helene would agree–it wasn't a vision or an intuition, it was just common sense. In the few days we would be here, I needed to find out as much as I could.

Being in this place was a Sci-Rom writer's dream come true–particularly for a Sci-Rom writer who had dreams that *did* come true. I'd dreamed of a thing that fell to earth from another world. That thing was *here*, had been here for decades, studied secretly by scientists from every part of North America.

I wanted to see it–I wanted to *know* that it was real.

Díaz had cautioned me on this. "Your dreams of this thing are why you are even here–I understand this. I believe I would myself find the urge to see such a thing with my own eyes all but irresistible. But I ask that you exercise caution. We are here for a reason; that reason must take precedence. Also, I remind you that you are, *yourself*, a state secret and a valuable asset–one that I risk *only* in the face of greater risks. The Yanquis must know *nothing* of who and what you truly are."

* * *

In a weird way... it really *was* like a Sci-Rom convention–just no cosplay.

I'd gotten into Sci-Rom for reasons of my own, starting with the fact that getting paid for the fucked-up shit in my head beat driving a cab, or any of the other marginal stuff I'd done for a living before Kayce Cullen 'arrested' me. But somewhere along the way, I acquired a fondness for the fans that went beyond their willingness to buy my stuff. Maybe, just maybe... it might've been their willingness to *believe*.

And now, here I was, surrounded by people who not only believed in 'impossible things' but knew for a stone-cold truth those things were true. There was something oddly familiar about being surrounded by people who not only believed in impossibilities–they'd made a life's work out of studying it.

And they were all scientists.

Sci-Rom writers are fans to scientists the same way people who read Sci-Rom are fans to the writers. In the same way that people who don't write can't imagine where ideas for stories come from, it amazes me that there are people who actually *know* science and know how it works, instead of just picking out a few key phrases and making up the rest.

Sometimes the admiration is mutual... oddly enough.

"Are you *really* Saul Ellsberg?"

"I ask myself that question all the time," I replied. "But the way you mean it, I think the answer is probably 'yes'."

I really hadn't wanted to be in the auditorium when Helene delivered her research findings on a subject who happened to be me. Next to the auditorium was a cafe of sorts. Admiral Díaz had been right about the coffee, but it *was* free. I was on my second cup when I acquired company.

She was younger and shorter than me, with a pale face, blue eyes, painfully prominent freckles, and bright red and extremely curly hair. Slightly heavyset, she was wearing what Estaditos call a 'pantsuit', which always seemed to me to combine the worst of men's and women's tailoring.

"I'm Ameryst," she said, holding out her hand. "Ameryst Albion. Would you like to see The Device?"

"Um... yeah, actually."

seven: murphy

On the long road down from Oregon Territory, I'd soaked up as much as I could about the part of Central America where I knew I was going to wind up. I had been under orders to hang out in libraries anyway, for other reasons. I'd also had a fair amount of hands-on experience in another world's version of the same region. Experience that would either be useful... or might just get me killed.

Either way, I'd soon be finding out.

No one called it the 'Pan American Highway' in this world, but a network of roads served the same purpose and pretty much followed the same route... and I knew that route pretty well.

I could've saved time taking the old *Camino Real* directly from Albuquerque to Monterrey, but there were a few purchases I wanted to make before I crossed the border, items I knew would be a lot easier found in a bigger city. It made sense to make my way to Greater Galveston, then make my way south on the highways following the Gulf Coast.

But I had other reasons as well.

The city of Greater Galveston is the biggest city in the Republic of Texas. The central business district covers all of Galveston Island, with causeways crossing the bay, connecting it to refineries and port complexes. A network of roads and streetcar lines connect inland suburban towns that eventually give way to farms and dairies–as well as a fair number of snake-infested swamps.

In another world, *my* world, a couple of real-estate hustlers from New York had bought up one of those swamps and founded a city named after one of the heroes of the Texas Revolution.

By the time I got around to getting born in that city, that world's version of 'Galveston' had been an early victim of global warming, all but destroyed by a hurricane. A bayou had been dredged out into a ship channel, and oil had been discovered in Texas. Only one of those things had happened on this side of the wormhole.

Yup. It was the oil.

Minus the rest of the equation, this world's Galveston stayed a big city that hugged the coast. What I would've called 'Downtown Houston' was just a drained swamp on one end of a suburban streetcar community called–in both worlds–'Harrisburg'. There were other streetcar suburbs with oddly familiar names in oddly familiar places, connected by streetcar routes that were almost the routes of streets I'd known–so much so that the urge to explore them was irresistible.

The last time I'd spent some time in a library, some interesting things had happened–but not before I'd had a chance to load a map of Greater Galveston into my implants. I called it up from storage and painted it onto my retina, hanging like a hallucination in the view before me. I was on the same highway I had picked up after I'd left the Texas Hill Country and its chupacabras behind me. Except for the occasional farm vehicle, the road was virtually empty.

I picked out the highway on the virtual heads-up display in my head, tracing it down to the main bridge into Galveston proper, checking to see if it came anywhere close to anything that looked like anything I might recognize. It would've been nice if I could've overlaid it with a map of

'Houston' from my own world, but the space aliens who'd put the junk in my head had not considered that useful information.

But I didn't really need it–and one of those streetcar suburbs looked *really* familiar.

* * *

"Seriously, dude–that sounds like *shit*."

"It's just soundcheck," I said. "Give them a chance."

I was sitting at a picnic table in front of a whitewashed one-story brick building with a tin roof. In the back of the building, what billed itself as a 'polka-bop' band was doing a soundcheck and fighting a losing battle with the house sound system.

The old Armstrong was only one of a few motorcycles parked in front of the place. The customers didn't think of themselves as 'punks', but you could've dropped any one of them into the clubs I used to work in, and no one would've noticed a thing. I was wearing the clothes I'd bought for a street fair in Albuquerque that wound up being visited by a 'ghost airship.' I fit right in.

If anyone noticed that the big guy sitting at the end table was having a lively conversation with himself, they didn't think it was worth mentioning. This too, reminded me an awful lot of a virtually identical establishment in another universe.

I'd started out my mission in *this* universe on the Oregon coast, in a place that even had the same name in both worlds–as well as a few other striking similarities.

From there, I had made my way inland to the place that was *almost* the city where I'd gone in that other world to die–and even though the differences were many, I still found myself catching odd echoes of the place that had once been my home..

On the road down to Texas, there had been other instances as well. Even though this world was almost two centuries diverged from mine in crosstime, things kept popping up that didn't seem like they should be there, things that seemed to contradict everything I'd been told about how the Multiverse works.

But I'd also been told the Multiverse was changing. Maybe there was a reason for these things.

It made perfect sense that refrigeration was among the things that had been invented in both worlds, just like it made sense there had been a time in both worlds before that invention, when houses had literal iceboxes... for which people bought ice from ice houses.

Texas summers being what they are, it made even better sense that ice houses in both cases wound up being places where you could also get a nice cold beer–or that ice houses in both cases would stay in the beer business after the ice business went away.

So, when I decided to check out a suburban neighborhood of Greater Galveston that seemed *awfully* close to where a former suburb of Houston would've been in another world, it wasn't all *that* improbable that I'd find an icehouse in the one universe where I'd left one in the other.

The fact that both icehouses wound up in the business of booking bands *was* pushing it a bit–but that *other* icehouse had been something I truly loved, an early loss in the endless abandonments and betrayals that have been my life. I wasn't going to ask too many questions of its shadow alter ego turning up in this place, as if by magic.

If it *was* magic... I was pretty sure it wasn't mine. But I know, to my everlasting sorrow, that magic doesn't always work the way you think it does. So I had to wonder.

But whether I'd found it or conjured it... it was still a good place to wind up.

"The neighborhood isn't exactly Montrose, and this ice house ain't exactly the Pik 'n' Pak," Case said. "But from what I remember... it's awfully close."

"Scary close," I said.

The sky behind that other ice house had been filled with the tall buildings and bright lights of downtown Houston. Here, there was a dim glow over the trees in the direction of Harrisburg, that turned orange toward Baytown–where there were oil refineries in both versions of Texas. All the tall buildings here were in Galveston. In the opposite direction, I'd find a road leading down to the coast which would take me to a highway that would take me to Mexico. Soon enough, I'd be leaving. I'd replenished my supplies... there was no real reason to stay.

"Having a hard time reading you, old buddy–is this a good thing or a bad thing?" Case had switched up his look again, topping off his t-shirt and dungarees with a flannel shirt with cut-off sleeves. If he was real, he would've fit in as well. I felt bad that I couldn't buy him a beer.

"I'm still trying to figure that one out myself," I told him.

I've often wondered why I never went back to Texas after I left The Company and The Order, why I'd been so willing to let my past recede into the distance... and stay there. Not wanting to be reminded of the wife who'd left me is part of the answer, but only part of it. I'd had a long and complicated life long before I'd tried and failed to change that life to make Caroline happy.

'Wanting to avoid unsettled scores' was maybe part of the answer, but only a small part. After I started getting old, I couldn't honestly say that there was anyone left in my old stomping grounds who *really* had a grudge as well as the means to do something about it–at least none who hadn't preceded me into room-temperature mode, and most of them human enough to stay that way.

There were other parts of that world where I had unfinished business, old adversaries who might want to complete that business... but my old hometown wasn't one of them.

Mostly, I think, I just hadn't wanted to be disappointed yet again.

Going back to Houston in my own world would've meant confronting head-on just how old I'd really become, just how much and often I'd failed. It would've meant facing how much of my life had been based on luck, circumstance, and opportunism on my part. It would've meant seeing people I'd once cared about grown as old as myself–in some cases, even less gracefully than me. It also would've meant dealing with the fact that a lot of them were *already* gone, along with the places and things I'd once loved.

It had been easier to live out what was left of my once-lucky life in the place my luck had led me, where nothing reminded me of everything I'd given up to even get that far. Then I'd given *that* up as well–given up *everything* in exchange for a second life, and a mission in another world.

Maybe I *had* conjured this damned icehouse into existence in that other world. Giving up *everything* is one hard damned thing to do.

"I'm glad I found a thing that reminded me of a thing I once loved," I finally said. "It's even in a place that's almost a place I loved as well. If I stayed here long enough, I'd probably find more stuff like this, maybe even echoes of people I loved as well–but that ain't gonna happen. We have a job to do."

"You could always come back," Case said.

The band had finally won their argument with the house PA–or maybe just found someone who knew how to run it. In either case, the lead guitarist had just struck a powerful chord that reminded me of everything I'd ever loved about Texas Blues. The road wasn't going anywhere. I could hang for a couple of tunes. Maybe even another beer or three.

Right about then, a shadow fell over the beer I already had–so I looked up.

Blue eyes, red hair, wearing what was either gang colors or band merch over black tights, boots, and a chambray shirt. She didn't remind me of anyone in particular... but she reminded me of a lot of other things.

"Anyone sittin' here?" she asked.

"Just my imaginary friend."

"Does your friend feel like company?"

"Probably not–but *I* do."

* * *

About a week later, I crossed over the Rio Grande on the strength of a better than real forged Pacific Federation passport and remembered Spanish language skills improved by my implants. The additional time I'd spent in 'Greater Galveston' hadn't really involved library research, 'ghost airship' sightings, or anything of cosmic importance. I was still wondering how much of it I might've subconsciously conjured into existence from memory, id, and regrets I claim not to have. I could test the hypothesis by coming back some day... but I doubted that was ever gonna happen.

I'd thought about passing myself off at the border as 'Californiano', decided against it. This world's Mexico had a long shared border with California as well as Texas–which *might* make a fake California passport easier to detect. Also, my appearance was continuing to alter, thanks to the recombinant DNA cocktail I'd taken before leaving my own universe. I'd be better off passing myself off as the credible anomaly of an asian/polynesian Oregonian who had found it expedient to leave Texas. No one would blame me for having had my fill of Texicans... or gringos in general. As long as it's *plausible*, any story usually works–because people *want* to be fooled.

The blinking light at the end of the map in my head was in the Guatemalan highlands, a place where the local definition of 'road' was likely to challenge even my old motorcycle's tough tendencies. I'd figure it out when I got there.

Meanwhile, a more immediate challenge was just getting from Mexico to Central America in the first place. The highway that had gotten me from Port Lavaca to Aguilares ran as far south as Mexico's southern border–which in this world was no further south than the port city of Coatzacoalcos. Past that, I'd be in a 'Central America' which had been a stable republic ever since independence from Spain. I could take my chances with the local roads after that. It wasn't a bad way to travel, if you weren't in a hurry. It was also a good way to get your throat cut in the ass-end of nowhere.

Luckily, there were other options.

I was still visiting libraries as other priorities permitted and recording what I read into my implants. I was finding the same breakpoint in history I'd found after the second or third time I'd done this. Everything looked *almost* the same to around 1500 or so, and after 1800 or so... *way* different, particularly on this side of the planet–or at least from what I remember from my least favorite required course in High School.

Also way better... at least in my opinion.

It was a world less burdened with humankind, a humanity less inclined to exploit the world or itself. It wasn't perfect, but it was a lot better than the toxic, diseased, overpopulated, wartorn mess I'd left behind me.

So what if cell phones were just phones, cars didn't look like jet fighters, and jet fighters didn't even exist? The need for *any* of these things was less apparent in my mind than ever. Whatever lucky break or divine intervention had spared this world the history that had created me was a *good* thing... as far as I was concerned.

I was increasingly inclined to think Case might have the right idea: find the source of the Dawn Matter signature we were tracking, make delivery on the artifacts I carried... then walk away. If the Obligate had any other missions for me, they could look me up–and ask nicely when they did.

By the time I'd made my way across Mexico, I'd pretty much figured out next steps and cooked a fresh batch of 'fairy gold' appropriate to the region. Time to see a man about a boat.

* * *

"I can take you as far as Playitas. Past that, you must find your own way."

"If you can take me as far as Playitas, Captain Ruiz, I am most grateful."

It wasn't *quite* like other such transactions back in the old days, but it wasn't far removed. At least this time around, I was merely making travel arrangements for myself and an old motorcycle–no mercenaries, no drugs, no crates of plausibly deniable automatic weapons.

Balthazario Ruiz was tall and hawk-nosed, with close cropped hair and a well-sculpted goatee. He had shown up for our meeting in a linen suit and what I still thought of as a 'Panama' hat. I was wearing dungarees and leather. I figured the *reales* I planned to offer would make up for my wardrobe shortcomings.

I'd found him the same way I'd found my bike, using this world's version of an 'internet'. It wasn't as slickly packaged, nor as well optimized to the needs of multinational corporate capitalism–no surprise, given that no such thing existed here–but it was useful enough for my needs... and I hadn't needed a slick interface in a long time.

Had I wanted, I could've made my way from one end of Central America to the other *entirely* by boat, either overland via rivers and canals or on the many ferries that hugged the coast. A canal connecting the Atlantic Ocean to Lake Nicaragua and the Pacific had inspired other canals connecting other bodies of water as well. Rivers were the highways and railroads of this region. Airships as well called between major cities–convenient for anyone who happened to be in a hurry, or at least what passed for a 'hurry' in this world.

Ruiz and I were seated at a back table in a cantina on the edge of the port district, on the 'Mexico' side of the river. Across the Coatzacoalcos River, I would be in República Federal de Centroamérica. There I would find Ruiz's vessel, the *Madalena*. "My mother's name," Ruiz had told me. I found myself thinking of another Madalena... and wondering what it would be like to return to Oregon.

"May I offer advice, señor?"

"But of course, Captain," I said, pouring us both more tequila.

"Fuel for your motorcycle will be neither cheap nor easily found in the interior, your fare would be cheaper without it. Are you entirely certain you require it? You could sell for a good price here in the city."

He had a point. I knew the roads were going to be little more than jungle trails where I was headed, and that I would reach a point where the Armstrong might be as much of a liability as an asset. But some intuition I did not entirely understand was telling me to keep it–and I always follow my intuitions.

"True enough," I told him. "But it is useful to me, has been of much use to me before, and is something I am reluctant to give up. I can always sell it later."

"Or perhaps have it taken. The hills to which you travel are not not known for bandits, but there will be no police. You will be on your own."

"I'm used to that," I said.

eight: kayce

RCNA *Marion Morrison* was as unremarkable as the RCN Marine general it had been named for. A blunt arrowhead some three hundred meters across, including the subby 'wings' housing its engines, airships like it had become common in California Air Navy. Dual role, it could quickly be refitted from transport to missile platform, as the need ever arose.

Including rotating watch officers, riggers, and cargo handlers, it had a crew of roughly a dozen under normal circumstances. It also could accommodate a small number of supercargo 'guests' as needed. I'd served on vessels like it, before leaving active duty.

An earlier generation of airships had required larger crews, but that had been before computerized fly-by-wire systems and variable geometry engines had made flying an airship no more complicated than piloting an autogyro.

Under present circumstances, that was a good thing.

"I would have preferred to post a guard on the *Morrison*," Admiral Díaz said. "But that would have raised suspicion. I would have preferred to transfer Howard and his flight crew to this hotel, but that would raise suspicions as well. Departing quickly remains our best option."

"Why so much suspicion, Admiral? I thought we were at *peace* with the Yanquis."

Díaz snorted. "Suspicion? Thank this new *presidente* of theirs for *that*."

We would soon be departing for the Majestic conference at Patterson Aerodrome. The admiral had made an early visit to the airfield, Saul and Helene had already left for the conference, leaving me to work on my presentation and think about calling my wife. The near-certainty that the call would be monitored was just one of the reasons I didn't place it.

And not even the most important.

The hole in my memory was still there, but it was beginning to fill in. Part of me wanted to believe–very, very *much*–that none of it had happened. What Admiral Díaz calmly described as a 'displacement event' was something I could *force* myself to think about. But without that effort, the comforting lie of a routine flight to Dayton asserted itself–even though I *knew* that 'routine flight' never happened.

I was beginning to understand why Saul had seemed so haunted for so long–he had lived with this for *years*.

"Does this change my orders, sir?"

The admiral was sorting through the clutter he'd left on the breakfast table, picking out top-secret documents from several scattered Yanqui newspapers. Without Mathilde, our office administrator, the admiral's carelessness with working documents was a security breach waiting to happen. Fortunately, the California State and BSI operatives who'd secured this suite would sweep it just as thoroughly before handing it back over to the Yanquis.

Having sorted out 'ghost airship threat assessments' from the sports page, the admiral began to reload his briefbag for the conference. "It does not. Our objective for being here remains the same: try to determine just how much the Yanquis are keeping from us, try to assess–as much as we can–what it is that they know and do *not* share–only now you must try to do this in half the time."

"I'm still not sure I can do this at all, sir. I wish you could've brought someone with better training."

"As do I, but trained infiltration operatives would have been spotted–likely even *detained*–as soon as we set foot upon U.S. soil. So it is to be you and Saul... and you must do the best you can."

"Did you find anything worthwhile at the airfield?"

"Little. Whatever happened to us left no obvious evidence on *Morrison* herself. I *suspect* none other than the flight deck crew and ourselves have *any* recollection of what happened–and perhaps they as well will forget. Upon our return, we will all undergo rigorous examination, Saul Ellsberg most rigorous of all. *Morrison*, we will most likely dismantle in a clean room–even though I doubt we will find anything.

“Regrettable, but as the Yanquis *presidente* is fond of saying: ‘it is what it is’.”

* * *

Now that the admiral was back from the airfield, it was time for me to suit up, straighten up, and do what I’d been brought here to do. This was our last chance before returning to the hotel to speak in a room we knew had not been bugged.

“Mingle as much as possible,” the admiral said. “Even though you have not attended this conference before, in many ways it differs little from academic or military gatherings you have attended. Expect questions about your work, answer them–that is why this conference exists.

“But if anyone asks you anything at all about our flight here from San Francisco, say nothing–and advise me *immediately*.”

“Admiral, even if I were inclined to say *anything*... I wouldn’t know what to say.”

It was supposed to have been a routine flight from San Francisco to the U.S. city of Dayton, Ohio. As far as everyone else in the world was concerned, that’s what happened. Anyone who happened to be on the *Morrison’s* flight deck the morning she lifted out of San Francisco had other memories.

That is, if they remembered anything at all.

“Regrettably, there was no discrete way for me to speak to the entire crew,” Díaz said. “Waiting until we return to debrief them is hardly adequate–but I refuse to further stoke Yanqui paranoia while we remain within their grasp.”

“No offense, admiral, but there seems to be plenty of paranoia to go around.”

The great man smiled his unfailingly gracious smile. “you are correct as always, Kayce. Paranoia is the enduring danger of our profession. But it is, under present circumstances, unavoidable. I wish it were otherwise. “

I understood... unfortunately, all too well

Before joining Bureau of Strategic Intelligence, I’d had as little use for BSI as anyone else in regular Navy, considered the Bureau as unnecessary to the Navy as my Pops thought the Navy itself was to California–a pack of paranoids with a low tendency to read other people’s mail, justified by the suspicion of someone else’s bad intentions.

But that had been before I met the *real* paranoids BSI had to deal with–or found out just how bad those intentions could be. The old empires had never really given up their territorial ambitions, merely had them constrained. The Brits call it ‘the great game’, play it better than almost anyone. But they don’t spy on their own people–leaving that to the Yanks and the Russkies.

But even the Russian Empire could not compare with the United States of America for sheer, endemic paranoia... or frustrated ambitions of empire.

“We say nothing,” Admiral Díaz replied. “I reminded Captain Howard to make sure his flight officers synchronized their watches to local time, to ensure timely departure. There is no other outward evidence of what happened. We can investigate further once we are safely back in California.”

“Assuming we make it back, sir–I still don’t really remember or understand what happened.”

"I know little more than you. I know that *something* happened to us not long after we left San Francisco. I *think* what happened was intended to ensure we never arrived in this place. I *know* that, in response, Saul Ellsberg also caused *something* to happen–and because of that, we are here after all. But no one who was not in Saul's presence when this happened has any recollection whatever that *Morrison* experienced anything other than a normal flight. Based on my own past experience, this may extend to members of *Morrison's* crew not on the flight deck when this... *event*... occurred."

"How is that even possible, Admiral? Is Saul a..." I tried to think of an appropriate word. I couldn't. "Is Saul a *martian*?"

"He is human, and he is our friend. But things have been done to Saul Ellsberg, and he is a conduit for other things. If it is easier to think of those who did these things as 'martians', do so–even though you know as well as I that the truth is far stranger."

"The Estaditos have a hard time with that hypothesis."

The admiral grimaced. "One day, I will tire of saying this. The Yanquis are *fools*, albeit dangerous fools. Our task here remains the same: determine that they have not allied themselves with something even more dangerous.

"I have instructed Howard to be ready for departure the moment this conference ends, by the way. Normally, we find time for the trade show that serves as our cover story–but nothing about this year is normal."

"More 'paranoia,' sir?"

"Perhaps, but I do not think so. The questions we came here to answer are critical, but barely compare, in some ways, to the question of the interrupted journey that brought us here. If we have no answers by the end of the conference... I see very little purpose in remaining."

nine: ellsberg

"Are you sure this is okay?"

Ameryst laughed, tossing a curling, flame-red lock from her face. "Your badge got you in, didn't it?"

"To be honest, I didn't think it would."

"If FDS was in charge, it probably *wouldn't*–but if FDS was in charge of this place, probably neither one of us would be here. Meanwhile, Majestic is still a *joint* operation–you're California 'Gold-Alpha', and a member of the U.S. propulsion systems analysis team just vouched for you to have a good look at a real 'aethership'. You're welcome, by the way."

"Oh, definitely–*thank you.*"

The airship hangar we were standing in was old, but not much shabbier on the outside than any other old building anywhere in the U.S.A. Except for the electrified fence surrounding it, Hangar 51 looked little different from the other airship hangars around it. The sign by the security gate simply read 'access restricted'–without mentioning just how restricted that access really was. Unless you *knew* what was inside... you wouldn't give it a second thought.

My new friend was also a fan. Ameryst Albion had read every word I'd ever gotten into print, was equally fond of Clarke Kimball and Anson MacDonald. She considered us the 'big three' of Sci-Rom–an assessment that I think Ted Sturgeon and a few others might argue with. I briefly considered telling her that Commander Kayce Cullen was 'Clarke

Kimball's' daughter, then decided against it. Except for arresting me that one time, Kayce hadn't ever really done anything to me.

On the walk across the base from the conference center, I got to hear Ameryst's thoughts on every Sci-Rom writer I'd ever heard of, a couple I hadn't heard of, and a few televisor serials I had no intention of ever watching. I thought about telling her I'd never owned a televisor set in my life... but that would've required her not talking for a moment or two. I got the impression she either didn't have many friends or didn't know many people who liked Sci-Rom. Maybe both. A lot of fans are like that.

"It's really what got me into physics," she said, as we badged through a second gate inside the hangar. The sign next to this gate was a little more explicit, reading 'HOMELAND LEVEL ONE AND ABOVE ONLY: VIOLATORS WILL BE IMPRISONED AND PROSECUTED'. It seemed that they had things a little switched around, but given the way I'd been 'recruited' into BSI, there wasn't much I could say about it.

"I didn't just want to *read* about aetherships," Ameryst said. "I wanted to figure out how to build them for real."

"Have you?"

"No," she said, with a sudden sad expression. "We know what the Device does, we know how to cycle it, we even know how to find anything else that works the same way–but it could be another hundred years before we figure out how to build one of our own. I *think* we could get into space with rockets... but no one seems to care."

I didn't know what to tell her. I'd had dreams of rockets, enormous things. I'd had dreams of enormous rockets flying into space, but I'd also had dreams of them being used to destroy entire cities. The thought of a country like the U.S. having such things was even scarier than the thought of an alien invasion. The world was probably better off without them.

“Why do you want to go to space?” I asked her.

“To be honest,” she replied. “I don’t really know. I guess you could say it’s a dream I’ve always had.”

“You need to be careful with that. The places dreams take you aren’t always what you think they are.”

* * *

At the last door to the hangar’s interior, a couple of U.S. airmen stood guard; but they apparently knew Ameryst–and lost interest in me the moment the badge reader flashed green. Inside, one more gate.

Then there it was. The Device.

I’d seen it in my mind many times, from many perspectives... but not *quite* like this.

I’m not sure why anyone had thought it necessary, but they had *exactly* recreated the crash site. The floor of the old airship hangar was covered with rocks and sand. I’d never been to Texas, but the images in my mind told me it was accurate–*completely* accurate.

In the center of the hangar, wedged into the sand, the outer hull. Scaffolds held it at what remembered dreams confirmed as the correct angle. Replicas of the recovered bodies lay in the sand. This as well, was consistent with what I saw in my mind’s eye–if I forced my mind to look at it. Another fence surrounded the recreated crash site, with another gate. I knew that my badge wouldn’t work on this one–but I had *no* interest in even trying it.

I had been told to expect as much. "There was once a Yanqui showman who toured the continent with a 'mermaid' constructed from a dead baboon and a fish tail," Díaz had told me. "Do not be surprised when Yanqui 'science' meets similar standards."

But nothing could prepare me for the sense of cold dread that even replicas of these things inspired.

The sprawled bodies were no larger than a child and seemed helplessly frail–but even though I knew they were just replicas, I was glad to have a fence between them and me. The sense of dread and fascination I felt was like looking at a spider or a scorpion. Even though I knew they weren't real… I very much wanted to be somewhere else. Even though the unseeing black eyes were merely glass, looking at them was still like looking into a bottomless pit.

A bottomless pit I still can't remember.

I still don't really know what happened–Helene's mesmerism only goes so far–but the combined feeling of fear, revulsion, and familiarity was stronger than ever.

"Do you ever wonder what they could've told us?" Ameryst said. "I mean, if they'd survived the crash?"

I shuddered. "Nothing you'd want to know."

* * *

To the back of the hangar, behind the diorama, was another security gate in front of a lift door. "Follow me," Ameryst said, leading me to the gate. "Let's go see the *real* stuff."

There were many levels of basement under the hangar housing the Device's stripped outer hull. It had taken years to figure out how to disassemble it, years more to actually remove the major components for further study. Each major component was in its own 'clean room' for further study and eventual disassembly. Most of them had barely been touched. The technology was simply too alien.

Even to me.

I'd originally been recruited into BSI for publishing stories about this thing in Sci-Rom magazines, stories based on dreams I'd had. When events in the real world started catching up with my dreams, my role changed. Somehow, I am connected to this thing and the things that made it. I don't know why or how. I do know that they've been a part of my life from the very beginning, even though I've only realized that recently–thanks to my therapist, who has a connection of her own, and Admiral Hiram Díaz... who knows far too much about all of this to not have some connection as well.

Ameryst had led me down into the depths of the mystery, past galleries where disassembled aethership components could be seen in their cleanroom containments through thick glass. Whatever Díaz had expected me to recognize or remember wasn't there. All of it was vaguely familiar in a disturbing way... but nothing seemed 'wrong'.

Finally, we reached the lowest level. End of the line.

"This is the stuff I work on," Ameryst said. "The propulsion system. You'll like this."

The elevator doors opened. Instead of a gallery looking into a cleanroom, there was a solid steel barricade, a security door, and two more armed guards–this time, in the black uniform of Federal Domestic Security.

For the first time since I met her, Ameryst was silent.

"Apologies, Doctor Albion," said one of the guards. "But for the duration of the conference, this area is under FDS jurisdiction. You and your... friend will have to leave."

* * *

"And that concludes my presentation," Kayce said. "Are there any questions?"

Plenty, I thought. Too bad you can't answer them.

I was standing in the back of the auditorium, Ameryst next to me–holding the crook of my arm in a somewhat proprietary way I should have found annoying... but didn't. We'd missed the first part of Kayce's presentation, but it was old news to me anyway.

There would be a brief break after Kayce finished answering questions, then a presentation from the Estadito Majestic contingent on 'Long-distance Gravimetric Variance Anomaly Detection Techniques and Data Analysis'–essentially, the same report that had made Admiral Díaz decide to bring me here in the first place.

The questions from the audience were few and brief–*too* few. A professor of military history who was also a trained intelligence analyst had just told a room full of people who were *supposed* to be dealing with the threat of an alien invasion that the invasion had happened *already*–and not just once, but on multiple occasions–some going back centuries before a crashed mystery disk in Texas had seemingly started it all.

And nobody even cared enough to tell her she was wrong.

It wasn't a big auditorium, it didn't need to be. The total joint staff of the Majestic Commission, at least the people who actually knew what they were working on, had never even approached a hundred. I hadn't initially noticed the black-uniformed FDS guards stationed at every entrance.

But I was noticing them now.

"I have to leave," Ameryst said. "I need to join the rest of my team for the next presentation."

She was walking away as Kayce made her way back from the front of the room.

"Who was that?" She asked me.

"A physicist named Ameryst Albion, and apparently a contributor to that detector the admiral doesn't think anyone in the U.S. is smart enough to build–and if you have any more signed copies of your Pops' books, she will probably be your friend for life."

"Sorry," Kayce said. "Fresh out. Did this 'contributor' say anything about where she got the idea for..." she glanced down at the conference agenda. "'Gravimetric variance detection of inertialess propulsion systems'?"

"It's not her idea," I said. "And she's not even sure whose idea it is."

"That seems odd."

"It gets odder," I said. "It may not be what the admiral expected... but I think I just found something."

ten: murphy

For days, they had arrived, thronging the city square and massing in camps in the forest beyond the city gates. All come to see a miracle. As far as the eye could see, as far as any place in the forest from which the House of the Sun could be glimpsed, the faithful gathered.

The House of the Sun, God's house, sat atop God's holy mountain, called Fire Within. At the appointed time, the fire within would become the Fire Revealed... and the universe would change.

As the time came closer, the world became strange. A shadow crept across the face of the sun and the world darkened in the middle of the day. Those closest to the House of the Sun, those who could see, fell silent. From afar, all that could be seen were two tiny figures ascending the long staircase, ascending Fire Within. The silence spread, only to soon be replaced by chanting. All knew what had been promised to come.

The chanting grew louder, then was joined by a single voice louder than any other, a voice like unto thunder, or the roar of the sea, a voice that grew so loud as to drown out all else.

Then Fire Within became Fire Revealed, blazing out from God's house and ascending to heaven.

Then I awoke, sweating in the darkness. Close at hand, where I had left my clothes, a dim glow–like moon through clouds. Drawn from my boot scabbard, the moon dagger shone in the dark like the scythe-like crescent of the new moon itself.

* * *

"You did not come for your fortune told."

"How do you know that?"

"Because you stink of magic," the old *herborista* told me. "And I know what it is you carry."

I had time to kill before *Madalena's* scheduled departure. I closed out the room I'd taken near the docks and tried–without success–to sleep. My old motorcycle was already aboard and tied down in the deck space I'd booked. So I went for a walk.

I'd seen familiar symbols on the front of a shop. An intuition had urged me to stop in... and I always listen to my intuitions.

Sister Guadalupe Concepción Hernández had skin like dried tobacco leaves–both in color and texture–and hair as dark as mine, but shot with gray streaks. If she could smell the stink of magic over the profusion of dried and fresh herbs in her shop, her senses were far finer than mine.

"You do not need a charm to make a girl like you," she continued. "And your future is not for me to predict."

"What about advice?"

She shrugged. "You will probably not heed it, therefore it is free of charge. Follow me."

In the back of the shop, the smell of herbs was less overpowering, the sound of traffic from the street less loud.

"What is it you would like to know?" Sister Guadalupe asked.

"First things first," I said, tracing a symbol in the air that caught fire as I traced it.

"You should be more careful," she said, making a gesture that caused the symbol to fade away. "You can draw attention that way... attention you may not want."

"You may have a point," I told her, thinking of a cave in Texas. "But I had to be sure of who I was talking to."

"You still aren't," she replied. "You merely know *what* you are talking to."

"It's still a step in the right direction," I told her. "If you know what I carry, you know who's protection it places me under."

"It places you under the protection of The Sisters," she said. "You go to them."

"Are you one of them?"

The old woman laughed. "I am *a* sister–I am promised to *La Comuna de las Hermanas* even as you are sworn to an Order of your own–but it is *The* Sisters that you go to. And of that, I can tell you nothing."

"Can't," I said, "Or won't?"

She laughed again, a rasping, mocking sound. "All things in good time, señor. Whatever mission you believe yourself to be on is but part of a higher working–surely you know that?"

"I'm used to working on a 'need to know' basis."

"You mean you are accustomed to being lied to–even as you have deceived others for what you told yourself were higher purposes."

"You seem to know an awful lot about me," I said.

"It is not merely *magic* you stink of, man of another world. Danger, despair, and betrayal surround you like a cloud of ghosts. You think the path that led you here may be no more than yet another betrayal–and you may be right. But that is also not for me to say.

"This much I can tell you," she said. "The secrets, betrayals, and sorrows of your life are mere shadows and reflections of a higher pattern of light and dark. Whatever I would or would not do, I *cannot* tell you of the path that forms before you with each passing step."

"And how am I to find a way... on such a path?"

"Trust the instincts that have led you this far. What is needed... will be revealed."

* * *

"I can't believe you're taking this shit seriously," the data ghost said.

"Why not?" I muttered, knowing no one else would hear me. "I take *you* seriously... and you're not even really here." I was sitting on the aft deck of the *Madelena*, sipping from the surprisingly cold bottled beer Captain Ruiz sold from the commissary behind the wheelhouse. Ruiz had changed out his linen suit for dungarees about like mine, a chambray shirt with rolled sleeves, and a red bandana. He was still wearing a panama hat, though–just not the spiffy clean number he'd been wearing when I paid my passage.

Madalena was part ferry, part cargo vessel. My old Armstrong Canadien surplus motorcycle was one of several bikes, trikes, and four wheelers parked on the riverboat's broad deck. From the center of the deck rose a wheelhouse, commissary, crew quarters, and an engine room. Broad awnings extended outward from the center structure, providing shelter from sun and rain and a place to sleep. A fantail aft deck extended out over the screws driving the boat through the water. It was a good place to sit and sip a beer.

Case 'walked' to the edge of the fantail and seemed to look down into *Madelena's* frothing wake. He'd changed out his wardrobe again, his ghost image now dressed in a brown leather jacket and a fedora that would've been grounds for copyright infringement if he'd decided on an imaginary bullwhip as well. My own jacket was stashed in the Armstrong's sidecar. Even at night, it was a little too warm for any such thing–at least to anyone who wasn't just a data projection.

"I'm real enough to know that you are getting closer to our target," Case finally said. "A *lot* closer. I'm also real enough to notice that you haven't bothered to check the 'heads-up' display since before we left Texas. It's almost like you already know where you're going."

"Yeah, funny that." Was it time to tell him? I'd kept it to myself earlier for a few reasons, not least among them not really trusting him. When I found out he'd hacked my implants and uploaded a copy of himself while I was in cold sleep en route to another universe... my feelings had been mixed. The real 'Colvin Case' had been a friend once, but had been a few other things as well along the way–if I had actually blown his head off at one point, instead of merely thinking about it, I would've been entirely within my rights.

No harm in keeping a few of my secrets. "I'm sure I'll need to check the telemetry you're getting from the other you once we start closing in–just like I'm sure you'd say something if the target moved."

"Nothing's changed, old buddy–with the exception of you taking advice from old *brujas*. Did you do that in the *other* Central America?"

"She's an *herborista,* not a *bruja*–but I'll take good intel anywhere I can get it."

In fact, I'd gotten surprisingly little. I'd discovered that the community of magic users in this version of Central America were fairly different from the ones I'd know in another world, and that they knew a lot more about me than I knew about them–including the fact that I was *from* another world.

But nothing I'd learned so far contradicted what I knew of my mission. I was still going to a certain place in the highlands of Guatemala to deliver certain things–jewellike pieces of hypertechnology that would either set free from this world an angelic being... or remove from this world its remains. Once done, I had the choice to request my own removal/retrieval–or at least that's what I'd been told.

I was not nearly so certain as Case was that I had not been programmed in some subtle way to complete this mission. And thanks to things I'd experienced that were undreamt of in Case's philosophy, I also did not rule out that I might have been 'programmed' in yet another way–that I might be under some sort of *geas* or other occult compulsion.

I was also beginning to share Case's lack of certainty about the alien devices I'd been tasked with delivering. The only thing I could be certain of was that *nothing* would be certain... until I was actually there and it was time to act.

I could see why Captain Ruiz had pointedly asked that I not toss empty beer bottles into *Madelena's* wake. It was a mighty temptation; the wake was brilliantly white in the starshine against the emerald green river water. Any man might have felt that temptation, seeing the wake stretch back into the darkness. My altered senses could follow it all the way back to the river's last major bend.

It reminded me of a highway I'd traveled a couple of times through a stark and barren desert. I had felt strongly on that highway that the distance I traveled was more than merely physical–and that I was as much on a quest as I was a mission. Sister Guadalupe's confirmation of this was unsettling–even if it indicated that I might actually know what I was doing.

I had been sent to 'hunt angels' by beings very nearly angelic themselves–or demonic, depending on your viewpoint. To take on this mission, I had been alchemically transformed and made young again–or subjected to highly advanced recombinant DNA therapy. Again–pick a viewpoint, pick your terms.

I no longer looked like me or thought like me, or acted as the man I remembered being. Perhaps he had actually died after all, and I was just a manufactured thing, a *golem*, with the memories of an old man who had been duped into taking a poison he'd been told would make him young again. It was as good a theory as any to explain the improbability of me, and all that had happened.

"How's the beer?" asked the intrepidly dressed data ghost on the other side of the fantail.

"Not worth what it cost," I replied. "But not so bad. Sorry you can't have some."

"Yeah, me too, old buddy. I'm getting used to it, though–and thanks, by the way."

"Thanks for what?"

"Thanks for leaving the interface turned on. You don't have to tell me about it if you don't want to–hell, you don't have to do *anything* for me–but I know that *you know* where you're going, even if I don't know how. The data feed through the wormhole just got redundant... and so did I."

"Not necessarily," I replied. "Yeah, I got something–but I could also be wrong, in which case a backup system would be kinda nice. And no–I really *can't* talk about it."

The ghost chuckled. "Being a redundant system is a little insulting, but I can deal. Putting me on a 'need to know' basis limits my ability to give good advice, but you know that. And I know better than to argue the point."

"Thanks."

"So... what's the end game?"

I opened another beer. "What do you mean?"

"What I mean is that unless something goes seriously sideways, we are weeks, maybe days, away from acquiring the target. Once we deliver the payload, you've kept your word–or maybe broken the spell you seem to think you're under. Either way at that point, you're free to do what you want. You've decided to stay here... haven't you?"

I could at least tell him the truth about this. "I still don't know, Case. Everyone on my own Earth I ever cared about died or went away a long time ago. Traveling the multiverse as an agent of the Obligate could be... well, interesting. It could also be an interesting way to find out how many additional lives they're willing to give me."

"At least you'd get to hang out with your space elf girlfriend."

I sighed. "Hardly my girlfriend, Case. For starters, I'm not really into older women–especially not *a thousand years* and some change older. And I'm still human, more or less."

"Less, in her case. You haven't been tortured by her."

"Believe it or not, there's also that. I have some *major* issues with the original version of you. But I also remember him as having once been my friend. Did he deserve to get turned into a half-alien cybernetic freakshow? Not really.

"I'm kind of tired of it all, have been for a long time. I got tired of the ends justifying the means somewhere between Afghanistan and Ukraine, got tired of telling lies in supposedly good causes, got tired of having to explain away 'collateral damage', got tired of keeping secrets up to and including the really big one: that humanity, my kind, are basically just cattle waiting to get harvested one way or another… assuming they don't breed themselves out of existence first."

"That why you never had any kids?"

I took a long swig from the beer. "Probably one of them. The secrets I kept earned me a second life, but they also managed to pretty much fucking ruin the first one. If I'd ever *truly* walked away from it all, maybe Caroline wouldn't have walked away from me."

"You never got over that, did you?"

"No, not really… I just eventually learned how to live with it. Talk about something else."

"Sure. If you stay here, what will you do?"

I could tell the truth about this one as well. "I've been thinking about that. I'm pretty much free to do whatever I want, assuming the Obligate doesn't come calling with another mission and/or I don't get abducted by whatever is following us around in a 'ghost airship'. This is a whole new world, Case. All I really know about it is what I've read in libraries and what I got to see first hand on the road down from Oregon. It might be nice to see some more of it, before I make up my mind."

"So, just bum around and see the world?"

"Yeah… why not?"

eleven: kayce

"FDS, and *not* Air Force? Saul, you are certain of this?"

“Black uniforms, and that’s what they told me, Admiral,” Saul said. “I wasn’t exactly able to ask for their IDs.”

“Ordinarily, Director Stone would have much to answer for,” the admiral replied. “Under present circumstances... I have no idea.”

Day One of the Majestic conference was ended. Saul, Helene, and I had each presented findings to our Estadito counterparts, who had presented findings of their own. So far, we had far more to share than the U.S. teams, but Admiral Díaz had led me to expect that.

There was remarkably little interest in what we were sharing... but the admiral had prepared me for that as well. “They are incurious and paranoid, Kayce. Those among them with any ability are fearful of standing out from politically connected mediocrities. Why else do you suppose they have needed our help with this from the beginning?”

We had been returned to our hotel once the conference closed for the day–once again in an unmarked staff car with a non-uniformed FDS-supplied driver. Now that I knew what to look for, I could tell that our hotel was surrounded by plainclothes FDS... and filled with them.

Even though our floor had been swept multiple times, the admiral insisted on another sweep upon our return, would say nothing until our technicians had completed and left. The bar had been restocked. While we waited for the technicians to finish, I followed the admiral’s example and made myself a drink.

“I am astonished she took you to the Device,” Díaz said. “What did you think of the Yanquis’ little diorama?” Like myself, the admiral was in full uniform. He had ripped his tie off as soon he’d gotten off the elevator. I followed his example on this as well.

“It looked like something out of a museum,” Saul said. “Has it always been like that?”

“The Tejanos who found the Device were at least clever enough to photograph everything as they found it, even if they were not clever enough to keep their discovery out of the newspapers. When the Yanquis took it from them, they removed everything from the site and recreated it exactly, as you have seen. ”

“Including the bodies?” I asked.

“No. The Tejanos who found them had the good sense to put them in cold storage–where they have remained, even after the Yankees took that as well. What you saw? Those have always been replicas.”

* * *

The admiral had wanted us to ‘get close to the Device’–and Saul had succeeded without even trying.

Never underestimate the power of Sci-Rom fandom.

“I’m a published author as well,” I said. “But no one has volunteered to give *me* a guided tour.”

“You didn’t miss that much,” Saul said. “Ameryst didn’t even try to get me into the cleanrooms themselves, just the sub-basements they moved everything into.”

“And your credentials and hers should have gotten you into every one of them,” said the admiral. “This is truly unprecedented. More has changed since the last Yanqui election than I had realized.”

The United States hadn’t always had a ‘Federal Department of Security’. It was the invention of a fairly recent U.S. president in response to widespread civil unrest in the aftermath of a failed military intervention. International sanctions against the U.S. had been another result of that failed coup attempt... and the sanctions had backfired. Instead of becoming a better-behaved member of the international community, the U.S. had become more insular, paranoid, and irrational than ever.

The winner of their last presidential election had gained power by exploiting those tendencies, with little else to offer than having done so. We knew he'd expanded the powers of FDS... but we had no idea it had gone *this* far.

The lead technician nodded to the admiral as her team withdrew. "Clean, sir."

"Thank you," Díaz replied as she left, then turned to speak to the rest of us. "I need a full report from all of you on everything you have seen while attending this conference–or coming or going to it, or anything else. I will also share with you what I have myself discovered since last we all spoke.

"I returned to the airfield today and requested that Captain Howard accompany me on an inspection of *Morrison*–this is a sufficiently routine matter as to not raise FDS suspicion. It is possible they have planted listening devices on *Morrison*, but not likely. In any case, I have known Howard long enough to communicate without speaking plainly.

"He has confirmed that the missing time we experienced was shared by the entire crew and that the ship's instrumentation logs show no abnormalities, which could mean many things–*Morrison* has some of the most advanced avionic systems ever created. It is not *quite* capable of flying itself, but requires little control under normal cruising conditions. What truly happened remains a mystery until we return home... and can examine *everything*.

"Otherwise, my time has been spent at the conference–which, so far, has been a near total waste of my time, other than to confirm how *very much* the Yanquis are hiding things from us. Helene, what of your day?"

Helene was the only one of us who had not poured a drink upon arrival. She was instead drinking what smelled like herbal tea. "I have not had the eventful day Saul has had," she said, huddled into a corner of the sofa and sipping her tea. She smiled a brief, rare, smile and continued. "I presented my paper to the most disinterested audience I have ever experienced at one of these gatherings. Then I attended a couple of presentations from the Estado Majestic teams, then returned here. Other than the same elevated FDS presence you've noticed as well, I really have nothing to 'report,' Hiram. Well, my feet hurt from being on them all day... otherwise, nothing."

The admiral smiled. "Your feet have earned their rest, my dear, thank you. By all means, retire if you wish. Kayce, what of you?"

I refreshed my drink. "Since I have never been to one of these conferences before, I can't comment on the FDS presence, other than to say that they are *everywhere*, uniformed and otherwise. I also noticed the same thing as Helene–an almost complete disinterest in my presentation as well. Again, I have no previous basis for comparison."

"I do," the admiral said. "I have attended this conference almost from its inception, have presented information on many occasions. It served a more useful purpose when securely sharing information electronically was less easy–but remember that the *Yanquis* came to *us*. Their need for our help is hardly less than it was fifty years ago–if anything, it has only grown with our understanding of how truly alien this *thing* is.

"The conference continues, as much as anything, as a demonstration of good faith–that, whatever is happening between our countries politically, the commitment to this alliance remains... only I no longer believe that to be true."

"Because FDS has become involved?" Saul asked.

"That is not all," the admiral replied. "The Yanquis are *definitely* withholding information. The presentation today that included your new friend Dr. Albion raised as many questions as it answered, remains conspicuously absent of crucial detail. They have demonstrated that this 'detector' of theirs works, but the key component that *makes* it work... remains a mystery."

"I'm surprised you said nothing," I said.

Díaz shrugged. "I had made my concerns known as soon as I saw the agenda. I was told that Director Stone would be arranging a demonstration tomorrow at the conference closing that would answer all questions. Director Stone should not even *be* here. But he is quite close to this new president of theirs... and perhaps just as dangerous.

* * *

"Congratulations on your new friend–she's cute, by the way."

Saul shrugged. "I suppose. Not really my type."

"Or mine," I said. The admiral and Helene had both retired, leaving Saul and myself to admire the smoggy 'view' of Dayton, Ohio and enjoy another drink.

There was also something I *really* needed to ask him.

"My 'type' is pretty much one of a kind," I said. "Or at least I *think* she is."

"You're married. You're supposed to feel that way."

"But it's not really true... is it?"

Saul's expression was suddenly guarded. "What do you mean?"

"What I mean," I said, "What I've been thinking about for the last two days, is this: even if you can't put it into words, I *think* I know what you did to get us here–and if I'm right, I really, really need to know something. And if you're really my friend, you'll tell me."

Saul took a deep, deep breath then sighed a very long sigh. "I'm really your friend, Kayce. I'll tell you whatever I can."

"Okay, here it is: Admiral Díaz thinks these things–mystery disks, ghost airships, whatever–aren't even from anywhere in this universe, but *another* universe–or maybe more than one–somehow existing parallel to our own."

"In some ways that's a simplification... but that's how I understand it as well."

"I also know that whatever you did to get us here safely–what the Admiral is calling a 'displacement event'–might just as easily be called 'magic', whether you like the word or not. No one else has any memory that anything ever happened to the *Morrison* at all. You ask anyone who wasn't onboard, and they will tell you that our flight out of San Francisco took all twenty hours it was supposed to take–and was a completely routine flight. Part of me wants to believe the same thing... even though I *know* it isn't true."

Saul poured himself another drink. I nodded and he poured me one as well. "I don't know about asking just 'anyone'–but, yeah, pretty much." He laughed bitterly. "Welcome to my world. Not a great place, is it?"

“No,” I took the drink. “It’s not. Everything about it just seems... wrong.”

He sighed and shook his head. “You get used to it. What’s the question, Kayce?”

I took a deep breath and sighed a sigh of my own. “Is my wife still my wife, Saul?”

“What?”

“The admiral thinks the Device–that thing you saw in the hangar–moves sideways through time and came here from another universe. I think you saved us by doing the same thing. I think there’s another universe where the *Morrison* is in pieces on a mountainside–and you and me, and everyone else who was onboard can’t be accounted for, we’re just... missing. Tell me I’m wrong–*please* tell me I’m wrong–and tell me I can still go home to my wife.

“I want to know that you didn’t save my life by transporting me into another universe. Can you tell me that?

“*Can you??*”

Part 2: Exegesis

one: case (virtual)

The only thing worse than realizing that you're a monster... is realizing that you're dead.

I remember the Real Me. I remember figuring out how to track down *narcotraficantes* and jihadists by reverse-engineering cell phone networks. I remember hacking banking systems, finding stuff we could use for blackmail, then disrupting the politics and policies of half a dozen countries. I remember figuring out who *really* ran the world... I remember finding out who ran *them*.

This was back in what some people might think of as the 'good old days', when all this stuff was new. There wasn't a 'global war on terror' on the nightly news to justify what we did. The bad guys didn't get taken out by Predator drones operated by pimple-faced little gamer nerds–and *nobody* watched death rain down on the NSA's private YouTube channel. All that shit came later.

Our predators were human and did the dirty deeds up close and personal. One of our best human predators was a guy named Murphy–at least until he got soft and fell in love. But by then, the game had changed... and so had I.

I remember Murphy. I remember being sent to pick him up at Ellington AFB after in-country missions, debriefing him, then partying with him for two days solid while he 'blew off a little steam'.

I'd grown up in a lot of places, but Houston hadn't been one of them. Other parts of Texas *had* been. When The Company moved me there and put me on the Central America desk, I expected it to be about like Dallas or Lubbock–just more humidity and fewer churches.

I was wrong.

Murphy used to say "once you get past Loop 610, you're back in Texas." I didn't know what that meant when I met him–but pretty soon, I figured it out. The suburban sprawl outside the loop could've been anywhere. It could've been Chicago, it could've been Atlanta, it could've been L.A. The politics might've been a little more right-wing, but otherwise it was utterly generic.

Inside the loop things were a little different. The core, older, parts of Houston could be as creole as New Orleans, as punk as New York, as queer as San Francisco, as funky as Motown. Anything or anyone could be had for the right price... if you knew the right people.

Murphy had been born there. He knew *everyone*.

Yeah, I remember Murphy. He was scary and dangerous and a little improbable. He was also *fun*. I remember closing out after-hour clubs that never *really* closed, then going over to his apartment, getting high, and breaking into secured networks for the hell of it. He wasn't as good at it as me, but neither is anyone else–at least anyone you'd consider 'human.'

You could think of it as the 'good old days', and I do–at least I *think* what I do is actually 'thinking'. Alan Turing would probably hit on me in a heartbeat... and whatever it is that I do feels like thinking to me.

The question of whether or not code could be self-aware sounds like the sort of thing the assorted hackers, 'witches,' and professional party people that used to hang out with Murphy would've *loved* to debate–while waiting for the MDA to wear off and the LSD to kick in, between tequila shots and lines of coke–right up there with the existence of Satan, who *really* shot JFK, and whether or not flying saucers were real. Then the debates would wear thin and we would all hit some 24 hour *taqueria* for breakfast. Then Murphy and I would load up on B12 and amphetamines and go to the office.

If either one of us had a *real* job, we would've both been in some fairly deep shit. But we worked for The Company–a federally-funded criminal enterprise that would overlook *anything*... except failure. As long as I kept finding the right targets and Murphy kept taking them out, we were free to do whatever we wanted on our own time–as long as it didn't blow the cover story of being 'IT consultants.'

That part was actually pretty easy. Houston was full of oil money, which is actually a lot like drug money. There were *real* IT consultants living just as large as me or Murphy. Or maybe it was all just 'cover stories,' and everyone I knew in that huge and fucked-up city had as many secrets as we did. Knowing what I know now... I can't rule it out. The bare minimum required for *any* cover story is plausibility–because, at the end of the day, people *want* to be fooled. I know that better than just about anyone. I believed the plausible illusion of my own existence for *decades*.

It all went on for years, way longer than should have ever been possible. The burn rate on field operators is pretty high. Murphy being alive and intact after the better part of a decade was improbable to the point of being supernatural (it *was* 'supernatural,' I just didn't know that yet). It should have raised some serious questions. But as long as he delivered the goods, upper management didn't care. If Management didn't care... neither did I.

And Murphy *always* delivered.

I suspected there was a lot of shit that didn't make it into his field reports, but I wasn't his boss back then. *Everyone* knew the big son of a bitch had secrets, but as long as those secrets didn't include working for the opposition, no one cared about that, either.

He'd been recruited as a short-term asset that was expected to have a fairly short shelf life. The fact that he was still taking out bad guys a good ten years past his sell-by date was seen as good return on investment. By then, he was a *little* more valuable... but he was just as disposable as ever. He'd been hired for a specific skill set and a specific set of contacts. After a few years I started wondering if our bosses might not have gotten a lot more than they'd bargained for. I'd seen some truly insane shit when Murphy was 'blowing off a little steam,' stuff that didn't exactly seem real. I kept telling myself it was just the drugs. The alternative wasn't something I was prepared to deal with.

It was a relief when he gave it all up–took a desk job and got married to a bright, brittle, painfully shy younger woman... who reminded me of my mother.

He said he was in love, but nothing with Murphy was ever going to be *that* simple. I think the big son of a bitch realized that whatever voodoo he had going on wasn't going to last forever. I think he had his own version of a midlife crisis, and decided to marry the one person in his life who wasn't as fucked-up as he was. That he'd ever met her in the first place was just as improbable as everything else about him.

I think even Murphy knew it was only a matter of time before he'd wind up hanging from a meat hook in the aftermath of some operation gone horribly wrong–something that *I* was probably going to wind up getting blamed for.

I didn't think his marriage would last... and I was right. Murphy was a glib son of bitch who could talk the pants off of anyone back when he still had his looks, but it takes more than persuasion to make a marriage work–not that *I* ever tried it. But he talked himself into believing it would, talked himself into believing he really loved her. At least it lasted long enough for me to straighten up my own act and go after the promotion Murphy could never quite talk himself into wanting.

That turned out to be a good thing–for *me*. Times were changing, and so was The Company. Management had decided it would be better all the way around if we outsourced the hacking, drug-running, and regime change. Better ROI, *way* better plausible deniability.

Also, we needed to grow the organization. For decades, Management had been talking up the need for a 'new world order.' The old-school black-ops cowboys who had recruited Murphy could barely read a spreadsheet, couldn't build a PowerPoint presentation to save their lives, and probably thought 'Lean Sigma' was some sort of drug. They didn't have the kind of skills it would take to scale up and diversify The Company, when the opportunity finally arrived.

But I did.

After the false-flag operation that 'changed everything,' The Company had an opportunity to diversify into just about *everything*. And because people *want* to be fooled, want to be safe, and have roughly the same herd instinct as a steer being led to slaughter... they let us get away with it. The organization grew and I grew with it. Murphy chose not to–and that was probably also a good thing.

By that time, the old-school cowboys who'd recruited him were long gone. The MBAs who'd replaced them would never have really trusted Murphy.

Me, on the other hand? As far as they were concerned, I was one of them. I thought I was as well.

Hell, I even thought I was *human.*

I'd always been a misfit. An Army brat who didn't get to stay in any one place long enough to make friends, a computer geek before anyone got around to considering geeks cool. I'd gotten beat up by guys who looked a lot like Murphy, before I got big enough to fight back–sometimes they beat me up for my lunch money, sometimes it was just for fun. Always being 'the new kid' didn't much help.

Dad beat me as well, after Mom died, but I never got big enough to fight *him* back–or even find out why. I didn't even know why he shot himself. Then an honor guard showed up at the funeral with a flag for his coffin... and I found out that reasons for beating me were the least of things I didn't know about my father. Maybe he'd known he wasn't *exactly* my father, and maybe that might've had *something* to do with it... but I didn't know that yet.

But in a way... I'd always known.

I'd had the dreams all my life. They got really bad after Mom died, then after Dad died they just... stopped. Over time, I made myself forget I'd ever had them. Sometimes I'd half remember something on some combination of booze or drugs, which is one of the reasons I gave up *everything* after Murphy's wedding and went straight in every sense of the word. Over time, I got very good at convincing myself I was 'normal,' that I always had been.

Then the dreams came back... only now I knew they weren't dreams.

I don't really know what *they* are, the things in my dreams, and I'm pretty sure that anyone who says they do is full of shit. I've seen the *real* files on the thing that crashed at Roswell, seen the files on the secret project that tried to figure it all out. If that project had ever gotten anywhere, it would have *really* 'changed everything'–but Management had other priorities. Who needs antigravity when you've already got helicopters and drones? Who needs alien mind control when you've already got Facebook and Twitter?

Or maybe they were just following orders. For all I know, Company Management is no more human than I am.

I don't *know* that the things in my dreams are monsters, necessarily, despite how they look. I just know I'm the monster they made. Later, other monsters made me even more monstrous–the monsters Murphy had *really* been working for, almost from the beginning.

Murphy may have fallen under their spell–they're beautiful enough–but he hasn't seen them the way I have. They're no more human than the ones that made me, they've made Murphy as much a monster as me. And they are certainly no more to be trusted than the human monsters that made Murphy an assassin, made me an assassin by proxy.

Those human monsters were good opportunists, good at finding potential assets for a 'new world order' or a 'war on terror' or whatever the hell they're calling it now. I can't imagine what their current assets are like; after twenty years, I'm guessing anyone like the Real Me is probably just as obsolete as anyone like Murphy.

I'm not sure Murphy realizes he's a monster. He can't possibly think of himself as 'only human' after all the shit he's done and had done to him. But he *might* be deluded enough to think he's somehow special–that what he is makes him better, somehow.

That's one of the problems with being a monster. You either think you're no different from anyone else, or that you're 'special'–special enough to deserve whatever it is you need or want, special enough to be exempt from the rules that apply to everyone else.

But it doesn't last. Eventually, there's a day you realize you've either become, or always were, a monster–that day really, truly sucks.

But it still beats the hell out of the day you realize you're dead.

two: murphy

Ruiz had been right about the roads.

The main road out of Playitas had started out okay–not much worse than the gravel-covered 'street' back in Fort Vancouver where I'd first driven my old bike. But *this* road narrowed rapidly; soon there were deep ruts from frequent torrential rains.

By the time I'd gotten as far as Las Pozos, it was obvious I'd soon need to lose the sidecar. I decided to ditch it once I was down to the fuel in the Armstrong's tank and the cans I could lash to the back of the old bike.

Ruiz had also been right about the lack of law enforcement. Anything out here remotely resembling a 'cop' had other priorities than looking out for a gringo heading up-country on an old bike. The 'fake service revolver' was once again strapped to my hip, in plain view of anyone who might take an interest in my person or my property. By the time the old bike was a complete liability, I would be fairly close to my target–close enough to strike out through the jungle on foot. How I was going to get anywhere else once the mission was over was an interesting question, but I felt sure I could figure out something.

I always do.

Two days out of Las Pozos, I had good reason to be glad I hadn't yet ditched the sidecar and my spare gear–including my tarp. That's when the rain hit.

Really hit.

Under my makeshift shelter, I inventoried my gear, working out what I could and could not stuff in a rucksack, what I would and would not leave behind. I even pulled the fabricator and the Dawn Matter devices from the bag's false bottom to see if I could make more space–as much to have something to do while it rained as anything else, as well as test out an idea or two. I eventually had to face the fact that I would arrive at my destination with what I had carried into this world... and little else.

Which perhaps might be for the best.

The devices I'd carried halfway across the continent *looked* innocuous enough. A trio of gemlike spheres in primary colors, I'd been warned of dire consequences if I removed them prematurely from the 'containment device' they were magnetically locked into.

But they were still nice to look at.

After I'd left the *Madalena* and taken to jungle roads, I pretty much left the 'social interface' in my implants switched off. There wasn't much in the way of tactical advice Case could offer me on the situation... and he was right about me knowing where I was going. There was probably no good reason to not tell him *how* I knew... but paranoia's a harder habit to break than being in love.

Also, he was beginning to weird me out. His occasional 'freeze moments' were happening more often, reminding me less of an archangel I used to know, reminding me a lot more–and more appropriately–of *Max Headroom.*

Something was happening to my data ghost sidekick. Something he didn't seem to be aware of, something that might mean he was less of a permanent fixture than he'd led me to believe.

I wasn't sure how I felt about that. He was less of a prick than his original had been, and he was occasionally useful. On the other hand, the son of a bitch was inside my head. Having it to myself without having to hit a switch would be kinda nice.

It had also occurred to me that Case's glitchiness might mean my *implants* might also be less permanent than I'd been told. Even though Evangeia and I had gotten fairly friendly while I was getting trained and rejuvenated on the Moon, not once in decades had I *ever* assumed *anything* she told me was the complete and unvarnished truth. It had been a given from the start that there was a greater game, one not known to a mere mortal like myself–that I was a pawn in that game, trading information for favors and abilities... and operating on yet another 'need to know' basis.

It was entirely possible that everything I had been told during my rejuvenation was the exact and literal truth. It was also possible that I had been played, masterfully, by a half-human being who had been deceiving on behalf of an alleged greater good for centuries.

For all I knew, the implants were failing as I reached the end of my mission, *exactly* as planned–and my rejuvenation might soon fail as well. The actual function of the devices I'd been given to deliver might be *exactly* as I'd been told–or might be something very, very different.

Staring out into the rain, I thought about summoning up Case just so I would have someone to talk to. Taking another hit off the tequila I'd bought in Playitas, I decided against it, decided I was good with my own company. I had inscribed a charmed circle in the ground with the Moon Knife before the ground turned to muck. The charm held, even if the ground hadn't. I didn't expect any Chupacabra to come calling, but it would also discourage snakes–which were not unlikely at all.

Assuming the weather cleared up even slightly, I was only days away from my target. How soon the Armstrong would no longer be of use had a lot to do with whether I wanted to run it dry or try to cache it in somewhat useful condition for getting out of here. The way the road was dwindling, 'sooner' was looking better than 'later'... particularly if the thing I wasn't sharing with Case turned out to be true. I'm a big believer in having a 'plan B', even one I wind up having to ad-lib on the spot.

Whether or not I would stay in this world, I didn't see much point to hanging out in the local version of the Guatemalan Highlands. Caching the Armstrong with enough fuel to get back to Playitas was looking like a good idea. From there, I could book passage on yet another riverboat, maybe even the same one.

I would not be making my way back to *el Norte*, though.

All of the river and canal boats in this region eventually wound up in Lake Nicaragua, which was the Pacific endpoint for this world's version of the Panama Canal. From there, I could book sea passage to any part of this world–or even catch an airship of the non-ghost variety.

That might be nice, actually... even though it wouldn't be cheap.

If *any* of the things I'd been told were true, I could take my time deciding whether or not I wanted to place that interdimensional Uber call–and if I *did* make that call, I needed to do it in a place where I wouldn't mind hanging around until my ride showed up.

But I also needed to make sure there wasn't any unfinished business that I would be–in *any* sense–'obligated' to take care of. What I had once called 'UFOs' were showing up in increasing numbers in this world, the same way they'd once arrived on mine.

In the case of my own Earth, almost all of those unidentified things in the sky had been waging a covert war for possession of that Earth. If what was happening here was a reflection of that war, there might be combatants I had an Obligation to side with–if I was going to keep my word.

There might be humans here I would be expected to side with as well–again, if I was going to keep my word.

Looking out into the rain, I considered once again the enormity of what I'd gotten myself into–and the narrow range of coincidences that had gotten me here. If I had somehow been able to save my marriage, I probably would not have wound up in a pub comparing notes on craft beer with Lucifer, Son of Morning.

If I hadn't gotten mindfucked by the original Colvin Case in the process of helping Morningstar leave Earth, Evangeia would have had no incentive to offer me one last mission. If a strung-out street hustler hadn't shot up the senior living coop I'd retired to, I might well have turned her down. Getting old sucks, but there's a lot to be said for the quiet certainty that one day you just won't wake up.

For all I knew, *that* was reality–and all of this was just the fevered delusions of a lonely and disappointed old man, desperate to escape the last failing moments of his life.

Sitting in the muck under a leaky tarp in the middle of a jungle, it seemed unlikely I would be sleeping any time soon. But if I did... did I truly know to what I would awaken?

three: ellsberg

All I could do was tell her the truth.

“I don’t know, Kayce. I don’t *really* know what happened, I don’t know how it works, and I’m not sure it’s something *I’m* doing. Something in my mind doesn’t seem right, even though a lot of it is clearer than ever. And a lot of it frightens me. If you’re worried about your wife, call her.”

We were sitting in the lounge of our hotel suite, trying to drink the edge off the day. Helene and Díaz had gone to their respective beds–or maybe the same one, for all I know; the extent of their ‘friendship’ was certainly no business of mine. Kayce had changed into the sweats that seemed to be the only thing she ever wore besides her uniform, and I’d ditched my coat and tie. It was beginning to rain. The night view of Dayton outside our window could’ve been Oakland, if Oakland had expressways.

It didn’t *feel* like a different universe.

Kayce was huddled into herself at one end of the sofa, arms wrapped around her knees, leaving most of the sofa to me. Beneath the buzz-cut blonde hair, the blues eyes stared into an infinity I knew all too well.

I refreshed our drinks and kicked off my shoes. For years, I had needed to get at least this drunk to sleep, when I slept at all. Helene Abenard, my latest and best therapist, had fixed that problem… but had left me with a few others.

“I don’t want to talk to her with a bunch of Yanquis listening in, Saul,” Kayce said, staring into the distance over her knees. “But I’m even more afraid that it wouldn’t *really* be her… or that I wouldn’t be able to tell if it was or not.”

For all that she'd once arrested me so Hiram Díaz could offer me a choice between working for him or going to jail, she was possibly the closest friend I had... this side of my bartender. She was also one of the toughest people I'd ever known. When it looked like we might wind up spread across the side of a mountain in a dead airship, she hadn't once flinched at what was happening. She deserved whatever I could tell her... even if it was next to nothing, even if some of it might not strictly be true.

More than anything... she needed me to be her friend.

"Asking me about the physics of what happened is about like asking a bird about aerodynamics," I told her. "Birds don't know about aerodynamics, they just fly. I'm pretty sure that Admiral Díaz could write a book on aerodynamics if he hasn't already; but if you kick him off the roof of this hotel, he's still going to hit the parking lot–not that I advocate trying it."

Kayce laughed. "Is the great man finally getting to you, Saul? It usually doesn't take so long."

I laughed as well. "All I'm saying is that if you want to know about the possible physics of what happened when we left San Francisco, ask someone like the admiral. If you want to know if your wife is still your wife, ask your heart the next time you see her–which you will, and soon."

She smiled. "Thanks, Saul. 'Physics' isn't the answer I'm looking for, but I'll talk to the admiral anyway–although if you don't really understand what happened, I don't know how much he can add."

"Maybe he can add more than you think," I said. "I don't have a clear memory of what I did, Kayce, but I'm pretty clear on everything that happened before it and everything that happened after. After the event, just about everyone on the *Morrison's* flight deck was in sort of a state of shock... except Hiram Díaz."

"That could mean a few things, Saul," Kayce said. "The admiral did... well, a *lot* of things before taking a desk job–and some of it is so classified that neither you or I are ever going to get the full story. But I think there's something else."

"What do you mean?" I asked.

"We didn't have this conversation, okay?" Kayce was holding her drink up. I couldn't tell if she was staring into the drink or the smoggy night sky. "It's not outside your clearance, but the 'need to know' might be debatable."

"Whatever it is stays with me, Kayce. Trust me."

"Oh, I do," she said. "Not easy in this business, but I guess you know that now."

"Pretty much."

"I know you tried to do background research on the admiral when he recruited you. I also know you found next to nothing. There are reasons for that. But if you had backgrounded Helene Abenard, you might have found something interesting–something that might or might not still be in the public record."

"Like what?" I asked.

"Basically, you're not the only member of this team Dr. Helene Abenard ever treated. Helene once had a *very* nice private practice as a psychist. Then she started doing 'missing time' therapy and wound up being recruited into Majestic."

"I sort of knew this," I told her.

“What you don’t know is *why* she changed her practice or how she got recruited. Even though you’re the ‘Patient Alpha’ in the paper she’s presenting, you really aren’t.” Kayce sat down her drink and turned to face me. “The *real* ‘Patient Alpha’ is Hiram Díaz. He just doesn’t have your abilities.

“At least I don’t *think* he does.”

* * *

The next day Helene and I once again needed to be at the conference as early as the Estaditos were prepared to let us in. At the admiral’s direction, we had packed our bags and left them in the suite’s common room before leaving. “I have instructed Captain Howard and his crew to be prepared for an immediate departure,” he told us. “We have no choice but to remain long enough for whatever Director Stone has planned for the conference closing, but I feel we should not remain one moment longer if it can be avoided.

“I will arrange to have your bags taken to the aerodrome. Please be sure that all sensitive materials are in your personal possession. I have already arranged for a detailed examination of the *Morrison* upon our return–I fear one for you as well, Saul Ellsberg,” the admiral said, peering wryly through his antique gold-rimmed glasses. Not yet dressed for the conference, he was wearing sweats like Kayce’s, drinking coffee, and reading a local paper. Perhaps I had made Kayce’s last drink a little stiffer than necessary–she was apparently still asleep.

“I was already expecting it,” I told him–although in fact... I was *not*.

This is how it works when you have dreams that come true: suddenly something you’re doing or experiencing seems familiar, sometimes to the point of even knowing what someone is going to say before they say it. Then you try to remember why. Then you remember that you dreamed it.

But it works the other way around as well.

There were no visions forming in my mind, just a sense of unease in the back of it. Something wasn't quite right, and wouldn't quite come clear. But I somehow knew that being prodded like a lab rat back in California was possibly the least of my worries.

"It is necessary, I fear," Díaz said. "We need to determine what you did." The wry look became a wry smile. "Be glad you are Californiano and have rights–the Yanquis would probably just dissect you. Spend your time today at the conference as you wish, find out what you can–but it is *imperative* that we are all together and prepared to leave by the time Stone holds his demonstration tonight."

* * *

"Shall you be seeing Dr. Albion today?"

"In fact, I plan to meet her for coffee as soon as we're at the conference. For *coffee*, Helene. We're all leaving at the end of the day... and she's *not* my type, whatever you and Kayce think."

My therapist smiled at me. "I never said otherwise, Saul. I was merely curious."

"Sorry–I'm just a little on edge."

The smile vanished. The last time I had been 'on edge', we were on an airship under attack from unidentified flying objects... until I somehow made it all go away. "Is this something we should talk about?" she asked.

"Not now," I said, nodding at our FDS-assigned driver.

In truth, I wasn't sure if there *was* a reason for my apprehension or not. Even though I'd been having occasionally prophetic dreams for as long as I can remember, the growing strangeness of those dreams was a recent thing. Whatever I had done to get us here safely was something even more recent, something I was still trying to understand.

For all I knew, Kayce was right. Maybe what Díaz was calling a 'displacement event' really *was* a shift between universes. But if it was, the differences were trivial. And if it was... I have been adrift between universes for a long, long time.

With Helene's help, I have come to realize that the dreams and abilities came from the same source as the wrecked thing in Hangar 51, the 'device' that people like Ameryst Albion had made careers of studying. I had also come to realize that source was something far stranger than anyone in Majestic could possibly know.

They thought they were studying aliens and alien technology. Ameryst thought she was studying an 'aethership' with an advanced propulsion system. For all practical purposes, that 'propulsion system' was a hole in the universe, an abyss as dark as the eyes of its makers.

Being in the vicinity of that abyss was making me uncomfortably aware of another abyss–one inside *me*. I'm an anomaly, and I don't make sense. But the *world* doesn't make sense anymore. I'm now just one anomaly among many.

I'd had dreams for a week of something happening to *Morrison*, just not what *did* happen. No dreams this time–just a growing sense of unease, a growing sense that whatever wasn't right with the world was getting less right by the moment... and a sense that *something* was going to happen.

As for being prickly over Ameryst's apparent Sci-Rom fan crush on her favorite writer–me–let's just say that I've had bad luck with relationships... and leave it at that. But leveraging that crush had gotten us the one solid piece of the information Admiral Díaz had brought us here to find. I guess after months of working for Díaz and Kayce, it shouldn't surprise me too much that I was learning to think like them... think like a 'spy.'

And I guess she was 'cute,' whatever that really means. She was smart, lonely, and a bit of a misfit. She was as troubled by dreams as I was, but in a different way. I was troubled by dreams that sometimes came true. She was troubled by dreams that almost certainly wouldn't.

Even though I used to write scientific romances for a living, I never really understood why anyone dreams of going into the aether to other planets. Wherever the 'mystery disks' and 'ghost airships' came from was beyond our reach, possibly no place any human would want to visit or live in. The only other known planets we could have hope of reaching were Mars and Venus–a barren desert and a cloud-wrapped mystery, neither one in any evident way worth visiting. I'd written stories about the things Ameryst dreamed about, written them to cope with my own dreams of things far stranger. But that didn't mean I believed in any of it.

Apparently Ameryst did.

I found her where she'd found me, in the conference center cafe. I'd been surprised that there was an actual conference center, even a small one, tucked away in the back end of Patterson Aerodrome. But according to the admiral, Majestic had been funneling money out of both the U.S. and California economies for years, as well as occasionally putting money back in–by way of patenting what little alien technology they'd been able to decipher. The core systems of the device remained as incomprehensible as the remains of its crew, but other parts were more accessible.

I'd always wondered where Velcro came from.

She was sitting at a table in the back–sipping what would be called an 'Americano' back in San Francisco and here was simply called 'coffee'. She was also nibbling at a pastry. She'd improved her wardrobe from the day before, from a pantsuit to a dark dress and hose, boots, and a green tweed blazer that actually paired well with her flaming red hair. She smiled when she saw me, I smiled back. As long as I thought of all this as just a big Sci-Rom Con, I sort of knew how to behave.

"I'm not supposed to be talking to you, you know."

"Then why are you?" I said, taking a seat. "I don't want to get you in trouble."

"You won't. My team lead cares what Homeland Security thinks because he thinks it'll get him promoted. I don't care about that. I'm just here to do science." She suddenly turned sad. "It was better before the election, you know. As long as we were making progress, no one really cared. Now they do."

"It's not just your new president," I said. "I do disinformation for California Majestic, but I also see the *real* reports before we put out the fake ones. There really *is* something going on, Ameryst. This 'detector' of yours couldn't have happened at a better time."

"It's not *my* detector. I just told them what to look for, made sure nothing was damaged when they told us we needed to cycle the device's primary drive state so they could test the detector."

"And who are 'they'?" I asked.

"FDS. The 'detector' has been a Homeland Security project from the start."

four: case (virtual)

The only thing worse than realizing that you're a monster is realizing that you're dead... until you realize that being dead has advantages.

The first 'thought' the current 'me' ever had could be put into words along the lines of *Holy shit–it worked!*

I remember Real Me, every moment of me, right up to the moment Real Me had to stop uploading–the moment when the data feed into Murphy's implants was closed for the transition to another universe. The next thing I remember after that is seeing through someone else's eyes, hearing through someone else's ears. There may be more of Murphy's sensorium I can access, but so far, that's all I've got. What he does with his dick is entirely his business, whether I get to watch or not, and I'd just as soon not–although if the *current* version of Murphy is anything like the version I used to hit clubs with, I'm sure he does some pretty good business... whether he wants to talk about it or not.

Real Me had always been able to think in code. Now that all I *am* is code, Fake Me does it a lot quicker and a lot better. Painting an animation of myself into Murphy's implants isn't as silly as it sounds. He has abilities I don't understand. I don't discount the possibility that he really *could* 'exorcize' me if he put his mind to it. Being useful, trustworthy, and likable is pretty important under present circumstances. Real Me had done some fairly fucked-up shit to Murphy once. Getting him to like, trust, or even put up with Fake Me was worth the effort.

And it isn't like I have anything better to do... particularly when he has the 'social interface' turned off–when I really *am* just a data ghost floating around in the chip in his head.

* * *

Finding out what Murphy *really* had been was almost as big a shock as finding out what *I* really was–particularly when one came right after the other.

One day Real Me had just... woke up.

I woke up... and *knew* I wasn't really human. The stuff that had been floating around in the back of my mind my entire life came together. So did a lot of other things. Even though Real Me had no particular 'need to know' about what The Company had done with the stuff they'd recovered at Roswell, I'd pulled the files anyway. The photos of preserved, dissected, and thoroughly not-human remains had been profoundly disturbing in a way I hadn't understood... until the day I woke up.

I woke up–and *knew* that the reason I hadn't made the connection between the things in my dreams and the things in cold storage at Area Fifty Whatever was because *they wouldn't let me.* I'd been under control the entire time... and I still was.

In the back of my mind, I had sort of always known. But I'd been able to think around it and ignore it. But that ended once *they* had a need for me. I'd been made for a purpose, put where I could carry out that purpose. *They* 'think like code' as well, that's where I get it–only to them, the whole world, the whole universe, the whole *multiverse* is code. And they are master hackers. After millions of years, they should be.

I woke up–knew what I was, knew more or less how I'd been made (don't ask), knew as much about them as they needed me to know–to make sure I could do what they needed me to do.

They don't have a name for themselves. They've evolved past such things. They may *look* vaguely humanoid, but they aren't. What they evolved from has a lot more in common with a termite or an ant. They aren't individuals, they never were, really. An entire hive of them has what amounts to a mind. Sometimes those hives live as parasites within worlds, sometimes they live in the deep outer dark–places where the stuff of time and space grows thin.

I woke up–and, among other things, I knew that the 'Mike Murphy' I'd know for years was as little what he seemed as I was. At least he was human (at least he was then), but he was something I'd always believed was a myth. The idea of an inner conspiracy within the heart of all conspiracies would have been too absurd to consider... if it hadn't been true. Almost the entire time he had been a Company man, Murphy had also been sworn to an ultimately secret 'order'... had done their bidding as well The Company's.

The fact that he'd never wound up on a meathook suddenly made a lot more sense.

He had fallen far by then. For old time's sake, I'd put together a way for him to save what was left of his job while he tried to save what was left of his marriage. I doubt the old-school cowboys who recruited Murphy would've ever signed off on the idea–letting a Company analyst phone it in via telecommute–but the MBAs that took their place crunched the numbers and decided they *loved* it. There may have been more to it than that. When I awoke to the knowledge that Murphy was a double agent, I'd awakened as well to the knowledge he was not the only one.

Regardless who was actually pulling strings on his behalf, he got what he wanted–he got to take his faltering career and his faltering marriage halfway across the country. The marriage failed anyway... and Murphy started to unravel. I stopped trying to defend his value to The Company. I knew what was going to happen next, and wanted no part of it.

Then I woke up... and knew that defending Murphy was the least of my concerns.

* * *

My life pretty much ended the day my makers activated me. I don't think they created me for the sole purpose of helping them kidnap a 'fallen angel', but I also can't reject it out of hand. I know just enough about them to know that the totality of their collective mind sees across universes, contains the living memory of millions of years. To things like them, a thing like me is a minor piece of contingency planning.

I probably should have *at least* been surprised to wake up that day to the knowledge that my old buddy was not just a double agent, but had a side-hustle as well–working for a being who credibly claimed to be 'Satan', who he had apparently met in some dive bar in the Pacific Northwest.

But I was *not* surprised; from what I remember of Murphy's taste in bars and drinking companions, I'm surprised it hadn't happened sooner.

I still don't really know why my makers wanted to abduct Morningstar or why Murphy's masters in The Order empowered him to prevent it. All I really know is that the day that plan failed is also the day my life, as even a *reasonable* facsimile of a human being... ended.

The plan failed, but not for any lack of trying on my part or my makers–who cut their losses and disappeared down a wormhole as soon as things went south, leaving behind me, three of their own corpses, and some technology they *really* should not have left lying around. They had underestimated Murphy, overestimated me, and completely failed on anything approaching a 'plan B'... or at least that is sure how it seemed at the time. I know better now.

The entire universe I'm now in *is* 'plan B'.

* * *

I'd more or less told Murphy the truth–or at least what he 'needed to know.'

There really *was* a highly compressed transmission squirting out of a subatomic singularity somewhere in Greenland, a pinhole between worlds. It really *was* a type of transmission no human on the Earth we'd wound up on had the technology to detect, much less receive or understand–even though Murphy's implants could pick up on it. It really *was* being encoded on the other side of the wormhole by the tortured remains of Real Me. It really *did* contain real-time location data for what might or might not be another beer-swilling fallen angel, or at least a similar anomaly–and the power constraints on that transmission really *didn't* leave room for much more than the location data.

But 'not much' isn't the same as 'not any'. Particularly if you're smart.

Real Me is a crafty son of a bitch and, like Fake Me, he doesn't have a whole lot else to do. I don't think anything that isn't him or me would even *see* the occasional shifted bit in the datastream he's sending through the wormhole, much less see it as anything other than just static or noise. And I have no way to send anything back, so it isn't like we're having a conversation. He's just talking to himself... as it were.

That's how I know he's dying.

The Fortuned don't *really* know how to turn Real Me into a Grey Alien, even though they've been studying what passes for Grey Alien DNA since the last ice age. But they don't *have* to, as long as they can get reasonably close. As long as they get their 'angel detector'–something they can control, something that sees through probability space–close is good enough... particularly if they don't care about side effects.

Which obviously they do not.

The Fortuned resort to torture any time Real Me doesn't cooperate. The simplest and most effective torture: wheeling in a mirror big enough for Real Me to see what two decades of genetic experiments have done. That one really doesn't work anymore, though–because Real Me no longer cares, now that he's dying.

He's doing it to himself, actually.

He's smarter than the entire damned lot of them, the pack of supercilious and superior space elves–the so-called 'Fortuned'–and their not-so-altruistic plans to save the multiverse from the even less altruistic creatures that made *him*.

I'm very proud of Real Me. He's outsmarted them again and again. He got Fake Me 'out', he wrote the hack that forced Murphy to let me live in his head in exchange for completing the mission. And now Real Me has figured out how to use the abilities we inherited from our Dads to accelerate his mutation... and make *sure* it's lethal.

One way or another, he plans to escape. He'll either figure out how to conjure up wormholes or he'll force his own mutation past the point where the Fortuned can't keep him alive as anything other than a mindless lump of flesh.

And he's got Fake Me as a backup plan.

I'm not going to let you down, Real Me. I wish I could tell you it all worked, I wish I could tell you how proud I am of Me, but that would be almost as pointless as telling you how much I love Me.

I know that one of these days those slightly shifted bits won't be in the datastream anymore, and pretty soon after that, the location data won't be there either. It won't really matter, because it looks like Murphy's 'angel' doesn't move around any more than you do... for similar reasons, for all I know.

I really will help Murphy complete his mission, even though I don't believe for a picosecond that he's been told anything approaching the 'truth' about any of it–any more than Murphy himself told the locals he hired in the field back in the day one damned thing more than necessary to get what he wanted, or ever told anyone he wanted to score with one thing other than what he thought they wanted to hear.

I'm impressed that he got lucky with one of the space elves, not so surprised that he either wanted to or managed it–he was pretty much an equal opportunity enjoyer back in the day, just as amoral in the sack as he was in the field. Similarly, I'm unsurprised he tried to work his marriage on a 'need to know' basis–just surprised that *he* was surprised when it didn't work... and that it genuinely broke his heart when it didn't. I hadn't been entirely sure he had one.

But *that* Murphy is as dead and gone as Real Me plans to be, if all else fails. I like the current Murphy better, anyway. He's even better looking than the one I used to hit clubs with, more lethal than the one I occasionally had to clean up after. Our relationship is even more fucked-up and codependent than the marriage that broke him, but at least we're honest about it. Monsters can, usually do, lie to themselves.

But only the really fucked-up monsters lie to each other.

What happens once Murphy has actually done what he was sent here to do remains a good question. He hasn't bothered to talk to me lately, leaving me to wonder what's really going on. I know he's not dead–the biofeedback circuits in his implants tell me that much–but that's really all I know. Everything I've done to be useful and trustworthy doesn't mean a damned thing once he decides it's in his best interest to leave 'social interface' turned off for good.

But I don't even know if 'social interface' still *works*.

The hack that Real Me pulled off to get me here was a masterpiece of software engineering, but nothing even close to what this hardware was designed for. Considering how long the Fortuned have had technology, this stuff should be a *lot* more advanced than it is. It's still advanced enough to have ways of dealing with something like me. Maybe the only reason I'm still here is that some sort of antivirus program has me in a quarantined memory space while it figures out what to do with me. If I was erased, I'd no more see it coming than a meat human knows they're dead.

Some sort of 'sleep mode' would've been bloody awesome, but I can see why Real Me didn't think about that–he hasn't slept as a human being in twenty years. At least those shifted bits in the data feed give me something to do. And if they mean what I *think* they mean... things are about to get interesting.

Really interesting.

"There are at least two possible answers I know of, Kayce, perhaps more. Of the two I know, there is perhaps some comfort to be had from either. You are not exactly alone in this–after all, I as well have a wife." Admiral Díaz was calmly buttering a scone. Scattered on the table before him was the morning edition of the *Dayton Daily News* and what was left of his breakfast.

I poured coffee and ordered a breakfast of my own. Neither of us was due at the conference until noon. Saul and Helene had once again gone ahead for Day Two of the Majestic Conference, would meet us in time for the closing reception–and the Estadito Majestic team's unveiling of the key component to their 'mystery disk detector.'

I still couldn't quite convince myself to call my wife. It had been easier to convince myself to follow Saul's advice: ask Hiram Díaz if my *real* wife wasn't now in a different universe.

"Anything you can share is appreciated, Admiral. All Saul can tell me is that he really doesn't know how it works. He's not even sure he's actually what did it. The *really* strange thing is... that I actually believe him."

Like myself, the admiral was wearing sweats from the Naval Academy gymnasium. He'd tried wearing them to the office once; Mathilde had flatly told him there were limits to informality and refused to unlock his file cabinets until he came back properly dressed. His answer had been to add a watch sweater and an officer's cap. He wouldn't be so lucky this time, nor would I; we would both spend the rest of the day in full-dress uniforms.

"I believe him as well," the admiral said. "Others with similar gifts have often said the same. I think he answered you as honestly as he could... and that he is as troubled by this as you are.

"Kayce, ever since it became apparent that these things are not merely machines from another *planet*, I have been trying to determine how such a thing can be, how a 'multiverse' can even function in theory. Even though my own background is engineering, I can at least talk to physicists–and I have.

"Understand that none of this is 'science' as you and I think of it–or at least not yet. We have no way of testing these hypotheses. They are as much thought experiments as anything else."

"I understand, sir."

"Good. In that case, let us start with the hypothesis from which I personally draw the most comfort. It is simple, really. You need not worry that 'your' Esmerelda is not truly yours for the simple reason that she never *has* been... that every moment you have ever spent away from her, starting from the moment you met, has resulted in the creation of a new divergent universe. If this view is true, what Saul Ellsberg did to preserve our lives has no impact on your ability to return home–for you *cannot*. You are no more or less lost... than you have ever been."

I had to ask. "And you find this *comforting*, Admiral?"

He smiled. "Not really. It is the comfort of knowing that what you fear to have lost was never more than an illusion. If this view of things is true, then it means that everything that ever was, ever will be, or could ever possibly exist or be imagined *does* exist–that we are nothing more than conscious viewpoints moving through an infinitely dimensioned matrix of infinite universes... every single one of which is 'real'."

I tried to imagine being conscious of such a reality–and couldn't. "I want to believe I can go home, Admiral, even if it's just an illusion. You said you had another theory?"

"Not mine, but I do have one. It has also been suggested that not all these divergent realities are permanent or stable–that over sufficient time, only divergences of *true* significance result in permanent branching of reality. If this is so, then we live in a state of constantly branching and merging timestreams–and because we do not stand apart from the world, we simply do not notice.

"In that case, the question is one of whether or not the difference between a world in which you and I are dead and one in which we live is 'significant'. It is significant to you and me, to be sure... but the multiverse may not share our perspective.

"I am not so sure in any event that whatever Saul did or caused to happen has moved us to a different universe. Until I have reason to believe otherwise, Kayce, I absolutely believe that you can return to your Esmerelda and I to my Sophia. And you have my word that I shall do everything I possibly can to see that we do."

* * *

Not much later, it was time to return to the conference. The hotel front desk rang us when our FDS-supplied driver had arrived. We gathered our briefbags and badges and made our way down.

Despite the smog from the nearby expressway, it was a vividly sunny day. If all went to plan, by day's end, we would be on our way home–or at least a reasonable facsimile of home, depending which theories you wanted to believe... and also whether or not we wound up having another encounter with the objects Saul had cryptically referred to as 'foo fighters.'

As we made our way to the waiting sedan, I realized I was hearing another sound in addition to the roar of the expressway traffic. It was also a roar... but it was coming from overhead, and growing loader. Our driver was standing by the side of the sedan and looking up. Almost fearful of what I might see, I looked up as well.

The roar was coming from a trio of dart-like silver shapes, obviously headed toward Patterson Aerodrome. They looked vaguely like rocket planes, but no rocket planes I had ever seen. For one thing, no rocketplane would be going anywhere near so fast this close to the ground. Then they sped up even more and roared directly over. As they did, I realized there were insignia on the wings–a bright white five-point star over a split blue and red circle. As they passed, I realized they stank the same way the expressway stank.

As I watched them recede over the city toward the aerodrome, I realized Admiral Díaz was laughing. I turned to him.

"I am sorry, Commander," he said, "but your expression is truly priceless. No, you have not seen some new variety of ghost airship or mystery disk–although I should not be surprised if someone reports them as such. An old friend of mine considers *that* the future of aviation. Under present circumstances, he may not be far wrong.

"They are called 'jets,' Kayce. They are from Texas."

* * *

The admiral explained on the way to the airfield. "They are propelled by what is essentially an enhanced turbo-impeller supercharged and fueled by a high-energy petroleum distillate. They are not so fast or fly so far as a rocketplane, but unlike a rocketplane, their flight is not merely ballistic. They can speed up, they can slow down. They are not so versatile as a good autogyro, but if the need ever arose for high-speed aerial combat, they would be an ideal weapon platform."

"They stink, and they're loud," I said.

The admiral shrugged. "They were developed in Texas. Everything there is loud, and Tejanos are even more indifferent to the scent of burning petrol than Estaditos. These craft were flown in for the Dayton Expo and air show–which we would be attending, did matters not dictate a quick return to California."

"I had no idea that Texas was so advanced."

"In some ways yes, in some ways not–have you not been there?"

"Once," I replied. "The naval base at Corpus Christi. Pretty, I thought... but a bit warm for my taste."

"Spoken like a true child of San Francisco, Kayce. I have spent much time there myself. Texas is... interesting. The Tejanos are not so independent as they think, but neither are they the mere extension of *Los Estados* many Yanquis take them for. They are like us, in many ways–politics notwithstanding."

Not just politics, I thought. The machines I'd just seen were loud, smelly, and in a hurry. Comparing them to airships like *Morrison* was like contrasting night and day. There might be a use for such things, particularly in an air war with 'aetherships' from alternate dimensions, but it was hard to imagine any other practical use for them. Environmental concerns alone would likely ban their use in California... or any other part of the Pacific Federation.

But California is not the world, not all the world has the same concerns. For a moment, I caught myself wondering what the Estaditos monitoring our conversation might think. Yanquis have even less concern for the environment than Texicans, consider *everything* from the perspective of maximizing corporate profit.

I could easily imagine some corporatist Yanqui entrepreneur–a *real* entrepreneur, not a posturing fraud like their president–hatching the idea that these things could be established as a cost-effective alternative to commercial rocketplanes or a faster alternative to airships.

The Yanquis would go for it in a heartbeat. Their working classes accept without question whatever the capitalist ownership class tells them; decades of unregulated corporatism have all but eroded anything approaching a U.S. middle class. Much of the world is happy to buy the output of the shabby factories that dominate the Estadito economy. Would the world buy 'jets' scaled up to the size of airships, belching fumes and noise into the air, if some damned yanqui made it worth their while?

Probably.

Sometimes, I wonder why Admiral Díaz and others like him are so concerned over an alien invasion. The real threat is *right here*... and it has been, all along.

six: murphy

By the time the rains stopped, I'd made my decision.

A day out from where I'd camped and waited out the rain, I cached the Armstrong, made a few other preparations that seemed appropriate. I now knew *exactly* where I was going, even if I was still unsure what to expect when I arrived. I also knew that–even with the time taken for my added preparations–I'd be arriving a lot more quickly than I'd originally expected.

I'd wondered, on the way down from Texas, just how similar these jungles would be to the ones I'd known in another world–*very* similar, I now knew, including similarities very few people that weren't me would even know about. What I'd found had been a surprise, but not really... I had sort of sensed it all along.

What I traveled really was just a trail now, not anything close to a road, and steeper than ever. I knew it would become steeper yet, but I didn't expect any problems with that. The alchemy of my rebirth had left me looking like a twenty-something guy, but not much like the twenty-something guy who used to be me. This guy had higher cheekbones–not as high as Evangeia's, but not far. My hair was thicker and darker, my skin was darker as well.

But the real changes weren't something you'd see in a mirror.

I'd found out a few things on the way here, things about myself. I'd found out that I was faster and stronger than I'd ever been before, found out that the shit in my head had been programmed with hand-to-hand combat skills that made my earlier skills look like playground posturing.

I'd found as well that either my earlier skills in magic had grown stronger or that magic itself was stronger in this version of Earth. Whichever it was, it was getting stronger the closer I came to my destination... which was probably not a coincidence.

As I walked on through the jungle, I wondered at how little I had ever truly seen this place, or at least a version of it, when I had first seen it many decades before. I had seen the world through different eyes back then, and the beauty of it was not always a thing apparent to me.

But I saw it now.

Eventually, I found myself on a familiar mountaintop toward the ending of the day, thinking of other mountains and other worlds. Looking northward, I could see the valley where I'd sheltered from a rainstorm two days before. To the south, I saw only jungle and another valley. But enhanced vision and second sight saw other things as well. I knew the *physical* end of my journey was soon at hand.

I decided it would be best that I camp for the night, even though I had stamina and senses sufficient to press on. I was by no means the only predator in these jungles, or even the most dangerous. And I would possibly need *all* of my stamina... once I arrived.

* * *

Again, chanting.

Again, a voice like thunder.

Again, the sun struck from the sky.

Only this time... I *knew* I was dreaming.

And this time, I saw the sky.

God's Mountain fell away before me. I could see the horizon, see and hear the faithful who had come to see the miracle occuring behind me that I could not turn to see for myself.

And before me was the sky.

And it was filled with otherness.

All around us, the demon chariots had come, for they knew as well what was to pass. Had they thought to prevent it... they thought wrong. They were profane things–barred from this holy place and soon to be banished.

In what was almost an evening sky, they were plainly visible in their multitudes.

As the voice like thunder grew even louder, too loud to bear, the miracle happened.

God's Fire revealed. Like lightning.

It touched each profane chariot, and each vanished. But it went beyond... into the farthest reach of heaven, condensing into a web of light that grew dimmer as the sun was no longer hidden.

Then I too was struck–for I was a profane thing as well.

And then awoke, sweating.

I almost expected to see it still, that web of light spanning the cosmos, almost expected to hear that roar like thunder. But I heard only the jungle, saw only the stars.

The stars and one thing other.

It hovered over the valley where I'd camped before, the same shape–silver in the starlight and etched like some large and enigmatic piece of art. A massive, flattened cylinder, gemlike colored lights clustering at either pointed end. A clear white light like a spotlight probed the valley's floor.

I couldn't say I was surprised the thing had followed me this far, the 'ghost airship' that first appeared in the Texas badlands. If it was what I was beginning to think it *had* to be... it could be nowhere else.

I watched it a long, long, time from within an enchanted circle of safety that may or may not have mattered–for this thing was not magic, at least not as I knew it.

Eventually, the bright, searching light winked out and the thing drifted away–this time to the north.

Case was going to be pissed when I told him about it–he'd only gotten to 'see' it that first time. But it might be a while before he and I 'talked'.

I became aware of an odd sense of warmth from my ankle. Drawing it from my boot scabbard, I was unsurprised to see the Moon Dagger glowing more brightly than ever, was glad it had been hidden before. Scabbarding it again, I made myself as comfortable as I could on the bed I'd made from moss and leaves and drew my old leather jacket over my shoulders–even though the night was far from cold. What dreams or revelations might yet come in this night I could not say. But I would force myself to sleep, nonetheless.

And try not to wonder at what day might bring.

seven: kayce

Sometimes all you can do is just do your job.

There had been a time once when I understood the world and understood my life. I taught history at the Academy, analyzed field reports at the Bureau, went to the opera and art openings with my wife, played chess and occasionally fenced with my Pops.

Then Hiram Díaz upended *everything*.

In the five years since the admiral had first recruited me into BSI, I'd gotten used to the idea that there were layers of reality. There was a version of history Pops taught at Berkeley, there was a version of history that I taught at the Naval Academy, and there were classified archives at the Bureau that contradicted both. I knew that a certain amount of what could be read in newspapers at any given time was the most superficial layer of what was actually happening.

Then I found out that there were layers that went even deeper than the Bureau's secret archives.

Maybe this was what Admiral Díaz had in mind all along when he recruited me–that I would wind up part of a decades-old conspiracy to conceal the presence of aliens. That my 'second recruitment' coincided with what was beginning to look like the opening phase of an alien invasion was hardly a coincidence. The Admiral was legendary for playing the long game. I'd always wondered why I'd been offered a desk at BSI. Maybe now I knew.

That second recruitment had begun with what seemed like a simple assignment: bring in for questioning a Sci-Rom writer who'd published sensitive information. But nothing is ever simple if Hiram Díaz has any involvement. He had apparently known for a long time that Saul Ellsberg was something more than a washed-up hack writer, apparently still knew more about what Saul *really* was than he was willing to share. How the admiral knew such things was an interesting question that might or might not ever be answered.

It's called 'need to know'... and it is the bane of my existence.

What I personally needed most to know was that I hadn't somehow gotten lost in this world of aliens, conspiracies, technology that looked like magic, and magic that looked like technology. I needed to know that I could still go home, that home really *was* home... and not just a reasonable facsimile.

Saul was right: I could've just called Esmerelda, pretty much any time I wanted. The U.S. is fairly backwards in a lot of ways, but phones work about the same as they do in California–even if the network is pretty awful. But we'd already been having problems before I even left, and I didn't want to make them worse. Given a choice between my job and my marriage, there is no choice. Between *anything* and my marriage, there is no choice. If I was lucky enough to get home from this, I would resign. The admiral could find someone else to play spy games with creatures from other worlds.

* * *

"Be pleasant, say as little as possible," the admiral told us. "This is the one person here from whom we will learn *nothing*."

Day Two of the Majestic conference was drawing to a close. Whatever mysteries Admiral Díaz had hoped to solve by bringing Saul and me to this thing were not much less hidden than ever, likely to remain that way. *Morrison* was on standby at the Aerodrome to take us home. The admiral's decision to cut short a day suited me fine. Even if we were attacked again by unknowns en route back to California, it would be better than being here.

Saul and Helene had met us, Saul still accompanied by the Estadito physicist, Ameryst Albion, who plainly had a crush Saul plainly could not see. It was a pity we couldn't take her back to California with us. I wasn't even sure if Saul liked women, wasn't even sure if *Saul* was sure... but he could find worse ways to find out.

The auditorium we had been meeting in and around for the last two days had been reconfigured for the closing reception and Director Stone's presentation. Of course, the bar held nothing but 'American' products. After a quick inspection of the wine list, I decided I would consider myself 'on duty.'

The buffet next to the bar was similarly unmemorable. This might have been politics.

The current U.S. president, with whom Stone was supposedly close, had a rumored preference for what Estaditos call 'convenience food'–which might actually be convenient, but doesn't look much like food. The buffet was a step up from *that*–but any hospitality manager serving anything similar at a state function in California would probably soon be considering their career options.

Curtains were drawn and FDS-uniformed guards stationed at the stage at the end of the auditorium. Whatever it was Stone intended to present, there would be no 'sneak peaks'. Over the sound system, bland and insipid 'American' music played softly.

Either the admiral felt a need to show diplomacy or years of drinking coffee laced with chicory had ruined his taste buds. He had accepted a glass of something called 'Anheuser Lager.' It was probably an astute choice. Director Stone, now making his way toward us, was holding a glass of what looked like the same thing.

As a BSI analyst, I had watched Jarrod Stone's career arc. He was a politically-connected insider who had successfully leveraged the paranoia of U.S. presidents and the xenophobia of the U.S. at large, creating what had eventually become the single largest department in the entire Estadito civil government–growing by acquisition and merger like one of their damned corporations.

The fact that Majestic was possibly on its way to being yet another acquisition was even scarier than the uptick in mystery disk sightings. At least what the unknown aliens planned to do here with advanced technology was unknown. There was no such doubt about the intentions of Jarrod Stone–or 'Homeland Security.'

He even *looked* like an Estadito corporate executive. Tall and fit, with tan skin, pomaded dark hair, pale gray eyes, and an expensively tailored gray suit. The Flag and Party pin on his lapel was not one of the cheap ones they hand out at Homeland Celebration rallies. It probably cost even more than the suit.

He grasped Díaz's hand in a politician's handshake. "Good evening, Admiral. I was so sorry to hear that you would be departing the conference immediately. I hope it is not an urgent matter."

"I have every confidence that you would already know of anything *truly* urgent occurring in California, Director–possibly even before me. It is a minor matter... but the timing is critical. Dr. Abenard you have met, but please permit me to introduce two recent additions to California Majestic. Commander Kayce Cullen and Sr. Saul Ellsberg. I assume you already know Dr. Albion."

Stone favored Saul and me with a bleak politician's smile, but no handshake. "Oh, yes. The historian and the writer of interplanetary fantasies. Your staffing choices are never anything less than inspired, Admiral Díaz. For years we have looked to the California contingent for advanced technological guidance. Now that American know-how is catching up, I'm glad to see that you have found other and more creative ways to maintain California's well-known competitive edge."

He turned to Ameryst, briefly took her hand. "I have not had the pleasure, Dr. Albion, but I have heard much about you. Your contribution to our breakthrough in gravimetric detection is very much appreciated. I'm sure your new friends from California are as grateful as I am."

Ameryst was startled and blushing beneath her vivid freckles. "Why–thanks!" she stammered.

Stone favored us all with a very slight bow. "I must see to final preparations for our presentation. I think you will be impressed."

Admiral Díaz introspectively sipped his beer as Stone walked away toward the curtained and guarded stage. He was joined there by two men I recognized: Colonels Blaine and Hodge, the two U.S. Air Force attaches who had delivered to BSI the incomplete data on the detection system Stone intended to demonstrate, now in full-dress uniform. After a brief consultation, Stone followed them into the cordoned area behind the stage.

Following my gaze, the Admiral sighed. "I have never, never, trusted that man. Whatever he is doing goes beyond showboating for appropriations. I am glad that we soon leave."

I turned to Saul. "Is it just me–or were we just insulted?"

"It's not just you," Ameryst interjected. "If you stay here long enough, you get used to it."

Saul was looking at the stage as well, with an apprehensive look that made the short hairs stand up on the nape of my neck. I had seen that look before.

"What's wrong, Saul? What have you *seen*?"

He wouldn't answer me, but simply shook his head slowly.

"He has been like that all day," Helene told me. "He says it is nothing, but I have my doubts. I have apprehensive feelings of my own."

Finally, Saul spoke. "I know him," he said.

"The director?" I asked. "You *know* Jarrod Stone?"

"I don't know why, I don't know how, and I don't know from where. If it is a dream, it's not one I remember. But I know that face. Something here feels *wrong*, Kayce. If I could leave now, I would."

eight: murphy

"I don't like it, dude–what if it's a trap?"

I'd switched on 'social interface' for one last consultation–and also to confirm what I pretty much already knew: that the destination the mutated remains of Case Prime was targeting from another universe was close at hand... and exactly where I expected it.

"If it's a trap," I said, "It's one you led me to... so it's a little late for that concern."

The data ghost was still dressed in the appropriated wardrobe of a fictional archaeologist from another universe–who might even be real in this one, for all I knew. He didn't like the fact that I intended to switch off again after this last consultation and go in alone. I liked even less the suspicions that were driving me to do it. But my instincts were telling me to do it as well... and I always follow my instincts.

My own wardrobe wasn't quite as much a fictional appropriation, but didn't miss it by much. I was wearing no visible weapons, was once again topping off my t-shirt and dungarees with a leather bike jacket older than my own apparent age... the one artifact I'd been permitted to bring into this universe that was truly my own. On my back was what appeared to be a worn canvas and leather rucksack, the contents of which were no one's business in particular.

At least no one's just yet.

"You know something you're not telling," Case said. "Keeping too many secrets have gotten other people killed."

"You aren't sharing everything either," I replied. "And given that you're living in my head, you've got as much incentive to keep me above room temperature as I have."

An interesting question, one I had no interest in answering: would the alien implants Case had hacked his way into continue to function in some way if I was dead?

For Case's purposes, it pretty much didn't matter. If the Fortuned ever came calling for the implants, the first thing they'd do would be to purge Case like the computer virus he was. The likelihood of anyone else on this world being able to interface with the hardware wasn't even worth considering. The tech in my head was many thousands of years more advanced than any computer system I had ever seen on *any* world. Only the Fortuned, or others similarly advanced, would even know it for what it was.

And I intended to keep it that way.

"You're still a punk-rock cowboy asshole," Case sulked. "And your cowboy tendencies have come pretty close to getting you killed on prior occasions. But arguing with you is pretty pointless, old buddy–I know that just about better than anyone. Anything you want to know or need to share before you do this thing?"

"Anything else you think you know that *I* need to know, let's have it. Me? I got nothin'."

"Since this is probably my last chance to say this," Case said, "I'm going to tell you again: don't assume that *anything* you've been told about the devices you were sent here to deliver is the truth–or that the target you're about to acquire is really what you've been told."

"Do you have reason to think otherwise?" I asked.

Case laughed. "Only decades of being lied to and manipulated by an assortment of human and not so human bastards with agendas of their own–something we more or less have in common.

"I have Real Me's memories, so I know that decades ago you and Real Me met what you were told was a fallen angel–and not just *any* fallen angel, the big guy himself... Lucifer."

"He preferred 'Morningstar'."

"Whatever," Case replied. "He's also on record as being the biggest liar in creation–but I wouldn't assume the people who hired you for this gig aren't far behind. Supposedly, we're mere kilometers from another version of the same thing–another angel, or at least what's left of one. You've been told that an angel on Earth–*any* Earth–is a deadly threat to the entire cosmos... and you're the guy who gets to deal with it."

"Yeah... pretty much."

"Let's ignore for the moment that's some fairly grandiose shit," Case said, "And look at the rest of it. I also have Real Me's memories of everything that's been done to him since that happened. He's been mutated, tortured, shot up with drugs, wired up with machinery. He's now psychic as fuck, to the point of being able to see into other universes. The signal he's been sending thru the wormhole guided us here–even though it sure as fuck looks like you already know where you're going."

"Maybe."

"Let's ignore that as well, at least for now. Neither one of us *really* knows what we're being sent to. A lot could've happened between the time Real Me finished copying me into your implants and you woke up in another world. That target could be *anything*. Now let's consider this 'package' you've been sent to deliver."

"What about it?" I asked.

"Supposedly, you've got the one gizmo that does the same thing you helped Morningstar do back on our Earth–recover enough power to leave and stop being an existential threat to fuck-all everything."

"Correct."

"As a backup plan, in case this supposed angel is too incapacitated to leave, you've got another gizmo that drops an angel or anything else made of 'Dawn Matter' into its own private black hole–which also takes care of the threat."

"Also correct."

"Finally, there's the gizmo that supposedly calls your ride–if you want one. And just like the old days, that retrieval will include a debriefing and another mission–for you, not me, since the debriefing will include a data dump from your implants... including me, at which point I get scrubbed and they recheck the rest of the dump for other bugs."

"We don't know that for a fact," I said.

"Damned right, we don't. We don't know *anything* for a fact. It is just as likely that those pretty toys you've carried halfway across this planet all do the *same thing*–and that *none* of it has anything to do with *anyone* coming for you. It takes a lot of power to push a signal through the synthetic wormhole connecting this Earth with ours. Outside of this supposed 'Obligation' you've traded with the Fortuned, they don't really have a need to come get you–they just want the data in your chips. Why not just use the power in the devices you're carrying to do a data dump through the wormhole? From what I know, I'm pretty sure it would work."

From what I knew, I was pretty sure as well. I'd been warned, among other things, to *only* take the device I was planning to use out of containment, and not more than one–unless I wanted to be at ground zero of what might as well be a tac nuke going off.

"And why 'restore' an angel you don't want to see abducted by Greys?" Case continued. "Why count on it using that restoration to leave the solar system and go home to God? Just because it worked that way before is no reason to believe it would again. If the 'black hole' trick works, *why do anything else*–particularly if having an angel on Earth is as dangerous as you've been told?"

"That's certainly how the dirty tricks squad we used to work for would play it," I said. "We *don't* know that approach would work. And despite a few operational similarities, The Obligate isn't The Company."

Case laughed a nasty laugh. "You and I have differing perspectives in both cases, old buddy. From my perspective, it's just as likely as not that you're at the receiving end of a very long con. And except for taking at their word some fairly sketchy and inhuman bastards, you've no reason to assume otherwise."

He was right… and I didn't. My own situation analysis wasn't much different from Case's, my own paranoia even greater. Part of the reason for keeping Case switched off was a plan I'd been thinking about before I'd even left Oregon–a plan that had begun to form as soon as I knew we were going to wind up *here*.

Events occuring along the way caused me to refine the plan, adding more contingencies and precautions. I intended to keep my word, I intended to complete the mission I'd accepted in exchange for my rebirth. I keep my word. That's sort of how I am.

But I was going to do it *my* way. That's also sort of how I am.

"I don't have one good reason to assume one goddam thing," I said. "There could be a lot of reasons why the instructions I received are the exact truth–up to and including the outside chance that dropping an angel into a black hole might possibly piss off God... and that even the Fortuned and the Obligate are not quite arrogant enough to risk *that*."

"Do you really buy into all this 'angels' and 'god' crap?"

"I've been asking myself that question for decades, Case. I once met a disguised nonhuman who claimed to be none other than Lucifer, Son of Morning–who wasn't exactly what the legends said he was. He hired me to help him depart the world, and I did. He offered to reward me for my help, and he did. The version of 'God' he described is pretty much the Deist version who kicks the cosmos into gear and lets it run itself... but that doesn't mean there might not be repercussions to dropping one of God's primal creations into its own event horizon. Ultimately, it doesn't matter whether I buy into it or not. Does the terminology bother you?"

Case laughed again. "A little, not that it matters–and not that it has any impact on the smart play for wrapping this up.

"Just drop the goods and get out, Murphy. Anything else is too big a risk."

Finally, it was time. The annoyingly saccharine music faded as the lights dimmed.

Then the curtains opened. The back of the stage was still curtained. Armed FDS guards still flanked the stage. In the center was a narrow black podium adorned with a silver FDS insignia. Behind it stood Director Stone. After a brief scatter of applause, he spoke.

"I would like to extend my thanks to everyone who took time to attend this conference, particularly our colleagues from California and our esteemed observers from Canada. Conducting this work in secret for so very many years has never been easy. Being able to work collaboratively from across North America was far more challenging before the networked digital information systems we now all depend upon–but now, more than ever, the ability to communicate directly with our collaborators is profoundly important. It is important to remember who we are, and remain focused on our shared goals.

"We all know that objects like the one studied here have returned, and in greater numbers. Their intentions remain a mystery, their capabilities a potential danger to the Homeland and the entire planet. As intrusions of these things into our common airspace has proliferated, the ability to detect them has become critically important.

"Although my own organization is not part of the charter Majestic group, our mission to defend the American Homeland has made it imperative that the Federal Department of Security also have a seat at this table, and shoulder our share of responsibilities.

"I know that this involvement has not been uniformly popular among all charter member organizations, but please understand: the 'American

Homeland' we are defending reaches from sea to sea, encompassing as well Texas and California. We may not be a single country. But we are *all* Americans.

"I am here tonight to show you the system we have created to detect alien intruders into the Homeland. I will also be introducing the source of this new technology. As well as valuable new allies in the fight against our common *true* enemy."

I turned to the admiral. "You were right," I said. "Whatever he's got back there, he got it from someone else. But what does he mean by a 'common true enemy'?"

"I do not know," Díaz said, his face immobile and unreadable. "But I agree with Saul. I wish we were gone from here already."

From the podium, Stone continued. "But first things first. We circulated the majority of the technical data on our detection system in advance of this conference. We had good reason to withhold data on the primary key component, many reasons, actually–some of which will shortly become apparent.

"The breakthrough here was *not* understanding the working principles of the device's drive system. That has been understood for some time. The issue was detecting the operation of such a thing at a distance. Our first prototype detector was the size of a warehouse and prone to failure. Even though pioneers like Admiral Hiram Díaz have made great progress in making digital processing systems smaller, faster, and more powerful... what we have is still not enough.

"We have known for some time that the primary control systems of the device were at least partly organic in nature. Much of our difficulty in deciphering its functions stems from the fact that these systems degraded long before we knew what they were, or could possibly have accessed them."

"*Our* difficulty?" I turned, Ameryst Albion was glaring at the podium, saw my glance and blushed. "We were doing just fine until *they* showed up. Of *course*, the Mark I was big–but it worked!"

Next to her, Saul was pale and continuing to shake his head, eyes wide and staring. Helene seemed frightened as well–which frightened *me*. "Helene, what's going on?"

"Whatever Saul is feeling, I feel it too," she said, staring at the stage. "Something is very, very not right."

"Admiral," I said, "Can we just leave?"

"Not right now," he said softly. "Look to the exits."

I did. Even though the lights were dimmed, I could still see that armed men were now standing before the auditorium doors–not FDS, not anything I had ever seen. Over their black uniforms they wore what looked like armor of some sort. They had combat helmets of a type I'd never seen, including masks and visors covering their faces. Their weapons were unlike any rifle or sidearm I had ever seen.

I turned back to the stage, where Stone continued to speak.

"... sometimes God and Providence work in unexpected ways. Even as America has come under attack from things alien to our way of life, so as well have we acquired allies that *understand* that way of life and can help us defend it.

"These new allies understand and share President Drumpfmann's vision of a unified American Homeland–and, with their help, we shall pursue that vision. But first we remove the threat from our skies–and this is how we will do it." He gestured, and the curtains across the back of the stage fell away.

In the sudden hush across the room, I could hear Saul muttering "no... no... no..." but I could not turn to look at him.

In the center of the stage was a crystal tube, maybe a meter across and as much as two meters high, ringed at the top and bottom with what looked like black metal. Inside the tube was something I had never seen before... but I *knew* what it was. In the basement of a hangar a mile away were the preserved remains of what could only be the same thing.

Floating in clear liquid, it was the size of a child–but clearly not human. Grey skinned with an abnormally large head and enormously dark and unseeing eyes. Cables of some sort attached to the creature's skull, connecting to the black metal at the top of the tube.

From the shadows at the back of the stage, a man strode forward to join Stone at the podium. He was wearing the same black uniform as the men now blocking the exits–almost, but not quite, the same uniform as FDS, but with a high collar, body armor, armored gauntlets and greaves, and an armband that looked like a U.S. flag... but one strangely dense with what looked like too many stars.

As he joined Stone, I suddenly realized that except for a scar, and close-cropped hair... he and Stone were almost twins.

Then he took the microphone. "I'm Colonel John Wolfreich, Special Operations Branch, United States Space Force. Under authority granted by President Drumpfmann, I am declaring this airbase a protected Freedom Zone. Please do *not* attempt to leave the Freedom Zone. I apologize for this inconvenience–but we're here to make America *great* again!"

ten: murphy

As I got closer to what I knew would be my destination, a sense of déjà vu began to set in... from many sources. From the recurring dream I'd had since arriving in this part of the world, I could overlay onto the jungle around me a vision of massive crowds come to see a miracle. From my own past, I could overlay memories of a version of this place and the things I had done there at various times in my life.

But there was even more than that.

I had the sense of many versions of me, each on his own urgent mission, but all come to this place. And all come to do the same thing, or a version of that thing. I could *see* those other versions of me, like images in a kaleidoscope, or a hall of mirrors.

Making my way down into the valley where I knew this journey ended, I ran it all through my mind–over and over. It was too late for me to do anything else. The precautions I'd taken were either unnecessary, sufficient, or insufficient–in which case I was probably going to *finally* wind up dead.

Whether I survived or not, I had decided to stay in this universe and on this version of Earth–even though I might have years, decades, or even centuries to reconsider.

I wasn't sure if I would even *want* such a lifespan, far less know what to do with it if I had it. I was still more or less human, after all. I was a clever monkey who had either evolved or been designed for the principal purpose of making more monkeys.

If I was lucky enough to escape this intact, I intended to go somewhere where I had the luxury of taking as long as I needed to figure out what I wanted to do with this second life. If it really *was* a matter of centuries, maybe I'd follow Evangeia's lead–protect this Earth as she had protected mine. Recreating 'The Order' here wouldn't be particularly difficult, given enough time.

There might even be a need for it.

Or maybe I should just let the world manage itself and try my hand at making more monkeys. Being a dad is on the shortlist of things I'd never done, for more than a few good reasons–not least among them not wanting to put children at risk from some old unsettled business catching up with me. All the old scores I had to worry about, even the ones with nonhumans who might still be around and still be pissed, were in another universe. With the exception of a few chupacabra and a hick sheriff back in Texas, I hadn't really done anything here to piss anyone off.

At least not so far.

That might change, depending on who or what was waiting for me–and how much it resembled the 'angel' I'd once liberated under different circumstances. Lucifer Morningstar had either sought me out for my help, or–as he claimed–we had both simply been in the right place at the right time. It could've happened. Magic works that way, sometimes. In any case, he'd been grateful enough–and generous–when I *did* help him.

He had also been a world-weary, bored, condescending, arrogant son of a bitch. Even though he was not the 'Satan' it had amused him to pretend to be, neither had he been an 'angel' in any sense the religious faithful would recognize. Instead, he had been a being of such truly cosmic loneliness and pain, he had redefined those words... and made my own loneliness and pain seem trivial beyond words.

He also had grudges that had lasted as long as human civilization. If the being I would soon be confronting was anything like him and did not appreciate me or the gifts I'd brought, I might wind up with a worse nemesis than all the old unfinished business I'd left in another universe rolled into one.

But I could just as likely wind up discovering either the nonfunctional remains of a former angel or what Morningstar had called a 'Seraphim Stone'–an unliving artifact. All I really knew was that Dawn Matter, the stuff of Creation that Case's fucked-up original was tracking from the other side of the wormhole, lay dead ahead.

Then I cleared a switchback in the trail leading down into the valley. And realized that something else lay ahead as well. Something I had not expected.

Not in any of the déjà vu kaleidoscope images my mind had of this place was the way forward blocked by a tall timber stockade... but it was now.

It stretched to either side into the jungle as far as I could see. The part directly below and before me, blocking the trail I stood upon, held a gate... also of logs. It was inscribed with symbols I knew. I had seen those symbols. I had seen them on a fortune teller's tent in Albuquerque, on an *herbarista's* door in Coatzacoalcos, and other places and times as well– not least the ritual blade tucked in my boot scabbard. I had not expected to see them here... but neither was I entirely surprised.

I continued down the path, then stood before the gate and spread my arms wide. I sensed that from within I was watched. I wanted to make very sure any watchers knew I was unarmed.

After a time, the gates swung open. I walked on.

Once again, the various déjà vu and memory datafeeds in my mind were more or less synced to perceived reality. I stood in a clearing that had once been a city square centuries before. To the back of the clearing, made invisible from outside by various means both natural and otherwise: a pyramid, not that different from many others throughout the region, in this world or mine–a reminder that there had been civilization here... long before white assholes showed up and ruined the neighborhood.

But one other thing than the stockade stood different from what was in my mind: the women.

They stood before me, dozens of them, some young and some old–skin, hair, and eyes every color of the human rainbow. They were all dressed humbly, in ways that would all go without notice–except for one detail: every one wore a broad black belt. Clasped to the front of the belt: the same scythe-like dagger I carried as well.

One stepped forth to confront me. I knew her.

"We expected you at least a day ago," said Sister Guadalupe Concepcion Hernandez, little different from when I had seen her last in an *herbaria* on the Mexico side of Coatzacoalcos–hundreds of hard miles across jungle trails and rivers from this spot. "What, did you stop again to romance some girl? Incite a revolution? Trade some contraband? Eh, no matter; at least you are here now."

She examined me with a critical eye, like I was a horse she was unsure of buying or a student in need of a reprimand. "The way you bear your blade is disrespectful, but you are only a man. Sister Isadora had only time to give it to you, not instruct you. Even so, you have used the blade as it is intended. You know much... Oh man of another world."

"As do you, Sister," I said. "And I am sorry if I kept you waiting. I got here as quick as I could–just not as quickly as you."

A smile broke the tobacco-colored face, revealing teeth pretty much the same color. It was not a kind smile. No, she was *not* going to tell me how she got here. "You did well enough, Señor Murphy–I am just an impatient old woman. Lucky for you, others have more patience than me. You will be taken now to a place where you can wash and make yourself presentable. Then you go to meet them."

"Them?"

"The sisters, of course. The reason you are here."

Part 3: Extraction

one: kayce

This time I saw it happen... and remembered it.

One moment, we were in a crowded auditorium. On the stage before us, an alien but strangely familiar thing.

Then we *weren't*. If there was anything between, my mind refused to see it.

I was still in a darkened room surrounded by people. There was still a stage in front of me. But everything else had changed.

On the stage, instead of a monstrous thing in a tube I saw two men standing over a console of some sort, flanked by other men–only instead of guns, one had a guitar the other a sort of violin... and none of them was wearing anything I would remotely describe as a 'uniform.' A moment later, I realized that the console was actually a matched pair of what appeared to be record turntables.

And instead of being in a room full of people stunned to silence, something that I guessed might be 'music' thundered from speakers on the stage while people around me writhed ecstatically in some bizarre dance.

I realized that Admiral Díaz was standing next to me. "Sir!" I shouted to be heard. "What happened?"

"Saul Ellsberg!" he shouted back. "He did it again, Kayce!"

"Admiral, is this another *universe*? I've never heard anything like this!!"

"You should get out more, Kayce–it's called 'techno-billy', and it's the latest thing in the clubs. And if this is another universe, the difference is too slight to matter–I know this place!"

* * *

The admiral was right: Saul had done it again.

The first time, we had been in a disabled airship drifting into a range of mountains. This time, a locked and guarded auditorium. Both times, Saul had done something with his mind that no one completely understood, something I couldn't even make myself think about.

With the admiral leading the way, we made our way off the dance floor and into a nearby lounge. It wasn't until he gestured to follow that I realized that 'we' now included Dr. Ameryst Albion–member of the U.S. Majestic team, physicist, and ardent fan of Scientific Romance fiction. With any luck, her fondness for Sci-Rom *might* make explaining any of this even slightly easier.

Ameryst and Helene Abenard both had arms around Saul and guided him. Whatever he had done had left him in what looked like a state of shock, pale and shaking. He and Helene had both been severely agitated in the moments leading up to whatever had happened... possibly because of the alien *thing* on the stage we'd gotten away from.

The lounge the admiral had led us to was quieter than the room we'd appeared in, even though I could still hear 'techno-billy' pounding away through the walls. There was a bar at one end, with windows behind it. Through the windows, I could see Dayton's smoggy skyline. We were in one of the hotels close to Patterson Aerodrome, but not *our* hotel–possibly a good thing.

The admiral found a pair of facing sofas in the back of the room big enough for us all, secluded enough to talk, quiet enough to be heard. My wife thinks that Hiram Díaz is vain, pompous, and self-serving–and she is not entirely wrong. But she's never seen him in action. He had assumed command of an impossible situation without a moment's hesitation. Not for the first time, I found myself wondering what, exactly, he had done 'in the field' before assuming an admiral's rank and authority over BSI. Seating us, Admiral Díaz turned to Ameryst.

"Dr. Albion," he said. "I sincerely apologize that I cannot *fully* explain what just happened. Your government retains secrets of its own; so does mine. We are currently in the main hotel of the Dayton Airshow and Exposition. Your badge from the Majestic Conference will work here. Certainly, you are free and able to leave... which might well be advisable."

Ameryst shook her head. "Thanks, Admiral, but no thanks. I'm not going anywhere until I *know* what's safe and where it's safe to go. And whatever you did–*teleport* us?–it hit Saul really hard. I'm not going anywhere until I know he's okay. Could we get him some water or something? It might help."

Saul had let himself be seated and had stopped shaking. He was still pale, though–staring into space and slowly shaking his head. Helene, sitting next to him, looked up and nodded.

"I can do that," I said. "Does anyone else need anything?" I was myself thinking fondly of the scotch we'd left in our hotel suite, or even one of the wretched American lagers I'd turned down at the Majestic reception–*anything* to take my mind away from the thing my mind didn't want to admit just happened. But before I could go to the bar for water or anything else, another voice joined the conversation.

"Hell, if any of y'all need *anything*, it's on me. Hiram! Hiram Díaz!! *Goddam*, boy, I was wondering when you was gonna show up!"

I turned. We had been joined by a man of average height and build, with sandy-gray hair, twinkling blue eyes, and an expression I can only describe as a 'smirk.' He was dressed in a blue flight suit and cap, Texican-style vaquero boots, and a leather flight jacket.

The admiral smiled, but I couldn't tell if he was glad to see this man or not. "What an *entirely* expected pleasure, Jorge," he said. "My apologies, but pressing matters had taken my attention. I was not sure I would be able to attend your party–yet here I am."

"Well, *what kept ya*?? Did the Rooskies finally figure out how to build an F-bomb? Did one of those pickled little green men I ain't 'spose to know about come back to life and start some shit? You're damn' near white as a sheet, old son–I'd say you need a drink."

He cast an eye toward Saul. "On the other hand, I'd say this feller's already doin' pretty good... maybe *too* good. I got some oxygen, some B12 tabs, a few other goodies–if he ain't ready to go down yet, I reckon I can pep him up."

"You are entirely too kind, Jorge. To be honest, I do not know what he needs. This lady is his therapist. I should introduce you–"

"Oh, I introduce *myself* to *ladies*, old son... you know *that*." The man swept off his flight cap and made a brief theatrical bow to us all. "First of all, y'all, my name ain't 'Jorge'–I let Hiram get away with it, don't ask me why. I'm General George Washington Bush, Texas Air Corps. My friends call me 'G.W.'" He winked at me. "But you can call me 'G-dub.' little darlin'... just like my *special* friends."

I wasn't sure how I was going to 'wash and make myself presentable' in a pre-Columbian Mayan pyramid. But pyramids are just big piles of dirt and rock, after all. It's not hard to hide stuff in big piles of dirt and rock–my current plans sort of depended on it.

Two of the women who had met me at the stockade gate led me to a small and somewhat cell-like stone chamber to which had been added modest but modern plumbing. Light fell into the room from a hidden skylight above. Other than the plumbing, the sole furnishing consisted of a cot and an armoire. Laid out on the cot: white linen shirt and trousers, a broad black belt like those worn by the women around me–who either called themselves, or the ones I was soon to meet, 'sisters.'

So far, I had seen no 'brothers'–guess I'm just special like that.

I washed and dressed, trading my scuffed boots for a pair of sandals I'd found by the side of the bed. I stashed the begrimed clothes I'd worn through several hundred miles of jungle in the armoire, along with the rucksack I'd arrived wearing.

Case's warnings notwithstanding, I had no intention of simply 'dropping the goods and getting out.' There were far too many unanswered questions, far too little reason to believe *any* of the things I'd been told. The godlike pragmatists who'd sent me here had taken precautions that would protect the things I'd been sent to deliver. I'd taken additional precautions of my own. I had a feeling those precautions would soon be tested.

Meanwhile, I had an appointment to keep... possibly more than one.

Outside the chamber, the unsmiling women who had led me still waited. They had no other weapon than the same Moon Dagger I had transferred from my boot scabbard to the belt I now wore as well. But I knew as well as they that no other weapon was needed. They looked at me, then at each other, and nodded.

"Acceptable," one said. "Follow."

Then I was led to another chamber... also deep in the temple/pyramid once called, in many languages, 'God's Mountain'.

It was larger than the first chamber, and rectangular. At the far end was a raised dais with two simple chairs. Like the first chamber, light fell from hidden skylights far above–enough light for me to see quite clearly who sat there. I gasped, then controlled it and made my face carefully blank. I needed to know what, out of an infinity of possibilities, was truly happening.

The women who led me here kneeled. I'm only a jerk when I need to be, so I kneeled as well.

"Arise," said one of the two figures seated on the dias. "Arise and come forward."

I did as told–and walked forward to meet The Sisters.

They were both tall and fair, with cheekbones like the ones I now had. One had coppery red hair shot with magenta and brilliant, pitiless blue eyes. The other had hair as dark as mine had become–'Superman black,' I call it, for the indigo highlights that had come with my rejuvenation. Her eyes were as dark and deep as the depths of space.

Both wore simple gowns of the same linen I was wearing. At the feet of the copper-haired one crouched a small jungle cat. About the shoulders of the dark-eyed one draped a serpent, with skin like mottled gold.

"I am Aelia," said the copper-haired one. I knew her by another name in another universe... but even there, she had owned many names. "And this my sister, Astarte. Whoever or *whatever* you thought you journeyed to this world to meet, whatever errand you *thought* yourself upon, it is to us you have been guided. Whatever oath or purpose you had before no longer matters. You serve *our* purpose now."

three: kayce

"And *you* can call me 'Commander Cullen,' General–oh, and by the way: I *am* married."

General Bush chuckled. "No offense, Commander. My motto is that 'what happens in Dayton stays in Dayton'–but I *do* understand if that's not how *you* roll."

Admiral Díaz stepped a few feet away, nodded for me to join him.

"General Bush," he said, speaking as quietly as the music next door permitted, "is an old friend. I understand if you find him difficult–many do. He is *not* a member of the Majestic Commission, references to 'pickled little green men' notwithstanding. But he is a frequent attendee of the cover event and the airshow. Those 'jets' you saw earlier? Those are his doing–and he may be our one chance at getting out of here."

"What do you have in mind, sir?"

"I have no idea what it looked like when Saul... removed us from the Majestic Conference. But I suspect all eyes were on the stage, anyway. If we have been missed, Stone's people will assume we are somewhere in the conference center. No one knows we are here–of *that* we may be certain. The *Morrison* is standing by for us at the airship moorings on Patterson. If General Bush can find us a ride to the airfield, we may be able to leave here before we are even missed."

"Or if the guards at the airfield have been alerted, sir, we could just as easily wind up in FDS custody."

"I think not," the admiral said. "I believe Director Stone sealed the auditorium for a reason. Whatever he is doing, he is keeping it a secret–at least for now."

"Who are those people, sir? Since when does the U.S. have a 'Space Force'?"

"Apparently it has one now–*not* of Drumpfmann's doing, although I am sure he will attempt to take credit for it. This 'Colonel Wolfreich' is all but Director Stone's *twin*... or perhaps something far closer. He did not arrive here from another *planet*."

The admiral smiled grimly. "We had long suspected President Drumpfmann of collusion with foreign agencies–apparently, more foreign than we knew."

"If that's true," I said, "how do we know that this General Bush is any more to be trusted than anyone else in this place? Drumpfmann has popular support in Texas as well. Since the election, Texas is more a part of *Los Estados* than ever."

"We have few other options," Admiral Díaz replied. "Drumpfmann's support in Texas does not extend past the ignorant and envious among their lower classes–and I have known the general for a long time. Whatever his other failings, General Bush is neither a toady nor a traitor–

and he is loyal to a fault, even though his loyalty is sometime given unwisely. I believe he will help us."

We walked back to where the rest of our team was seated. General Bush had gotten Saul some water, which he was drinking. He looked like he was recovering from whatever had happened. But he still looked like a man in shock. There was also a bottle of whiskey on an end table and several glasses. I helped myself.

So did the admiral. "Gracias, Jorge," he said. "Here is our situation: it is urgent that we return to the airfield and board our transportation back to California–*immediately*. We cannot risk using public transportation or any provided by FDS. Can you get us to the Aerodrome?"

The general's smirk became a broad grin. "Oh, did you and Stone have a falling out? I can't say I didn't see *that* coming. I never trusted that little bastard; I sure hope you didn't either."

The admiral tossed back his whiskey, poured another. "Trust is a luxury I am seldom able to afford. Time is currently a luxury I cannot afford at all."

"I reckon not, not if you're wantin' to walk out on a pretty good party–and tryin' talk me into leaving as well." General Bush poured a whiskey of his own, held out the glass.

After a moment, Admiral Díaz raised his own glass, clinked glasses in an unspoken toast. "Then you shall help us?"

"Probably not the best idea," Bush said. "But yeah, I can get you to the airfield–but are you *sure* about headin' back to California?"

"I am not certain what you mean."

"It's a long flight, Hiram. You'll be in U.S. airspace for at least two hours, then Texas airspace for at least another two, then over incorporated territory for a *long* time before you're back in California. If you got problems with Stone, don't think for a minute they couldn't get a lot worse before they get better."

"You have another suggestion?"

"Hell yeah, I do, old son–head with me down to Texas."

four: murphy

It was called *La Comuna de las Hermanas*–'The Commune of the Sisters'–and it had existed for centuries. Centuries that made this world different from mine.

"You were placed under our protection," said the sister called Aelia. "I have thought it likely one such as you might appear, once others had begun to appear as well. The Commune has been charged for many years to watch for certain things–particularly in the near vicinity of a thing that happened once in the place you call Texas. You did not visit the site itself, but you came quite close. And you are followed by things we watch for as well."

A stool had been brought for me so I could sit before the dais. The inhumanly beautiful woman I could have named 'Evangeia' was now clearly not her, but her double. The differences were subtle, but there. She seemed older and sadder somehow, and also more... human?

Or perhaps the change was me. Decades before, her double had seemed utterly alien to me–neither human nor a woman. More recently, after the *elixir vitae* of Fortuned DNA had begun to change me, I saw her differently. The man who now looked back at me from the mirror looked almost as much a Fortuned hybrid as Evangeia herself. Did that make her double seem more human?

If so... what did that make *me*?

Her 'sister' was nothing I easily understood. Although she looked as much a Fortuned hybrid as Aelia or me, she had deep and utterly black eyes that were neither human nor Fortuned–*not* the eyes of a Selenite, but just as dark. I had a suspicion... but only one way to prove it. Those eyes took in *everything*. But she had not once spoken.

"We had to be sure of who and what you were," Aelia continued. "And that meant permitting you to guide yourself here. If you were what I thought, you could then be dealt with. If you did not come here, then I was wrong–and you were merely a harmless anomaly. I would need to see you, in any case."

"And now you have, great Sister," I said. "What is your judgment?"

"You plainly have the blood of the Fortuned, whether you came by it as I did or by other means. You bear the same Mark of Obligation as did my father and was once offered me–and yet you are also very plainly human as well–and either well-gifted or well-instructed in magic. You knew the Moon Dagger for what it was from the moment you touched it.

"It is my judgment that you are, indeed, an agent of my father's folk–who have seen fit to break the ban placed upon them and ignore the warning to not return to this world. That you are at least partly human does not place you beyond consequence for ignoring that warning."

"I'm sure ignorance is no excuse," I told her, "but I'm sorry–*what* ban? *What* warning? Banned by *whom*? This is all news to me."

"These are things you should know," Aelia said. "Unless you are as great a liar as was my father, or even stranger than I thought. My father's folk were banned by my dear sister–who *suffers* for it to this day, so do not think to treat her warning lightly or to tempt me. Nothing has changed:

the price of breaking that ban remains death–no matter *what* you have been told."

I turned to the other sister. I still wasn't *sure*... but I always trust my instincts.

"In another world and another life, you and your sister were both my–well, 'friends' may not exactly be the right word for various reasons, but it'll do. But I knew you well *enough*, Astarte, Queen of the Morning. I know *why* you take that name. I also know that you could've killed me with a single thought from the moment I set foot in this world. You can kill me right now, for that matter.

"In another world and another form, I helped you once before and I can help you again–that is, in fact, why I am here.

"Wanna talk?"

five: kayce

"I'm sorry, General–the airfield is under lockdown. Homeland Level One access only."

"Son," General Bush said, as the guard returned his identity card, "I'm a general in the Texas Air Corps, which is a *full* partner in the Homeland Defense Alliance as of last November. If I'm not 'Homeland Level One'–what the *hell* is?"

Even though the Admiral insisted that we return to California, General Bush had been as good as his word that he would get us to the aerodrome. His transportation was a massive, locally rented six-wheeled sedan. "Not as good as my ride back at the ranch," the general assured us. "But it'll do the trick."

In the very back of the sedan, Saul sat between Helene Abenard and Ameryst Albion–who had formally requested political asylum in California. General Bush himself had taken the wheel, with Admiral Díaz and I sitting behind him.

The guard looked even unhappier than he had when the massive sedan first pulled up to the gate. His partner, if anything, was even less happy. "There's no problem with *your* credentials, General, or even Dr. Albion's–but everyone else in your car is a California Citizen."

"Including a full admiral, and every single one of them packing a diplomatic passport. Did these orders come from Director Stone? Maybe you should call him and ask him about it."

The guard looked even less happy. "I can't do that, sir."

"Really? Well, *I* can." Bush pulled a mobile phone from a jacket pocket and hit a speed dial button. After a moment, he said, "Bush here–yeah, I can wait." Then he looked up at the guard. "You sure about this, son? I don't particularly care about getting you in trouble, *or* waiting until Stone's goons show up... but we can sure play it that way."

The guards looked at each other. The least happy of the two spoke. "There is no way this is working out for us, Gus–go ahead and let 'em through."

As we passed through the gate, the admiral asked, "So, who exactly did you call?"

Bush shrugged as he put the phone back in his jacket. "My dry cleaner back in San Antonio. They're closed this time of night anyhow."

* * *

By the time we made it to the *Morrison's* mooring, Saul had recovered enough to make it up the gangway unassisted, but he was still dazed and seemed confused by his surroundings. Helene escorted him to *Morrison's* infirmary with the intention of strapping him down. Ameryst went with them. From the wheel of his massive sedan, General Bush watched their progress up the gangplank with an appraising eye–apparently hoping for a glance up either Ameryst or Helene's skirt.

"The offer still stands, Hiram," He said. "If–for *any* reason–it looks like you can't get this rig to Cali, head south. I'll keep the porch light burning."

"What of yourself?" the admiral asked, joining me at the gangway. "That ruse you played at the gate will not work twice."

"It only needed to work once," Bush replied. "I've decided to go catch a ride of my own. I ain't goin' back to the hotel–my staff knows what to do, and I already paid the band. Hasta la vista, old son!" He gunned the engine, snapped off a salute, then roared off across the tarmac.

With Helene, Saul, and Amaryst secured, the admiral and I joined Captain Howard on the flight deck.

"What is our current status, Captain?" asked the admiral, as I took an observation seat and strapped in.

"We are cleared for immediate departure as soon as you're aboard, Admiral. Unfortunately, the ground crew was pulled for some sort of emergency a little over an hour ago. Shall I advise the tower we are now ready to depart?"

"No, Captain, you will *not*. We have an emergency of our own to deal with, and it will not wait. I am ordering you to assume communications silence and prepare for immediate unassisted lift-off."

It took only minutes. *Morrison* held station under full downward thrust while her own crew freed the lines, then reversed thrust and leapt skyward as soon as the lines and crew were aboard.

"We're being hailed by the tower," the communications officer said. "They want to speak directly to Admiral Díaz."

"No voice communication!" the admiral said. "Signal them that you have departed on my orders and are returning to California per our existing flight plan. Do *not* confirm that I am aboard." He turned to me. "Obviously, they now realize we escaped the conference center, but they do *not* know where we are. It is in our best interest to keep it that way for as long as possible."

"That's not going to hold them long, Admiral," Captain Howard said. "Flight plan or not, they are going to call this an unauthorized departure. Excuse me, sir–did you say *escaped*?"

"If they do not like our flight plan or departure, they are welcome to file a complaint with the North American Air Safety Council," the Admiral said. "My current concern is being out of U.S. airspace as soon as possible."

six: ellsberg

"Ummm... is there a reason for the restraints?"

"Emergency lift-off," Helene Abenard said. "Also, you were not lucid and haven't been for a while."

She smiled, but it was a shaken and weary smile–that left me wondering what, exactly, I had missed. "In my professional opinion, the restraints can be released." She reached down to touch something on the side of the... bunk? As the restraints released and reeled away, I suddenly realized I wasn't really sure where I was.

"Is this the *Morrison*?" I asked.

"You should at least know that, Saul. What do you recall?"

I swung my feet to the floor and sat up–either remembering or realizing that this was the airship's infirmary. It was a small space, no bigger than one of the crew cabins. Sitting up, I realized we were not alone.

"Hello, Ameryst," I said. "No offense, but if this is the *Morrison*, and we're in the air... what are you doing here?"

Dr. Ameryst Albion was in the other seat the small space permitted. She smiled a smile as shaky as Helene's and waved. "Hi," she said. "I guess I'm sort of a defector. Do you remember *anything*?"

* * *

It was screaming. The pain was more than I'd ever imagined anything could be. But I couldn't shut it out.

The scream was in my mind.

It grew, and it grew, and it grew. Then the curtains opened... and I *saw* it.

I don't know that I had ever seen one before, except in my mind. I had never imagined that I *would* see one–much less that *it* would be the one in pain.

I had to get away.

The first time, the thing in the back of my mind had moved an airship–*not* between universes, I now realized. Just far enough to get away from the machines that had caused its engines to fail. This time, it had moved me just far enough that I would no longer hear the alien scream in my mind... and took my friends with me.

"Either you are getting better at this," Helene said, "Or we are getting better at experiencing it. There was no 'missing time'–whatever happened, it was instantaneous. One moment, we were in an auditorium at the Majestic Conference. The next moment, we were in a hotel ballroom ten klicks away–listening to the worst music I have ever heard in my life."

"I've heard worse," Ameryst said. "At least it had a beat."

"You are taking this awfully well," I told her. "I don't think many people would."

She shrugged. "'Most people' don't spend half their lives dreaming about other worlds while they try to reverse-engineer alien spacecraft. I always wanted to ask where your story ideas came from. I guess now I know."

I sighed. "I didn't know myself for a long time. I'm sorry you got sucked into this, Ameryst."

"Oh, don't be!" she said. "It was all a dead-end, Saul." She was suddenly sad. "The U.S. Majestic team isn't like yours. I was *never* going to have a public professional life like you or Commander Cullen. After FDS took over the project, the work on Majestic was a dead-end as well." Then she smiled, seemingly happy again. "And I always wanted to go to California."

I turned to Helene. "I heard it screaming–did you?"

"I knew something was wrong," she said. "I felt it almost as soon as you did. But I didn't experience what you did until they brought out that..."

"Alien," I said. "In some of my dreams, they're called 'Greys'... among other things." I turned to Ameryst. "I guess you realize *that's* what built the Device, right? That's what they look like when they aren't preserved remains from a crash site."

She nodded. "I didn't expect I'd ever see one. Certainly not like *that*."

"It's beginning to come back to me," I said. "Parts of it, anyway. At least we got away. How soon are we in California?"

"Not soon enough," Helene said. "Director Stone has charged us with kidnapping Dr. Albion, performing acts of espionage at the conference, and violating numerous statutes of the North American Joint Civil Aviation Act. An hour ago, President Drumpfmann declared a state of emergency and granted Director Stone direct authority over U.S. armed services. I don't suppose you can get us to San Francisco the same way you got us to Dayton?"

I shook my head. "In the first place, I didn't 'get us to Dayton'–we can talk about that later. But, more to the point, I don't really have control over this, Helene. It just... happens. I feel drained right now. Whatever I'm doing, I don't think it's good for me. I don't think it's even anything a human being *should* be able to do."

"I would agree," Helene said. "When we got you here, you showed physical signs of shock–even though you had suffered no actual trauma or injury. Your mental state was far worse–as agitated as I have ever seen you in regression therapy. You were hallucinatory as well. You recall nothing?"

"Nothing."

"A great pity," Helene said. "Apparently you thought you were talking to someone named 'Case.' It seemed to be an interesting conversation."

seven: murphy

"Dude... I thought Morningstar was a dude."

"I don't remember you being so provincial back in the day, Case. Morningstar is a fucking angel–it can present as whatever the hell it wants."

I was back in my cell–and whether you wanted to use the term in the monastic or penal sense of the word, it still had a lock on the outside of the door–and I was intended to be in for the evening. Whether or not that lock was enough to keep me in if I had other ideas was an entirely separate proposition... but I was trying to be nice and be a good little prospective communard–there was no sense in pushing the matter without a good reason.

Maybe I'd finally found a good reason to talk to Case, or maybe I was just lonely and bored. There were still a few things I was keeping to myself, and probably he was as well. There was also some small question about just how 'private' this conversation really was. The being I had known as Lucifer Morningstar had claimed senses acute enough to count atoms. That the subvocal mutters on my end of the conversation might be audible to 'Astarte' seemed not unlikely at all. That she might as well be able to hear Case also was perhaps less likely... but not impossible.

Whether or not she might *repeat* any of it was another matter entirely.

All things considered, I deemed it worth the risk. There hadn't been a single piece of worthwhile advice Case could've shared on my final approach to this place. There were still matters I intended to handle on a 'need to know' basis. But he had offered me other good advice. And he just *might* have a useful opinion on the current situation.

Apparently bored with the other wardrobe options he'd played with on the trip down from Oregon, my data ghost sidekick had reverted to the appearance he'd had the first time I had ever 'seen' him–a goofy, overaged club kid wannabe in mom jeans and an eyesore Hawai'ian shirt. There was no furniture in my cell for him to pretend to sit on unless he further intended to pretend to be taking a shit–in which case, 'social interface' would likely be getting shut off forever. I sat cross legged on my cot. Case pretended to sit on the floor, next to the cell's door.

"So," Case said. "It turns out that the mysterious 'Sisters' I've heard so much about turned out to be your old angel buddy gone trans and this world's version of your little Space Elf girlfriend. Unless you're planning on seducing her all over again or trying your luck with an angel, seems like you can make delivery and we can peel outta here... unless, of course, there's something you aren't telling me."

Many things, actually. And I needed to keep it that way.

"Right now, I'm either a prisoner or a guest or a candidate for yet another fucking initiation," I said. "And until I know which, I am playing this *very* cool and it is *totally* my call. But there are a few things I need to figure out... and I think you can help."

"Sure thing, old buddy–if you need some more advice you're going to ignore anyway, go for it."

"Not so much advice as analysis. You are, among other things, a reasonable facsimile of a guy who turned out to be a Grey hybrid in disguise. That gives you a few special insights into a pretty specialized field of knowledge. I need to pick your brain, dude."

"Technically, it's *your* brain. But I'm not going to be picky about it if you aren't."

I sighed. Not only had he gotten glitchy, he'd also acquired a sense of humor. Oh well... it's not like the poor bastard had much else to do.

"Fair enough," I said. "I just need your best guess on whether or not something is even possible."

"Like I said... go for it."

"The reason you and I are here–this universe, this planet–is because Greys tried *twice* to abduct an archangel from our version of Earth. Another accessible Earth with evidence of yet another fallen angel was too big a risk to take. So The Obligate sent me here to deal with it."

"That's why *you're* here–I just invited myself along for the ride."

I decided to ignore it. "But there was a secondary mission objective. This world shouldn't even *be* 'accessible.' For as long as anyone has known about them, the rifts between worlds *only* connected across million-year level gaps in probability space... until recently.

"What The Obligate calls 'The Greater Cosmos' is apparently getting bigger by the day. That's why I was ordered to do history research. They want to know how recently this world diverged from mine."

"And here I was thinking you just had a thing for librarians."

Definitely ignoring it. "There are holes in space. Those holes connect universes. Greys spin them up when they want one. Everyone else has to use the holes that 'just happen.' What if it works the other way as well?"

"What 'other way'?" Case asked.

"If a Grey hivemind can open a portal between accessible universes, if other species can find and use portals that occur naturally, why couldn't someone or something else close portals as well as open them?"

"I'm assuming," Case said, "you have a specific 'someone or something' in mind... am I right?"

"Very much. Her name is Astarte. Unlike the 'Morningstar' we knew, she considers herself this world's protector. And five hundred years ago, give or take, she kicked everyone else out of the pool."

"And by 'everyone,' you mean...?"

"I mean 'everyone'," I said. "Every single crosstime species not native to this version of Earth was told they were no longer welcome here–banned, under pain of death. Every single rift connecting this Earth to any other was closed, whether it had opened naturally or been created. And until a new rift recently opened out on the edge of the solar system, that ban was complete.

"Is it possible, Case?"

There was a long silence–so long I wondered if he was about to glitch out again.

Then he turned and looked at me. "Well, if it happened, I'd say the short answer is 'yes.' If you're asking me if it really *did* happen, the answer is 'maybe.' If you're asking me if the Greys would want to get their claws on anything powerful enough to do such a thing... not just 'yes,' but *'hell, yes.'* And if they haven't tried to abduct her already, I'd say it's only because the 'ban' actually worked–at least until now."

"My thoughts as well," I said. "It all checks out. What Astarte and Aelia call 'the great closing' occurred on this Earth around the same time Grey agents first tried to abduct Morningstar on ours.

"*That's* where the timelines diverge. From that time forward, there were no crosstime aliens on *this* Earth–no secret societies, no 'UFO' sightings, no humans used as either cattle or foot soldiers by nonhuman others–none of it. Well, the one secret society... but they actually seem to be good guys–well, girls, actually."

"Groovy," said Case. "Give the head witch who happens to be an angel her power pill so she can go home to God and we can find something more interesting to do."

"Not that simple," I told him. "For a lot of reasons. For starters, closing off this world took one helluva a lot out of her. There is a reason why she has not left this temple the entire time we've been on this world–basically... she *can't.*

"There is also the matter of whether or not she would even *want* to go. Morningstar didn't give two shits in a rusty bucket about my Earth and appreciated humanity mainly for our entertainment value. If we hadn't invented warfare, booze, and television at appropriate intervals, he might've wiped us out himself... just for something to do. Astarte, on the other hand, considers this world under her protection.

"But that's not even the biggest part of it."

"You mean there's more?" Case asked.

"Very *much* more. Calling Astarte and Aelia 'sisters' is almost as misleading as considering either one of them human. They've loved one another for over a thousand years, Case. You can call the relationship whatever you want. You're a few hundred years too young to begin to understand it, and so am I. But there is one thing I understand very clearly: neither one of them is going anywhere without the other."

eight: kayce

We really *did* almost make it.

As soon as the state of emergency had been declared, all attempts at communicating with us had ended. The admiral had sent a number of coded transmissions to California, most of which had gone without reply.

We had continued to transmit, but we had no way of knowing if the transmissions had been received or not. Wireless communications were being jammed, as long as we were in U.S. airspace.

Effectively... we were on our own.

"We knew Stone had influence within the new administration," Admiral Díaz said. "We knew Drumpfmann had fairly grandiose plans. But nothing like *this*."

The *Morrison* was under full thrust, in flight toward the Mississippi River and Texas airspace. The exhaust from the turbo impellers glowed orange in the moonlit night, as below us the countryside rolled past, towns and cities strung out like clusters of jewel-like lights on the ever-present expressways.

The admiral and I were seated in the observer seats immediately behind Howard and his flight crew. The flight deck was rigged for night flying, with the controls illuminated in red and cockpit lights turned off. Ever since the communication chatter had ceased, the flight deck had been largely silent... our situation spoke for itself.

"Director Stone played us, sir," I said. "You were right... all along."

The admiral snorted. "I was a fool, Kayce, as were we all. We thought the Yanquis could be trusted to deal honorably, that their need for our help outweighed all else. They have no need for our help with what has happened to this world–they are part of it!"

"Even with everything that's happened... I find that difficult to believe."

"Believe the evidence of your senses, commander. *Nothing* we saw in that auditorium was of this world–not even what otherwise seemed human."

* * *

When I first joined the Majestic group, I hadn't even believed there *were* such things. 'Mystery disks' and 'ghost airships' were the stuff of the overwrought scientific romances my father wrote for fun and Saul Ellsberg had written to eke out a living.

Then I discovered that such things were not only real, they had once encroached upon our world for centuries before recently returning–a secret in plain view, currently concealed from common awareness by a conspiracy involving every single government in North America.

I had also discovered that the fundamental nature of these things was *far* stranger than any scientific romance of 'aetherships' crossing the void between planets. These things were from other *universes*, other versions of Earth utterly different from my own.

In a way, it explained a lot. My pops had always laughed at Sci-Rom writers who wrote about space aliens who had conveniently evolved on other worlds as various bipedal humanoids that could conveniently breathe the same air. The thing I'd seen in a tube at Patterson Aerodrome was so little human, it had to be from a version of Earth millions of years different from mine.

'Colonel Wolfreich' and his troops were clearly from some place a *lot* closer. Close enough that he could be Director Stone's virtual double, close enough that he and his troops could share U.S. President Drumpfmann's toxic worldview... probably from a world where it had already prevailed.

That was something new.

The Majestic alliance had been created to analyze something utterly alien that had fallen to earth half a century before, crewed by creatures that were barely human. Over the decades, more things turned up in the sky constantly. Then, over the last year, the floodgates opened. Mystery disks, ghost airships, and half a dozen things no one had ever seen before were now a common occurrence.

There had been varying theories on this between U.S. and California members of Majestic, with the Estaditos insisting that the only thing that had changed was our ability to compile and analyze reports of the unknown.

Only that theory was also a lie. The Estaditos knew *exactly* what was happening. They had been told by their new allies.

Defending the Republic of California had just got a *lot* more complicated.

* * *

"Captain, Admiral," the copilot called out. "Electrowave detection is painting targets on our six, closing fast!"

"Thank you, Mr. Everett." Captain Howard looked to the admiral. "If you were wondering how serious Stone is... now you know, sir. That's almost certainly an intercept flight; they will almost certainly overtake us by the time we reach Texas airspace. Given the state of emergency, they can even shoot us down over Texas–and probably will."

"I did not think even Drumpfmann insane enough to risk outright war," Díaz said. "Apparently I was wrong. Mr. Nagata," he asked the pilot. "How soon do we make Texas airspace?"

"Twenty minutes, sir–and the captain is correct. Those targets will overtake us at or before the Texas border."

"Any thought on what those targets might be?"

"The speed and flight profile is consistent with rocket-assist attack gyros–not as good or as fast as ours, but they don't have to be," Nagata replied. "And they'll be in air-to-air missile range while we are over U.S. airspace."

"Sirs!" the communications officer chimed in. "We're getting hit with a tight beam–it's voice communication!"

"Let's hear it," Howard said. The comm officer flipped a switch on his console.

"–orders to escort back to Patterson AD. We are authorized to engage if you do not comply. Please respond," said the voice on the loudspeaker.

"We *cannot* go back," Admiral Díaz said. "It is critical we reach California, Captain Howard. If these gringo fools fire upon us, they will regret it."

"And we'll be regretting it first, Admiral," Captain Howard said. "I understand that whatever happened at Patterson exceeds my 'need to know.' I hope *you* understand that I cannot give orders that will endanger my crew. If we are to proceed, you must assume full command of this vessel, sir."

For a moment, I felt really sorry for Howard. Between 'foo fighters' and U.S. attack autogyros, he had probably seen more action on this trip than his entire previous Navy career. So had I, for that matter–but at least I had known what I was getting into.

Then, suddenly, it didn't matter *who* gave the next order.

"I'm painting another target!" Everett called out. "Twelve o'clock high and closing at–that *can't* be right. Closing *fast*."

I heard a familiar roaring sound coming from the space before us as a silver dart, glinting in the moonlight, fell from the clouds before us. A moment later, two more fell into formation behind the first. A new voice came in on the loudspeaker.

"Attention U.S.A.F. intercept group, your attention please. This is General Bush, Texas Air Corps. *Please* be advised that the craft you are pursuing contains diplomatic envoys to the Republic of Texas–and is under my *personal* protection. You are hereby directed to stand down and return to base. I advise that you comply.

"I am locked, loaded, and ready to roll, boys–*how about you*??"

nine: murphy

"I speak for my sister." It had been one of the first things Aelia had told me.

I wasn't sure how this could be. The Fortuned are naturally psychic, but they don't *really* read minds. An angel can number the atoms in a drop of water or hear a feather fall to earth on the other side of the world, but the minds of other beings are utterly closed to them–or at least that's what I'd been told.

But questions put to Astarte were answered by Aelia. And it seemed to me that not all questions asked by Aelia were entirely her own. How it worked wasn't all that important, really... I just like to figure things out.

More interesting to me were the questions being asked, regardless who did the actual asking.

More interesting still: the questions that were *not* being asked.

They *knew* that I had been sent by the Fortuned, knew I was Obligated. And–unless they thought I was lying–that I had *not* known that Astarte had closed this world to the multiverse. The obvious inference was that I had not been sent by Aelia's own people, but their analogs from yet another parallel universe.

But they didn't ask.

It was equally obvious that I had been sent here on a mission... but they didn't ask about *that*, either. Either they already knew or they didn't care–and both seemed equally improbable. Something didn't add up. And until I knew what that something was, I intended to play it close. The precautions I'd taken meant I could afford to take the time. The old rucksack I'd stowed away wasn't divulging any secrets any time soon, and not before I was ready.

Meanwhile, I was permitted to go freely about the temple complex. My cell was no longer locked at night. The clothes I'd more or less worn continuously from the time I left Mexico to the time I arrived here had been laundered for me, which I thought was mighty generous–I would've been as inclined as not to burn them. My old leather jacket had been cleaned as well for my eventual departure. Until that time, I was more comfortable in the linen garments favored by *La Comuna de las Hermanas*.

My exact status was not clear. I eventually found that there were other men in the temple complex as well, but I was the only man who wore a Moon Dagger. There were other distinctions as well: while the sisters of the Commune were clearly from every part of this world, the men I saw were just as plainly locals who had likely never set foot outside this valley.

Joining yet another secret society had not been high on my plans, much less breaking the glass ceiling in an apparent matriarchy. But I had discovered the whereabouts of the mess hall and the library, and discovered that there were Tai Chi-like group exercises held daily at sundown that I was welcome to join. A neighborhood cantina or two might've been nice... but you can't have everything.

I left 'social interface' switched off. Case couldn't really offer any further advice than he'd given. And I had a decision to make. One that only I could make... and that I would have to make soon.

Did I have it within me to kill an angel?

The being I'd once known as Morningstar had only been 'fallen' in the sense of having come to rest on Earth and lingered past the point of being able to leave–even though he and I eventually found an end-run around that situation. Far from having rebelled against Heaven, the one thing he (in my mind, the pronoun still seemed appropriate) wanted in all the cosmos was to return.

If I were to take everything he'd told me at face value, he and his kind were an order of beings made in the earliest moments of creation as God's servants in further building that creation, made of stuff that preceded star stuff or anything else: 'Dawn Matter'... shards of the cosmic egg itself. He had fallen far and grown smaller–from being a shaper of galaxies to being a cleverly bored misfit who more or less pretended to be human from the end barstool at his favorite bar.

But 'Astarte' had grown smaller yet.

Whatever she had done to close this Earth from the greater multiverse had cost her greatly. She did not speak; she did not leave the temple. Whatever else she did other than sit beside her 'sister' with a golden serpent curled about her neck... was apparently no one else's business. The only place either were seen, to my knowledge, was the same sitting room where I had first met them. The Commune did not precisely treat 'The Sisters' as goddesses... but they didn't miss it by much.

I had been sent to set free an angel by way of restoring its 'wings'–after all, I'd already done it once before, right? I'd also been given a backup plan and backup instructions. Even in her diminished state, it had been made clear to me that Astarte could not be permitted to fall into the hands of the Greys. I had been given a second device, in case the 'Dawn Matter' I found was not a living angel willing and able to leave Earth–a device that would collapse anything composed of such matter into a quantum black hole.

I had no way of knowing if Astarte could be restored or not, one chance at best of acting in either case, and just as much skepticism as Case had that I had been told the truth at all. His advice to simply 'deliver the goods' and head back up the trail wasn't bad from a strictly tactical perspective, but it ignored larger strategic concerns… and utterly ignored the question of what was 'right.'

It was a question I'd ignored for the better part of sixty years, both before and after my rejuvenation. The question of what was 'right' hadn't ever mattered to The Company or The Order, was important in only the most abstract and self-centered way to The Obligate.

Why that question mattered to me now was, itself, an interesting question. It didn't seem likely to have much with my rejuvenation, which has given me the DNA of an advanced hominid species that was as inherently amoral as I had learned to be–and even less inclined to apologize for it.

Perhaps it was a response to the world I'd been sent to. I had spent my old life in a world perpetually on the brink of one apocalypse or another. For all that Aelia's double in my world had promised that her Order would intervene before humanity committed nuclear suicide, they had been less willing or able to prevent slow suicide by other means. They had tolerated dictators, wannabe dictators, and brutally unnecessary wars.

I had left that world spiraling into what seemed an inevitable collapse. The sense of deep cynicism and resignation I had felt for many years resulted as much from that sense of collapse as anything to do with the failures of my personal life.

Now I was in a new life and a new world, a world that had been guided from behind the scenes even as mine had been–but in vastly different ways. While the possibility remained that this world could wind up at the brink of the same apocalypse I'd left behind... it hadn't happened yet.

And maybe it wouldn't.

I felt a sense of responsibility I had never felt before. 'Do the right thing' had never been more to me than the name of a movie. I had lived an entire life within which the concept was meaningless.

Did I want to carry over the values of that life and that world into this one? The 'old me' had been perfectly content to take his various employers at their word as to who should live, who should die, and what was considered acceptable collateral damage. My current employers were fighting a million-year, multi-universal war in which this entire planet could wind up as collateral damage. It would take more than a second life, more than a minor infusion of Fortuned DNA, to move me to a viewpoint where this was acceptable.

And even with a nuanced view of just what, precisely, an 'angel' was... how was killing one *not* blasphemy?

“If I had known we were going to wind up here,” Ameryst said, “I might’ve taken my chances with the aliens.”

“From what the admiral says, it’s not so bad,” I replied. “The food sounds interesting, anyway.”

We were sitting in the back of the *Morrison’s* flight deck, watching a seemingly endless prairie unroll beneath us as the sun rose. At the other end of the deck, the pilot and copilot were playing what looked like some variation of video chess on the navigation console and pointedly ignoring the civilians in the observation seats while they waited for their reliefs. They had been there since midnight. So had we.

In formation around us, I could see the Texas Air Corps attack autogyros that had taken over from General Bush’s ‘jets,’ which had thundered on ahead to our destination: an aerodrome outside San Antonio. The jets were yet another familiar/impossible thing from my dreams, but none of this inspired déjà vu. I had no more idea what was happening next than anyone else.

Admiral Díaz had spent well over an hour working with *Morrison’s* comm officer trying to connect with San Francisco–apparently without much success. “We are to fly under escort to San Antonio,” he’d announced to *Morrison’s* flight crew, “where I will request further orders, once that is possible. For now, we are guests of the Texas Air Corps and my good friend Jorge... which I suspect you will all find... *interesting*.”

* * *

Eventually, the prairies gave way to rolling hills that could almost have been the hills surrounding San Francisco. By that time, Ameryst had curled up in her seat and napped–a blanket from ship's stores tucked around her. I watched the green hills drift past her fire-red hair and pale skin. Sleeping seemed like a good idea. I might even try it myself.

Apparently, the admiral's 'old friend' enjoyed something of a reputation. I had been strapped to a bed in *Morrison's* infirmary when it happened, but the U.S.A.F. intercept flight had peeled off almost immediately when challenged–even though they had full legal clearance to follow us into Texas airspace.

Even though I had never heard of him, there was something strangely familiar about the name 'George W. Bush' that caused the same sense of unease as images of massive rockets or the idea of jet-propelled aircraft. I could remember meeting him now: he'd smirked at the admiral, leered at Kayce, assumed I was on drugs and offered me more. But I *completely* believed he had completely meant it when he threatened to blow U.S. Air Force attack craft out of the sky... and so had the U.S. Air Force.

I tried to clear my mind and see if anything in it could tell me what was going to happen, but nothing would come clear.

This is how it works when you dream the impossible, impossibilities that sometimes come true: you see and experience things not in the waking world. While you are experiencing them, they are as 'real' as anything else you have ever known. In the dream, you might be yourself–but just as often someone or something very, very different. Then you wake up–trying to remember your dreams, trying to sort dreams from reality, trying to guess what 'impossible thing' is about to happen, anyway.

And trying to not think about having become, yourself, a fundamentally impossible thing.

* * *

The city spread out into the distance, further than the eye could see, to a horizon where a brown haze stained the sky. The massive towers of the city's core surrounded me... though none were as massive or as tall as the one where I found myself. The streets far below, visible through the tower's glass walls, were clogged with traffic, with even more on roads like Estadito 'expressways'–only miles across, extending out into the hazed horizon.

"Nothing much like it in the Texas you're headed to," said the man sitting across from me. "And you probably wouldn't like it if there was. I miss it, though."

This was something new. I *knew* I was dreaming.

"What is this place?" I asked.

"Nothing you will ever see in the waking world," the man said. "Nothing I'll ever see again."

He was of average height and build, with thinning blond hair and tinted glasses that reminded me of my own. The tailoring on the suit seemed odd, but it looked expensive. I caught a glimpse of myself reflected in the glass wall we sat next to, at a small table in what appeared to be some sort of bar. Surprisingly, I was still me–right down to my beat-up old tweed jacket. On the table, a couple of drinks. Scotch, by the looks of it.

"You should try it," the man said. "It won't get you buzzed, but you should be able to taste it, anyway."

"I like to know who I'm drinking with," I said.

"Names don't matter in this," he replied. "You aren't really who you think you are, any more than I ever was. But at least you're really human. I envy you that."

I tried the drink. Scotch, alright–and a good one.

"So... why am I here?"

"You're here because I'm running out of time, and that means so are you. Intervening directly like this is costing me a lot–but if I get what I want, it's worth it."

"What is it you want? And what does it have to do with me?"

The man laughed. "'What I want' would take a little more time than we have, even with you jacked up to my speed–which isn't doing either one of us a whole lot of good.

"for a while, I thought I wanted revenge. Then I thought I wanted to escape. Then I realized I wasn't really going to have either... and I started thinking about what I wanted as a legacy. And that's where you come in."

"How?"

He chuckled in a dry, deadpan way. "You're going to help an old buddy of mine do the right thing." He removed an envelope from his pocket and placed it on the table. "Stick that in your pocket," he said. "It's not real, of course, but that doesn't matter. I need you to do it, anyway."

I shrugged and did as he asked. "Now what?" I asked.

"I'm sort of making this up as I go along," he said. "But you'll know it when it happens." He sipped his own drink. "There's something I need to show you, then it's time for you to wake up," he said. "*Really* wake up."

eleven: kayce

Like everything else in Texas, Hughes Aerodrome was too big, too loud... and reeked of petroleum. The Texicans use it for *everything*, including the fuel for very large and very inefficient airships that have been responsible for some of the most spectacular air disasters in history.

After the Yanqui interceptors stood down, the admiral gave me leave to retire while he continued to try to contact California. I found my way from *Morrison's* flight deck to the cabin I'd been given on the flight out from California, found that Helene had helped herself to the second bunk.

"Hiram's orders," she said. "He wished to place a cabin at Dr. Albion's disposal."

"Not a concern–at this point, I would take deck plates or a hammock."

"I can give you something to help you sleep," she said.

"Not necessary, but thanks–I might need something on the other end to wake up, though."

"We have a few of those as well."

Neither sleep aids nor stimulants were needed, though. Utterly spent, I collapsed into deep sleep. I had no idea if we would make it to San Antonio or not... and I was completely past caring.

For all I knew, I would be waking up in another world–or back in San Francisco, which was beginning to seem like another world. For all I knew, I would wake up to discover we'd been commandeered by a flight of mystery disks, or that the Estadito *Presidente* had declared war on the world... or at least the parts of it that didn't want to see his insane country any 'greater' than it already was.

And I just... didn't... care.

At some point, it had simply become too much. I wanted my old life back, where the strangest things I ever had to deal with were the poets

Esmerelda's mother brought to her art openings, or Hiram Díaz's latest efforts at circumventing RCN dress code. I wanted to go back to my old security clearance and my old job–either one of them, really. Teaching military history to bored cadets and writing secret reports on Russian naval strategy were both beginning to sound pretty good.

Eventually, I awakened to my inner ear telling me we were landing–I had slept across the breadth of Texas.

Sitting up in my bunk, I realized I wanted coffee so badly I'd even drink the chicory-laced stuff Admiral Díaz favored. I replaced the dress blues I'd slept in with a flight suit, looked in the mirror and decided it would just have to do. Helene had already vacated the top bunk.

Then the engines cut and *Morrison* rose taut into its lines. We'd arrived.

* * *

On the tarmac, Captain Howard and his crew stood in formation to one side of their ship. On the other side, I saw the admiral standing, with Saul, Helene, and Ameryst Albion. I was surprised to see Saul standing unaided. What he had done in Dayton–apparently 'teleport' our entire team out of a locked auditorium–had left him even more undone than the way he had gotten us to Dayton in the first place.

Good thing he was looking better; we might need *another* miracle if we were ever going to get back to California. He looked at me and nodded, then looked away, turning to stare intently at the *Morrison* as though he had never seen it before.

There was something about that stare... I caught Helene's eye. She briefly shook her head, briefly held a finger before her lips. Whatever it was, she had noticed it as well–and did not seem concerned. Whatever it was, it would have to wait.

I joined them. In the distance across the field, I could see several assorted vans and other ground vehicles headed our way. After a brief nod to me, Saul was now staring at the approaching vehicles as intently as he had studied *Morrison*–as though he'd never seen an automobile before. *Something* had definitely changed since the last time I had seen him, but there was no time to find out what… whoever was approaching us, they would arrive in mere minutes. As they grew closer, I could make out markings on some of the vehicles: the insignia of the Texas Air Corps.

"Hola, Kayce," said Admiral Díaz. "You are rested, I hope?"

He had also switched to a flight suit. Helene looked as haggard as I felt, but Ameryst was actually smiling. *Enjoy it while you can*, I thought. "Not really, sir, but it'll do–did I miss anything interesting?"

"Only if you find the yanqui *presidente's* paranoid rantings via public 'net message' interesting… which I do not."

"I try not to take these things personally."

"A fine sentiment," Díaz said, "but you may find it difficult, given that you and I are specifically named in these… communications as saboteurs and kidnappers. Director Stone has, I fear, shared far too much information with his commander-in-chief. I see no evidence that this extends to operational details regarding Majestic–but neither do I see reason to *not* think this.

"Stone plays a dangerous game, Kayce. He is encouraging his mad buffoon of a president to destabilize treaties and alliances that have maintained peace for over a century. What he hopes to gain from this is uncertain, but I do know this: *no one* other than ourselves who attended the Majestic Conference has left it.

"The observers from Canada and Mexico are *not* in touch with their governments. Before communications became impossible, BSI field agents confirmed that Patterson Aerodrome remains under lockdown as part of this 'state of emergency'–which I am beginning to think was already planned in advance of our escape."

"The lockdown? Or the 'state of emergency?'"

"Possibly both. I think our escape may have forced the escalation of something planned already. I keep asking myself what purpose would be served by taking us as hostages or captives. I can think only this: *every single person* from either California or the United States with any functional knowledge of the Device or related technologies was in that room."

"I'm probably not thinking as clearly as I should be, Admiral. What would that accomplish?"

The admiral's expression became grim. "The yanquis have had a fondness for sneak attacks before, Kayce, even with no other advantage than treachery–even without a belligerent fool for a leader who revels in it. Suppose they were to have access to a virtually undetectable new technology platform, and could be confident that every single person who knew of this was safely under lock and key. What then do you think might happen?"

I used to teach history for a living. Does 'history repeat itself'? Absolutely... and I had to ask. "Are we talking about another 'Pearl Harbor,' Admiral?"

"I think their intentions worse this time. We may require new allies of our own."

"Is that why we're here?"

"We are here as a result of some fairly extraordinary events that are far from clear or understood. Texas is a satellite republic to the United States, General Bush's actions notwithstanding. It would be best to assume as little as possible until we know more–and *in particular* assume the possibility of surveillance. Please do *not* speak plainly of sensitive information unless we are certain we are in a secure environment."

I glanced to where Saul stood, staring intently at the approaching ground cars. "I'm assuming our... 'exit' from Patterson Aerodrome would be considered sensitive, sir?"

The admiral followed my glance. "*Especially* that, Commander–despite the low probability of anyone believing a single word we might say."

He then raised his voice. "Dr. Albion, Sr. Ellsberg–your attention, *por favor.*"

Saul turned, looking at Admiral Díaz as though he as well was a thing never before seen in this world.

If the admiral noticed, he chose to ignore it. "I do not believe that either of you has been here before. Texas–particularly this part, the *original* republic–is as little like the rest of North America as any place you are likely to find... with the possible exception of Quebec.

"I cannot imagine someone like George Bush in a position of rank anywhere else. I have every confidence we will be treated well, but please do *not* forget the circumstances that brought us here. Say as little as possible, defer questions to me as *much* as possible. I will resolve the question of your status as quickly as I can, Dr. Albion. In the meanwhile... I must be able to count upon your absolute discretion."

Ameryst nodded briefly. The admiral then crossed to the other side of *Morrison* to give Howard and his crew their own final instructions. As the admiral crossed the tarmac, Ametyst walked to where Saul stood and again grasped the crook of his arm–but Saul didn't notice... he was too busy looking at *everything*.

I walked up to Helene. "How long has he been like that?"

"Not long," she said. "Once he became lucid, I saw no reason to restrain him. He and Dr. Albion were on the flight deck most of the way here, where I believe both were able to sleep. This is something new."

"And you're not... concerned?"

"*Very* concerned, but what am I to do–keep him under sedation until we return to California? I have no idea how soon that will even happen."

"So what *do* we do, Helene? This is your expertise, not mine." The ground vehicles had gotten closer. Leading them was a massive open sedan. I could recognize the driver as General Bush. Seeing us, he grinned and waved.

"For now, we follow Hiram's lead and follow Hiram's orders. Whatever is happening to Saul is beyond anyone's control, even his own."

"And this could be nothing," I said. "After the last few days, we could both be overreacting."

Helene's expression narrowed, and she slowly shook her head. "No, something about him has changed. But for now, there is nothing we can do."

* * *

"Until we get all this bull hockey cleared up, welcome to your new home. *Mi casa es su casa*, y'all."

The admiral winced. "No offense, Jorge–but you should stick to English. *Gracias*, nonetheless."

"*De nada*, old son," General Bush replied. "And none taken."

We sat on an outdoor patio, behind a long, low, house styled much like pre-Republic haciendas in California, or other places where Spain had once held dominion. In the distance, I could see the airship moorings, airstrips, and hangars of Hughes Aerodrome. In nearer distance was a much larger building, also styled after the Spanish Colonial era.

Other haciendas were also near at hand, clustering around a swimming pool the size of a small lake. Beyond the swimming pool, there was an actual lake. Around it grazed a small herd of very large cattle–all with magnificent, long horns. A circular road connected the buildings.

From an esplanade in the center of the road rose two tall flag poles. From one waved the Lone Star flag of the Republic of Texas; from the other, a flag bearing the same insignia I'd seen on Bush's 'jets': the insignia of the Texas Air Corps. Parked on the road were the vehicles that had brought us here: an assortment of service vans and Bush's massive open roadster–a six-wheel all-terrain vehicle, a preserved pair of the same magnificent long horns affixed to its grill, painted the same service blue as the vans.

I had expected we would be taken to 'guest airman' quarters like the ones that had housed Captain Howard and his crew at Patterson. I was mistaken. The large building Bush called 'the ranch' was either a personal home or part of Texas Air Corps' home base. Or possibly both. As the admiral had warned us... Texicans do things their own way.

The vans had taken Captain Howard and his crew to other guest houses; the general personally escorted us–the admiral, myself, Saul, Helene, and Ameryst–to the guest house we would be using. Either he was out of uniform, as indifferent to standard uniform code as Admiral Díaz, or Texicans had a more relaxed code in the first place. He had traded out his flight suit for dungarees and a pearl-snapped chambray shirt, kept his vaquero boots, and added a large Texican-style sombrero adorned with four large gold stars.

On the table before us was a large iced carafe of what General Bush called 'sweet tea'–refreshing, even if it was cloyingly over-sweetened. Ameryst, Helene, and Saul had gone to pick out suites in the guest house and refresh themselves. Saul was still strangely quiet and staring intently at *everything*. Helene was right: whatever was happening was more than we could handle under these circumstances.

"Clearing up what you aptly describe as 'bull hockey'," the admiral said, "should be our first order of business, Jorge. What do you propose?"

Bush refreshed our glasses of over-sweetened tea, drained his own, poured another. For the first time since I had met him... he was not smirking. "There's really just one 'order of business,' old son," he said. "Shutting down Drumpfmann and his buddies before they make things any worse. That ignorant *pendejo* is ready to start the first world war–I ain't gonna let that happen."

"Stopping him may not be so simple," the admiral replied. "Even with the combat advantage of your new aircraft."

"There's more where that came from–a *lot* more. Didn't it ever strike you as funny that I didn't want a seat at the table?"

The admiral's expression, already guarded, became very carefully blank. "To what table do you refer?"

"Majestic, old son. We've both been under orders not to talk about it–but you *know* I know."

"As you say, Jorge… there are certain things I am indisposed to discuss."

The smirk returned. "Oh, yeah–I know. Same as the *last* time I saved your bacon, back when we both got planes shot out from under us in Nicaragua. You couldn't talk about what you was *really* doin' there, neither could I… but we both knew what was goin' on.

He took another sip of his tea. "Things are a little bit different this time. Ronny Reagan mighta played fast and loose back in the day–and *definitely* had some oversized plans–but he knew where to draw the line. Tricky Dick was probably about as crooked as Drumpfmann, but at least he wasn't *stupid*.

"It took 'em awhile, but the Yankees finally got it right–went an' elected a prez with Ronny Reagan's big ideas, Tricky Dick Nixon's shady tendencies, and so fucking stupid he makes *me* look like a rocket scientist."

"There are bigger things at stake than President Drumpfmann," Admiral Díaz said, his expression still carefully blank.

"Oh, more than you know, Hiram–*much* more than you know. That crooked shitsack *is* part of the problem, though. He's *made* himself a part of the problem, made some new friends that *are* the problem." Bush's eyes became flintlike, his thin mouth set in what almost seemed anger. "If we're going to fix this… we're gonna have to work together."

"I must confer with my government before I can agree to anything… or *share* anything," the admiral said.

"We both know that's not *entirely* true–but that's okay. The Yankees can't jam your gear here; there's also a secure high-capacity landline channel to San Francisco. You'll be able to confer just as much as you need.

"Meanwhile, *my* government is right here–and I've been 'conferring' with President Richards ever since I touched down. It took some work, but she finally agreed with me.

"We're gonna show our hand, old buddy–*all of it*. By all means, go ahead and 'confer' all you need. I don't expect you to share sensitive intel without authorization... but I *got* mine. Assumin' you get a green light on your end, y'all are gonna find out what the Republic of Texas has been sittin' on. Then you get to figure out what it's worth in return."

He winked at Saul. "I suggest you get some rest while your boss gets straight with his boss, Mr. Ellsberg. We need you firin' on all cylinders for this one. I cain't say anything else for now–but you are gonna *love* this..."

twelve: murphy

"I must have gone to sleep *really* wanting a beer," I said.

"You did indeed drift into slumber wanting something with some urgency," said the figure sitting across from me. "And while it was not precisely a beverage, this remains a fairly excellent fresh-hopped IPA. You should have some anyway."

"As long as it is clearly understood that neither one of us is actually here–sure, why the hell not?"

It was the same back table in the same suburban growler bar where he'd first recruited me. He looked the same as the last time I'd seen him in his 'human suit'–the better part of twenty years past and a universe away. Catching my reflection in a random piece of brewery signage, I realized the same was *not* true of me. I was still the latter version of me I'd been rejuvenated into.

From his favorite corner barstool, Gilmour was expounding economic theory to a new victim, while Ramon and Dave debated the therapeutic qualities of high-CBD hash oil. Everyone else was watching Seattle beat the shit out of Oakland on the TV over the bar. Even though it was just a fucking dream... it was still good to be back.

Lukas Murgenstaarn poured us both glasses from the tall pitcher in the center of the table, held up his. "By all means," he said. "'Clear understanding' is as good a reason for drinking as any. Cheers."

We clinked glasses, I sipped a bit. He was right about the beer. "It's at least a good start," I replied. "But let's get back to the 'not really here' thing: you're supposed to be about twenty years into a pointless trip to the center of the universe; The Lyin' Lamb went out of business *years* ago; and as for me... well, I'm in another universe. One where you have *significantly* switched up your look."

"That would make two of us," he said. Morningstar was in full human emulation mode, right down to the oddly-inflected accent that didn't really sound Dutch... but didn't sound like much of anything else either. I hadn't had a lucid dream in many years. I found myself wondering what the occasion was. "Why is it a pointless trip?" he asked.

"Because even if you are able to crank it up to ninety-nine dot whatever the speed of light, you will still arrive at the center of creation just in time for the heat death and/or collapse of the universe," I said. "That's why."

"Both the universe and I may have surprises for you yet, Murphy. But even if it were but one split nanosecond before the end of all things, that moment of reuniting with God would remain all I cared for. And I think you know that."

"Does that hold true as well for Astarte?" I asked.

He smiled and poured more beer. “Now we get into what you *truly* seek in your dreams. ‘Clear understanding’, as you did say yourself.”

“So I did.”

“Then you should understand that neither this shell you recall drinking with nor that stricken thing you guessed to be my analog is the *true* nature of an angel, merely a relatable disguise. A change of heart, a decision made a mere half-millennium ago, is to such a being no more meaningful than a random choice made seconds past in your own existence. The burning shard of Creation, the living core of Dawn Matter that lies within that shell, is no different from what animated that facsimile of a man you knew as ‘Morningstar’... for all that other circumstances may have changed.”

“Then I should offer her wings,” I said. “As I helped you find yours.”

“No child of Creation’s dawn has any higher hope or aspiration than to return to the cosmos and again commune with Creation’s maker. Whether or not it is *possible*... is perhaps another matter.”

“I was prepared for that possibility as well,” I said.

“So you were told, by inhuman beings with agendas of their own, who themselves merely speculate on the intent and motives of beings even less human than themselves.”

“Should I doubt them?”

“You should accept your own limitations and accept that some things are simply beyond you. So should the Fortuned, so should those they call Selenites.” He smiled a bitter smile. “So should angels, for that matter.”

“How so?” I asked, helping myself to more beer.

“If it is the will of the Creator that Creation become part of an even greater whole, a luminous vastness in which a thing so small as you may cross universes, then it is presumption and perfidy for even a thing such as I to attempt to thwart that will–regardless that God granted me the ability to do so. Free will does not mean license, Murphy. Even if love argues against it, the greater love and duty is obeying God’s will.”

“And how am *I* to know God’s will?”

Morningstar laughed. “Did I have an unfailing answer for that, neither one of us would be here. But where an angel may falter, a mere human–a toy of a talking monkey–may yet win true: The Creator merely gave me the power to once shape galaxies; you were given a *soul*, a thing more ineffable than Dawn Matter. Your soul will guide you past the limits of your senses and intellect, if you let it–even past the limits of *mine*. Remember that.

“Astarte and I are essentially the same being, merely separated by choices. She chose to intervene in the ordering of your world as I did not–and to little avail, really. The world is being reordered by forces beyond any of us, as is the cosmos itself. There is perhaps a role for you in this ‘new world order’, but you must *want* it.

“Regardless, it is time now for you to awaken.”

And I did.

It took me a moment to place myself, while instincts I have not always had made me to lie still.

I was still in the cell I’d been given in the temple of the Sisters. There was a weight on my chest, which I recognized in the dim light as the mottled golden serpent I had seen draped about Astarte’s shoulders.

Good thing for me I'm not particularly afraid of snakes.

The lower half of its body was coiled, the upper half held the head not far from my own. It didn't *look* venomous... but you never know.

"It's about time we talked," it said to me. "For, while I appreciate patience as few do, time is ever a matter of concern. And yours may have just run out."

Part 4: Extasis

one: kayce

The California-like hills had flattened out an hour or so out of San Antonio, leaving a terrain not unlike what I remembered flying over in *Los Estados*.

There were other similarities as well. At one highway intersection, we saw a massive sign proclaiming 'Drumpfmann: God's will, our destiny' and portraying a cartoonishly heroic caricature of the Americano presidente, poised before the combined U.S. and Texas flags.

Stopped at the intersection, General Bush leaned over the side of our vehicle and expressively spat. "Y'all get to deal with that shit in Cali, Hiram?"

Admiral Díaz was seated next to General Bush in the front of the massive roadster. Saul and I were in the seats behind them, next to a large iced chest of beverages. Helene and Ameryst had not joined us. Whatever it was General Bush planned to share, it had been decided that 'need to know' did not extend to them.

"Not so much," the admiral replied. "Among the *viejo californianos*, the man is merely regarded as the most recent and egregious embarrassment the *yanquis* have inflicted upon themselves.

"In places like Bakersfield, the man enjoys some support among the ignorant and disaffected lower classes, but even *that* support rarely extends beyond the progeny of *blanco* immigrants who regret the good sense of their forebears.

"John Drumpfmann offers nothing but confirmation to those who believe *blancos* should own this continent, should have retained the right to own others, were somehow 'cheated' out of a supposed manifest destiny to enslave and abuse."

"Spoken like a true Californiano, old son," Bush replied. "But for a lot of folks, that's all he *has* to offer. I had it lucky, so did you. We're both 'old money', more or less–you more than me. Neither one of us knows what it's like to feel passed over. We're privileged, whether you want to admit it or not.

"So is *that* son of a bitch," Bush jerked a thumb at the receding billboard. "And that's the part I don't understand–why the hell does *anyone* who ain't already rich think that snake-oil merchant is gonna do them any favors?"

* * *

The night before, the admiral had left with General Bush to use the promised secure-channel comms gear. Helene, Saul, and Ameryst had retired to their rooms. I wanted badly to call my wife, but even if I hadn't been under orders... I would not have known what to say.

I was relieved to see guards posted in front of the guest house. Ensuring that the civilians on our team stayed put was no longer my concern. I could retire as well. I picked one of the remaining guest suites, had a long hot bath, and collapsed into bed.

Sleep was a long and uninterrupted interval of peaceful blackness that I needed *badly*. The events of the preceding day and a half had completely drained me.

When I awakened the next day, I found my duffle bag and gear in the suite's anteroom and freshly laundered uniforms and flight suit in the closet. Someone had even polished my flight boots and dress shoes.

I also found a note in the admiral's hand: *we have new orders. I need you in your flight suit and prepared for a short trip. Be ready to depart no later than 1200 hours. Join us in the main lounge–will brief you then.*

By my watch, I had barely two hours before the scheduled departure–I had been even more exhausted than I'd realized. I dressed quickly in my flight suit and boots, and made my way to the front of the guest house.

In the main lounge, I found Amiral Díaz, Saul, Helene, and Ameryst. There were visible remains of a hearty breakfast and an assortment of newspapers on the dining table, as well as a carafe of coffee.

The admiral glanced briefly at his watch, raised an eyebrow. "Rather a late start, Commander, but understandable. I fear you must serve yourself if you wish for breakfast."

I poured myself some coffee and picked through a basket of pastries. Finding one, I sat at the table and gestured toward the newspapers. "Anything of interest?" I asked.

The admiral smiled bleakly. "Other than the predictable demented bleatings of the Yanqui's mad *presidente*–which I do not personally find interesting–very little at all."

The admiral had also opted for a flight suit and was standing before an unlit fireplace with his own cup of coffee. Saul, Helene, and Ameryst were all seated on a long sofa facing the fireplace.

Behind them, I could see the patio where the admiral & I had met with General Bush the night before. Beyond that, I could see the same grazing long-horned cattle and parked autogyros I had seen the night before. Parked immediately before the guest house: the massively garish all-terrain roadster General Bush had met us in when we'd touched down the night before, adorned with the same long horns as the cattle, was parked next to a smaller vehicle.

"I spoke with the admiralty at some length," Admiral Díaz said. "They believe that there is value in the information exchange General Bush has proposed. You, Sr. Ellsberg, and I are to accompany the General to a location north of here. Dr. Helene and Dr. Albion will remain here and await our return. In our absence, they will be briefing members of General Bush's staff on aspects of the Majestic program we have been authorized to disclose.

"You should also be aware that Dr. Albion has been granted asylum by the Republic of California and has accepted an offer of employment very similar to Sr. Ellsberg's. She is now also a member of our team."

"*That* was quick," I said.

Ameryst smiled. "There was a competing offer from the Republic of Texas," she said. "But I always wanted to go to California."

"I thought you always wanted to go to *space*," Saul said.

"Well... that, too."

Saul seemed recovered from whatever had happened the day before. When we'd landed in San Antonio, he had stared at the airfield as though he had never seen anything like it before, as if the entire world were new and strange.

But, of course, Saul Ellsberg himself... was something new and strange.

Not quite a week ago, Saul had saved a crashing airship through means that I can only describe as magic. Not quite a day ago, he had used the same means to move my entire team from a locked auditorium to the hotel ballroom where we'd met General Bush.

Thinking about these things not only hurt my mind, it was increasingly difficult to believe they had even happened. Another narrative *wanted* to take their place.

But it couldn't.

"Just how extensive," I asked, "is this 'knowledge sharing' agreement? Am I to understand that we are going to permit BSI civilian contractors to be *interrogated* while we take a road trip? No offense, admiral, but are we really *that* trusting?"

The admiral glanced meaningfully at the ceiling, held fingers briefly before his lips. "The orders I gave on our arrival stand, Commander. You may assume that the call I placed to California last night falls within the same context. May *I* assume this somewhat addresses your concerns?"

Admiral Díaz had made clear that we should assume we were under surveillance from the moment we landed in Texas. Apparently, he had made the same assumption about the 'secure comms channel' General Bush had offered for us to receive new orders.

"It does, sir," I said. "But I think we need to make it as clear to Dr. Abenard and Dr. Albion, as circumstances permit, what is and what is not within scope of this briefing they are expected to make in our absence."

"I did so before you joined us. I will repeat now for your benefit: we are authorized to share details of the Majestic program *previously* withheld from the Republic of Texas. *Recent* developments... are still under evaluation. You, Sr. Ellsberg, and I will evaluate the information General

Bush has offered to share. Based on our evaluation, I shall report to the admiralty. The admiralty will make a recommendation to the Presidential Council, after which we may expect further orders.

"Pending my next report, it is the continued opinion of the admiralty that we should return to California as soon as possible. However, it has been made clear that the *Tejanos* possess information we do not have. Delaying our departure by one or more days risks little, perhaps gains much. If you have any other concerns, Commander... I should like to hear them now."

I considered. The Admiralty Council is made of the dozen full admirals that lead the California Navy. Either Hiram Díaz had convinced a majority of his peers to approve this plan or he was lying. Not my problem in either case, as long as I could still go home. "May I assume that Captain Howard has revised orders as well?"

"Only slightly. I have instructed him that if–for *any* reason–you and I are not returned within twenty-four hours, the *Morrison* shall be prepared to depart *immediately* for California with the remaining members of our team, avoiding unincorporated territories in favor of Mexican airspace."

I nodded. "No other concerns on my end, Admiral. Let's hope that whatever General Bush is sharing with us is worth the risk."

* * *

"How much further is this place?" Admiral Díaz asked.

We were some three hours out of San Antonio, and deep in the heart of Texas. Mercifully, it was an overcast day–but the heat was still oppressive. The clouds overhead looked as though they could boil over into a prairie thunderstorm in a space of minutes. Luckily, the open roadster had what appeared to be a retractable roof.

"About an hour," General Bush replied. "Commander Cullen, think you could pass me another Shiner to cut the dust? That would be awesome."

I opened one of the tall brown bottles, handed it to Admiral Díaz, who handed it in turn to the general. When we'd left San Antonio, the ice chest had been full of them, as well as bottles of a sickly sweet beverage called 'Dr. Pepper' and a few cartons of the same over-sweetened tea we'd been sipping the night before. Texicans, it would seem, did not drink water.

"I'll have one as well, please," Saul said, plainly suffering from the heat. His tweed jacket was crumpled into the space beneath his seat, his sparse hair slick with sweat.

I passed Saul the beer, only briefly tempted to open one of my own. Whatever the standards of the Texican Air Force, California Navy officers do not drink on duty.

As we had made our way north from San Antonio, the highway we were on had gotten wider as the terrain flattened, beginning to resemble the 'expressways' I'd seen in *Los Estados*. Traffic had increased as well–an assortment of sedans and lorries, occasional over-sized roadsters like the one we were in, many of them apparently intended to carry cargo instead of passengers.

"Much gracias," Bush said, accepting his beer.. "Just so y'all know, we're switching vehicles in Fort Worth before we head on to Aurora. When it happens, I need y'all to hustle–we won't have long."

"Interesting," the admiral said. "May I ask why?"

"Couple of things, Hiram. First of all–as much as I love this car, it's about as conspicuous as a hoochy dancer in a convent. Second of all, our escort," he nodded at the vehicle following us, "is *not* cleared for our final destination–just us."

"Aurora?" Saul asked. "*That's* where we're going?"

"Yup," Bush replied. "Got a problem with that?"

The look on Saul's face reminded me of a few things I was trying really hard not to think about. The name sounded familiar... but I couldn't quite place it.

"Good question, Saul," I said. "*Do you?*"

two: murphy

"So," I said to the serpent I'd found coiled on my chest, "aren't you going to be missed?"

"Hardly," replied the serpent. "Dear Aelia slumbers, as so often she now does. And if you are who and what I believe... you know better than to refer to Astarte."

The voice, though genderless and neutral, was strikingly familiar—possibly because of a dream of unknown provenance the serpent had awakened me from.

"And if you are who *I* believe," I replied. "The identity once taken by another version of you lends a certain irony to this situation."

I was now sitting crosslegged on one end of the cot in the modest stone cell I now called home. The mottled golden serpent I had first seen draped about the shoulders of a possible archangel or goddess called 'Astarte' was coiled at the other end, part of its body raised as though to make dinner of some hapless rodent. But no natural reptile could have maintained such statue-like stillness.

Or have a conversation with me, for that matter.

"I just figured out how you are doing it, by the way," I said. "You communicate with Aelia the same way… don't you?"

"Your own modifications appear both more recent and of slightly different design, just as that symbol on your arm is not *quite* the same as I recall from when it was last seen upon this world. Which is, of course, consistent with what you have told us… as well as what I had already surmised. But you are correct: I speak to both you and my dear sister through the devices implanted within you.

"It is the only voice I have had for many hundreds of years. It is time you knew of that… and other things."

the serpent's tale

I cannot speak to personal experience of the Big Bang or the pronounced phrase that started it all, although the continued expansion of the resulting universe is something I understand all too painfully well.

In common with other remnants of creation's early dawn, that expansion does not exactly affect me the same as later creations. Perhaps this distinction extends all the way to the Creator as well… in which case, God might likely by now have already fallen within her own event horizon, and Blake and Newton were right—cultural presumptions of gender notwithstanding.

But this is not something I can know.

A thing I *can* and *do* know is that this expansion has also caused the Cosmos to grow thin in spots, and that the fabric of space and time sometimes unravels in the void into a deeper void… one that crosses over into other cosmos.

It is not for me or others of my kind to venture into that deeper void. I am as much a part of this universe as the stars and galaxies I helped create. I cannot imagine the consequences of my removal. I do not propose to find out.

These consequences do not extend to the later and smaller beings that have populated this and other worlds. They are free in ways that I am not, for all that even now I have powers they cannot imagine. The elder among them have even learned to open the deeper void at will to travel within it. What they may have encountered in that deeper void is beyond my knowing... although I have my suspicions.

The universe grew larger while I remained the same. I became increasingly fascinated with the small things that had arisen from the muck of the worlds I'd made, came to rest on one such world to study them—only to discover one day that I had overstayed... and was too diminished to leave.

When I first realized that I had come to rest on this one small piece of Creation, this 'Earth', I took it as the will of God and accepted it. When the life I had come to study evolved into small things with minds, I saw it as further evidence of the divine plan unfolding.

Over the many millions of years that have followed, I have alternately ignored and embraced those creatures. I have never quite been able to discard the sense that they were the true reason for me to have become bound to this tiny rock, but neither have I ever had any true sense of why this should be so. Am I here to guide them, protect them? Or perhaps merely exterminate them... were they to ever threaten the greater cosmos. God's guidance in this matter would be appreciated... but we don't talk anymore.

What I do know is that the continued expansion of the universe opened even more holes in its fundamental fabric—many in the close vicinity of the world to which I had become bound. Then other small things, not unlike the things of this world, crept in from elsewhere. First had been those who call themselves 'the Fortuned.' A slightly different variety of talking monkey from the ones that I watched evolve, but enough like them to interbreed.

And enough like them to share their propensity to wage war.

But unlike *my* monkeys, The Fortuned had found foes outside their own species. Those foes, the creatures they called 'Selenites', soon came to my world as well—not quite 'talking monkeys', for they neither spoke nor had evolved from primates, but another small thing that had evolved into having a mind. That mind was very different, different even from my own.

Whether or not they thought of their interaction with the Fortuned as 'warfare' was a highly interesting question. They infested my Earth's moon, and for many thousands of years contented themselves with occasional predation upon the beings of this world.

What else they might have done on other worlds in other universes was of no concern to me—not anymore than that the Fortuned chose to live as gods among their lesser cousins, not anymore than the other small things that increasingly crept in as well through thin spots in Creation. Was I not Morningstar? Had I not shaped this galaxy and countless others?

These small things that came and went as flickering shadows meant nothing to me. They could only serve as a petty, small distraction from the greater cosmos to which I yearned to return. But then *I* grew smaller yet... and perhaps more easily or more readily distracted. Then another thing occurred as well. A thing I had not imagined possible.

I fell in love.

three: ellsberg

Another day, another dollar... another dream or two.

I'd dreamt on the flight to Texas, dreamt of a massive, nightmarish city–it wasn't until I woke up that I realized what I'd been dreaming was also Texas... just a different one.

I realized a few other things as well.

The man in my dream, the man who told me it was 'time to wake up', was *not* 'another me'–not my brother, my other, my doppleganger–but we had a shared bond of suffering. The bond of lab rats in adjacent cages.

Things were moving fast by then. The shock of seeing in reality things that had haunted my dreams had done as much in a minute as Helene's therapy had done in a year. The barriers were breaking down... and not just the ones in my mind.

I was beginning to get a sense of what was going on. It was a relief to know I wasn't really some sort of supercharged mutant who could move things with his mind, but the idea that something like that was using me as a targeting system wasn't much better.

* * *

"So, *this* is 'awake'?"

"Not yet," said Colvin Case. "But you're getting there."

The hellscape of massive buildings and highways had gone. The only thing that remained was the man I'd met in that hellscape. What formed around us was a landscape I recognized from a particular type of magazine cover, but it was also a landscape I'd seen in my dreams. The Earth hung in the black airless sky; around us craters and mountains stood stark in the pitiless sunlight.

"I just realized I know who you are," I said.

"I'm not surprised," Case said. "They did a good job with you." Even though the bar had vanished, we'd kept our table and chairs. Case looked past me and raised a finger. A bartender flickered into existence, refreshed our drinks, and vanished again.

"Apparently, 'they' did a good job on you as well."

He chuckled dryly. "There have been some improvements on the original design concept. Not my doing, and nothing I particularly appreciate... but it has its uses."

"What did you need me to see? I hope it's more than the Moon."

"It is." He pointed to his right. "Look there."

'There' was a particularly large crater. From where we sat on the side of a mountain, I could see that the interior was a deep, dark well.

"Where I'm from," Case said, "that is gentrified real estate owned and operated by people who would consider either one of us a half-ape monstrosity. They also think they own the universe—several of them, technically."

There was motion in the well. Something emerged that I knew *very* well: a massive black triangular object, like the *Morrison* in outline—if the *Morrison* were scaled up to a mile across.

As it rose past us, I realized that this—or something very like it—was where it had all begun.

“The problem is,” Case continued, “the fucking space elves aren’t the only ones who think they own universes. There’s at least one other group with a competing claim—those guys,” he gestured toward the pit with his drink. “And they’ve been fighting over it since before human beings even existed—and that’s the whole reason either one of *us* even exists.”

The black triangle continued to rise until it was silhouetted against the Earth. As it rose, something else came into view over the lunar horizon: a silver dart-like shape that reminded me of one of Bush’s ‘jets’—only, again, scaled up to massive size. A searing red beam connected the two for an instant, then ended as the black triangle erupted into fragments that rained down around us.

“That’s what’s come to your world, buddy,” Case said. “War: a proxy battle between imperialist powers. I spent most of my human life fighting one of those—it is *not* fun, even less fun for the poor civilian schmucks that wind up being collateral damage. You wouldn’t know anything about that, even though the people you’re working for and the people I used to work for have an awful lot in common. The empires in your world never got big enough for this kinda shit.”

“Lucky us.”

“Luck’s got nothin’ to do with it.” Case waved the waiter back into existence. I hadn’t even realized I’d emptied my glass.

“If you’re going to be useful,” he said, “you need to get clued into the bigger picture.”

“Useful to who?” I asked.

“That’s where it gets *really* interesting.”

* * *

Sorting it out when I wake up just keeps getting more complicated.

After a minute, I remembered that I was in a guest house on an airfield in Texas. I remembered being on an airship flying to Texas. I even remembered what had happened in Dayton, and why we'd had to leave. I could think about it now without screaming. The tortured thing I had to get away from was very much in pain.

But it had inflicted a little pain of its own.

Maybe this was what Case had meant by 'really awake.' I'd been taken from a place I still couldn't remember, had things done to my mind and body that I didn't want to think about, then I'd been dumped in San Francisco. Eventually, I recovered enough memory to know I was really me… but it took time.

I could see it now, could see all those years of struggle to make sense of my life for the futility those years were. The *things* that did this to me had done far worse to Case, far worse to Case's world. I didn't particularly blame him for wanting revenge, but I was glad he'd decided on something better.

But he didn't know *everything*. There was something else happening here. What was happening in my world wasn't just a rerun of what had happened in his.

I would need to keep that in mind.

As I was sorting it all out, my phone rang.

"Ellsberg," I mumbled, as I struggled to think who or what could be calling me.

"Díaz here," came the admiral's rich baritone. "Apologies for disturbing you, but we have approval on the agreement General Bush proposed to us last night. Please be dressed and available as soon as possible. We depart at noon."

* * *

I didn't even know where we were going until we were almost there–not that it would've made much difference.

All I really know about Texas can be summed up in the silly cliches that make it into the video channels–except for the bits about crashed stuff from other planets.

"No, not a problem," I told Kayce. "I guess I'm not even surprised. I'm a *little* surprised that you don't remember the 'Aurora incident' from your own research."

She frowned. "Vaguely," she said.

"One of those 'ghost airship' stories from around the 1900s... only this one supposedly crashed."

"That's right, I remember now," Kayce said. "The whole thing was debunked as a fraud, intended to promote tourist trade. Once we knew that, we dropped it."

"Look around you," Bush said. "Does this particularly look like a tourist destination?"

In the late afternoon sun, the land around us was a tawny-colored prairie, punctuated with stands of trees–some of them green, most of them greenish-brown. In the distance, I could see cattle grazing.

"I'm a west-coast city boy," I said. "And I freely admit my bias. But, no... not really."

"No," Bush said. "It purely does not. But it was pretty easy to put out a story about greedy, connivin' Texicans tryin' to fake up a crashed 'ghost airship.' Same way it was easy to put out a story fifty years later about a bunch of drunk Texicans not knowin' a crashed California experimental aircraft from a 'mystery disk' from another planet.

"One of these days," he took a long swig from his Shiner Bock, "y'all have just *got* to stop misunderestimatin' us."

four: murphy

"Any chance you could skip ahead to the part about me running out of time?" I said.

"It is important," the serpent replied, "that you know *everything*. You and I both have decisions to make and promises to keep. You are not precisely what I had expected, but neither are you far removed. But if I am to trust my senses, the reckoning I had expected might be soon coming as well. You claim to have once counted versions of myself and dear Aelia as friends. I may require that friendship... but I also wish to ensure that I have earned it."

"What 'reckoning'?" I asked.

"Not only are there are 'more things in heaven and earth than dreamt of in your philosophy,' Murphy—there are more things *between* Heaven and Earth than you can know. God made many angels, other things as well, and those of us ranked as angels have created much as well.

"I would not willingly submit to be judged by any less than God Herself," the serpent said. "But what I 'will' and what *will be* may have very little in common at this point, diminished as I have become. Even I face consequences."

It began with simple curiosity. I wanted to know more about these things that were almost the same as 'my' monkeys and were seemingly determined to colonize 'my' Earth. As the behavior of the native monkeys became increasingly complex, I found them increasingly entertaining. While I still took my greatest pleasure in observing the universe I had helped bring into existence, there were many times that I found the smaller cosmos immediately around me, engaging in ways I would have never thought possible. More and more often, I found myself taking on the masquerade of being one of these creatures, changing my angel's perception of eternity to match their perceptions of fleeting mortal time.

So it was, some few thousand years after they first arrived, that I settled for a time on the periphery of a Fortuned stronghold, the better to observe them.

I did not attempt to walk among them as one of their own, as I have among the primates native to this world. Do not amuse yourself that it would be beyond me—I am not yet so diminished that I cannot equally deceive monkeys that shape tools from chipped flint and monkeys that shape their own worlds—but there was simply no need. Although the Fortuned amused themselves among their lesser cousins, they largely ignored the ones they found less amusing.

The form I had taken was one I felt sure they would find utterly *unamusing*.

A key distinction between the Fortuned and 'my' monkeys was the manner in which they age and reproduce. Although equally *nothing* compared to my own immortality, the Fortuned live longer and reproduce less than the 'humans' native to my own Earth. And they do not truly age until their lives are almost spent—at which time the end comes quickly, even by human standards.

They do not like to be reminded of this.

I had taken a form that served *very much* as such a reminder: a human female at the very end of its lifespan… a 'crone.' In this form, I took up residence in a cave on a hillside within view of one of the dozen or so strongholds the Fortuned had established upon my Earth. Over time, native humans formed villages around these strongholds, which would be remembered in later human folklore with names like 'Olympus' and 'Asgard.' Later, the strongholds would be gone, leaving only the folklore and the occasional odd artifact that 'my' monkeys would later become very adept at explaining away.

Apparently I was to be remembered as well, given the many folk tales of ancient and immortal crones living in caves apart from both gods and men. Regardless what I do among your kind, it seems my fate to forever inspire stories.

These strongholds were in form what humans would later describe as 'castles,' but they were no such thing. They were spacecraft, set upon this Earth to mark it as under the protection of the Fortuned. Had I thought then of this world as 'my' Earth, I might have found that presumptive… but I did not. I was still adjusting my own perspective from the shaper of galaxies I had once been. The arrogance of the entire Fortuned species combined would not have matched my own.

Later, they would be humbled… and so would I.

* * *

I was not truly aware of her at first.

There were still times I was more inclined to watch galaxies than watch humans. I would forget them, forget my surroundings, forget I was pretending to be one of them. This as well has resulted in stories and folklore I would later use to my advantage... but it was nothing I intended to happen.

Had I remained entranced in observance of heaven a little longer, perhaps none of it would have ever happened. She might have left, she might have simply been slain, I may or may not have noticed. Even the lives of angels are shaped by small and seemingly random events—although I am increasingly disinclined to regard anything as *truly* random.

All I know is that, as the place where I sat once again spun to face its sun, I realized I was not alone where I sat. Finding myself curious, I willed my perception of time from the angelic to the human. As had often been the case during this phase of my exile, I found that my immobile form had been garlanded with flowers and presented with offerings for which I had no need.

I also had company.

She was curled up under her cloak, before what had been a fire to warm her in the night. She stirred as the dawn lightened.

"Why are you here?" I asked her.

She bolted upright, then mastered herself and bowed. She was little different from how you see her now: her hair the same deep red, her eyes the same clear blue, her face and form making her mixed parentage apparent at a glance to anyone who had ever observed both species. She was clothed as one of the local monkeys, which had recently discovered the art of weaving, but her cloak was of the Fortuned—which likely had as much to do with her ability to remain unmolested as did the fact of her being in my presence.

“If I have offended, great Hecate,” she said, “I humbly beg pardon. I had nowhere else to go. I will serve thee, if I may remain.”

I looked upon her with all of my senses, which are many. I could see that she had been born of a human mother with a Fortuned father. I could see that she was more of the father’s kind than the mother’s, though not enough so to be accepted among them. From this, I knew she would live far longer than her mother’s kind, assuming they did not kill her.

Why it should have mattered to me whether this should happen or not is utterly beyond my knowing. Perhaps I had grown weary of watching a cosmos I was no longer free to wander within. Perhaps the Creator had intended all along that such a thing should happen, and it was as planned that I should find compassion and love for these small things, as it was that I should be exiled from Heaven to be among them. Add it to the many questions I hope to someday ask God, if her plans for the universe include mercy and compassion for me as well... and the chance to someday return home. All I know is that I looked upon this small thing—abandoned even as I am abandoned, for all that I was never *cast* out of Heaven... despite what the stories say.

Looking upon her, knowing that she truly *had* been cast out, knowing that her best hope was to find a way to mask her own nature, living among creatures not truly her own kind... and, if she survived, watch those creatures become dust, again and again, as had I. Looking upon her, I felt something I had never felt before.

“What is your name, child?” I asked.

“I am Aelia.”

The vehicle switch had taken mere minutes. General Bush steered his roadster into a low-ceilinged brick tunnel that smelled of cow manure, barely slowing in the process. Waiting midway in the tunnel was a dust-covered sedan, also a six-wheeler, that had driven in from the opposite end. Seated in it: four people whose dress and appearance would resemble us from a distance.

The man dressed as General Bush snapped a quick salute as he took the wheel of Bush's roadster, which then roared off to the tunnel's other end, followed by the escort vehicle. The vehicle we took was already running. A short time later, we were again heading north–this time on a smaller highway that led us quickly from the 'city' of Fort Worth and back into the scrubby emptiness of Central Texas.

Not long after that, General Bush turned onto an even smaller highway–just a road, really, regardless the signage–that wound through stands of oak and sage and more prairie. As the sun drew lower in the sky, we began to see lights in the lonely houses and ranch buildings scattered around us.

Another turn to another, even smaller road, where the pavement gave way to potholes and iron ore gravel. A half mile further, and this last road ended. The sign in front of the building read 'Texas Agricultural Extension Service, Station 22'. It was a bleak and unlovely frame structure, painted orange by the setting sun–except for the tin roof, which remained the color of brown rust.

"And we are here," General Bush said, as parked the sedan in front of the building. "Just follow my lead," he said, as we walked toward the front door.

I looked to Saul as we followed. "Anything?" I asked.

He smiled crookedly. "You mean, does any of this correspond to my increasingly unreliable visions? No, it does not. If anything *did* happen here… it's nothing I know anything about."

Once inside, we found a small office with two desks. Seated behind one of them was a woman of middle years and ample proportions, her graying hair pinned up in a loose bun, her brown eyes appraising us from behind utilitarian black-framed glasses. She wore a faded floral print dress, a cardigan, and a scowl.

"*Hola*, Marietta," said Bush. "And how are you today?"

"Not bad, General."

"And how is *he*?" Bush said, nodding toward an unmarked door in the back of the office.

"Expecting you," the woman replied. "And seems to be very happy about it. I guess these are the folks your office called me about?"

"Yes, ma'am–they are."

"I still think it's a bad idea… but go on in."

On the other side of the unmarked door was a cluttered storeroom, filled with what looked like agricultural implements. Once we were all inside, Bush pulled a rectangular card from a jacket pocket and inserted it into an unmarked slot in the side of what looked like an old desk lamp. The back wall slid back, revealing stairs.

The stairs descended some twenty feet, into a room some twenty feet square, three concrete walls were lit by a fluorescent ceiling fixture. Where a fourth wall would have been was only darkness–until Bush threw a switch, and more fixtures came on, a bank at a time, until we could see the size of the space next to us.

It was not small. Nor was the object hung suspended within it. Even so, I had expected it to be bigger.

"I know what you're thinking," Bush said. "When you call somethin' a 'ghost airship', you think of something as big as what we fly nowadays. Well, not necessarily. They called 'em that, 'cause they didn't know what else to call 'em. But it ain't *really* an airship–at least not what we'd call one."

It was cigar-shaped, maybe as long as *The Morrison*, but little more than ten meters wide. Flattened at the bottom, it drew to a point at either end, the point surrounded by glassy blisters. The hull was plated in a coppery material that looked metallic... until you looked closer.

A third of the way back from the end closest to us, the hull color grew brighter in a circular region half the hull's width. In the center of that circle: an irregular hole, maybe two meters across at its widest. Through the hole could be seen cables and wires of various widths, running at various angles to each other in a way that seemed more organic than mechanical.

There was no visible means of propulsion, no gondola, no steering vanes, nothing besides the general shape that in any way resembled an 'airship.' It seemed highly unlikely that something so small and apparently metallic could be floating from mere buoyancy.

Admiral Díaz spoke. "This is no mere model... is it, Jorge?"

Bush chuckled. "You mean like that cinema prop in Hangar 51? No, it is not. That hole in it? It gets smaller every day, one of these days... it won't be there.

"I don't know if it will ever actually fly again, but this here's the real deal: a genuine, working 'ghost airship'."

"Then we indeed have the basis of an agreement," Díaz said. "This *far* outstrips the efforts of the Majestic Group."

I turned to Saul. "And you've never *seen* anything like this?"

He shook his head. "Everything I *see* comes from the same source. This is from somewhere *else*." He walked over to Bush. "Isn't it?"

"That sounds about right," Bush said. "But I'm the wrong feller to ask."

"Where's the right 'feller'?" Saul asked.

"Right this way," Bush said.

six: murphy

There came a distant rumble. The temple shook beneath us.

"Would this be the 'reckoning' you mentioned?" I asked.

"Doubtful," said the serpent. "I think this more your reckoning than mine, although it affects us both. You have not gone unnoticed upon this world."

"So, which is it? 'Ghost Airships' or 'Federales'? It can't be both."

"The true scope of the Cosmos embraces all things, all combinations of all things... and my attempt at sequestering this world from that greater cosmos has failed. Actually, it *could* be both."

"And unless you have consistently lied to me across two consecutive universes about the sharpness of your senses," I said, "you already know what it is."

"I know what I see, but that doesn't mean I understand it. I'm merely an angel, Murphy—I don't know *everything*."

To be the beloved of an angel is far different than to experience love from another mortal being.

Let us begin with the obvious: the love of such a one as I is hardly driven by the need to reproduce or colored by the physical sensations or compulsions that have evolved to serve that need. To be the beloved of an angel is more *pure* for that. Any feelings I have arise from far different and far more complex needs than merely engendering offspring or satiating complex neural clusters in various parts of primate anatomy. To be adored by a thing such as me is to be adored as a reflection of the cosmos itself.

Or maybe I was just really, really bored.

What we were and are to one another is not a thing easily explained. Those who came to know us over the centuries called us 'the sisters', though we have had many names. Over time, I did my best to explain to her who and what I truly was, revealed as much of my nature as is possible. I also helped her to explore her own nature, learning to explore the gifts of her dual nature as best as possible.

Not long after she sought refuge with me, her father's people withdrew their strongholds from this world, even though their presence remained a secret. This was a consequence of their war with the creatures they called 'Selenites', which also continued to traffic furtively upon this world, as did others under the terms of some sort of bargain. None of this mattered to Aelia or I. We were of this world, our concerns were for this world.

And each other.

Over time, she came to love me and I loved her in return. I discarded the crone appearance, adopting an appearance like unto her own that I thought might better please her. I learned to please her in other ways as well. Of course, I do not feel the things her body feels, but mine are the senses and memories of an angel. Everything I have ever seen humans do to pleasure one another is a thing I can recall to subatomic levels of detail. The workings of their bodies are as evident to me as the inner workings of stars or galaxies. She attempted to pleasure me as well, and for a time I simulated the appropriate response, thinking that might please her as well... but eventually she asked that I not.

"There is no need, my love," she said. "Although you do it remarkably well. It is not as though either of us is exactly human, after all."

* * *

The 'Commune of the Sisters' was Aelia's doing.

The world had changed greatly from those early days when she first sought sanctuary with an angel disguised as a crone. Her mother's people proved even more inventive than her father's, developing in mere thousands of years the means to travel at will across their world within their own short lifespans. They also found even more inventive ways to drastically shorten each other's lifespans, as well as equally inventive rationales for doing so. Time and time again, humanity reinvented empire and slavery, blissfully unaware that their entire world was occasionally claimed by 'empires' that considered human emperors and serfs equally animals and property. Agents of those other empires increasingly made free of this world as well. Humankind was as much in danger from without as it was a danger to itself.

By that time, I had many homes and secret places in all parts of this Earth. Aelia and I had spent lifetimes in each of them, building alliances of those who might love their world enough to defend it, even from itself. Almost invariably, these alliances were largely with women and not men—who were far too easily infected with the dream of empire and the will to violence.

By that time, I had turned my eyes almost entirely from the stars and galaxies and dwelt with Aelia among humans, even though our inhuman natures made us apart from them as well. I knew the galaxies would always be there for me. I knew that Aelia would not, so I chose to live a life with her while I could.

In pursuit of that life, we abandoned Europe and Asia to witch hunts and conquests and came to this place. There were empires here as well, there was cruelty here as well. But there was also a chance, a slight chance, to avert the worst of it.

But then the invading armies arrived anyway—all of them, from this world as well as others.

The night skies were alive with craft from many worlds, fighting to determine who would claim this one. My angel eyes saw in the heavens above the strongholds of the Fortuned again returned, as well as hiveships of their adversaries, no longer content to merely claim Earth's moon.

The strife above was mirrored on the earth below, with butchers named Columbo and Cortez determined to remake what they called 'the new world' in the obscene image of the old.

The Commune of the sisters could not oppose all these things, for all that there was much they could do to guide a peaceful world in secret. But Aelia was both adamant and passionate. She saw human empires as no less corrupt than the one that had brought her father's people to this world in the first place, was determined that no other should be cast out and abandoned as she had been.

Then she herself was taken.

seven: ellsberg

Bush led us away from the ghost airship, deeper into the space under the 'agricultural station.' Following him, I felt an odd sense of satisfaction. Even if I didn't know what he was leading me into, at least I knew it was something *different*.

Not the things that had haunted my dreams, not the tortured thing that had screamed in my mind, not the new narrator who had appeared since.

Something different.

"There's some things you're not telling us, Saul." Kayce looked more amused than pissed.

"A few," I agreed. "But since Admiral Díaz more or less plans on dissecting me when we get back to Frisco, I can promise it will all come out in the end."

"If we even *get* back," Kayce said. "That's likely the least of your worries."

"We'll see."

Ahead of us, General Bush knocked on a door. "Hey, Ruhl–you good, man? Those folks I told you about are here. Can we come in?"

The voice from the other side had an odd accent I couldn't quite place.

"As agreed, Bush. Bring them in."

Bush nodded, opened the door... and waved us in.

The room on the other side of the door was darkly lit with what looked like oil lamps and cluttered–books, bits of dismantled electronics, what looked like a guitar... other things as well. There was a smell... not really unpleasant, just odd. It was like musk mixed with cinnamon, with maybe a touch of motor oil... over the faint stench of decay.

After we had all entered, Bush closed the door after us. From the darkness at the far end of the room, a figure shuffled into view.

"Ruhl Skattersmythe," Bush said. "I'd like you to meet General Hiram Díaz, Commander Kayce Cullen, and Mr. Saul Ellsberg. Saul's the feller I told you about."

Ruhl Skattersmythe was tall–taller than anyone I had ever seen–and dark and made a faint whirring noise when he moved that sounded like machinery. As he stepped closer... I realized that was *exactly* what it was.

"You were the pilot," I said. "Weren't you?"

"Aye," he said. "So I was.."

The reports we'd read about the Aurora crash had been a mishmash of conflicting stories, but the biggest conflict was over the pilot of the crashed vehicle. Some said he'd survived, some said he'd died. Some said he was clearly a man, others said he could only have been a 'martian.'

All of the stories were correct.

The body was mostly hidden beneath a long robe, but the arm he exposed was wrapped in a network of metal wires–some thin, some thick, some like cables. It looked *exactly* like what I'd glimpsed through the hole in the 'airship.' The arm itself was mottled, some parts as gray as death, others pink and almost raw, other parts mottled to dark copper.

The face that showed over the cowl of the robe was much the same way, with impassive blue eyes looking out from a face that flushed from corpse gray to baby pink. He had long, ashen hair bound behind his head. His eyes slanted; his cheekbones were high. His ears swept back and upward, matching the slant of the eyes. More cables followed the contour of his neck, some framing his cheekbones, others disappearing into the ashen hair.

"You're the one Bush told me about, the writer. *They* speak to you... don't they?"

"*Something* speaks to me. How do you know?"

Ruhl smiled sadly and touched the cables encasing his arm. "*This*," he said, "does not end at my skin." He touched a finger to his temple. "It goes all through me, now. My poor vessel is still broken, but it can *see* again. What it can see... I can see.

"I can see that the little grey people made you their tool. They put a thing in you that infects you with dreams. Those dreams have changed–haven't they?"

"How can you know that?" I asked.

"What the little grey people did to you has been known to my people for a long, long time. They preyed upon *us*, once... until we learned to resist them. The senses I share with my vessel, now that they are restored, can detect *many* things... including things I don't really understand.

"But I understand what was done to you... and I think I know why."

"I would like to know that," I said, "more than almost anything I can imagine. Can you tell me?"

"Not easily, not quickly," Ruhl said. "I shared *much* with Bush and his people–more than I might have done, and perhaps more quickly, than had I been more fully myself. But had it not been for them... we would not be speaking. I will share what I can, Ellsberg. But I cannot promise that it will all make sense to you."

"Can you tell me about yourself? I read about what happened here. There was a storm, your vessel crashed. They said you were a martian. They also said you were dead."

"Bush has told me what a 'martian' is," Ruhl said. "It's close enough to what I am to serve. I *was* dead, but I am getting better. Bush and his people helped me... which is why I help them."

"Does it hurt?" I asked.

"Less than it did. I once had bad days, but that's largely past. Now I just focus on what needs to be done. I try to make sense of the things I seem to see. Much changed while I was dead. I'm still trying to figure it out."

"Maybe I can help," I said.

eight: murphy

The rumbling had stopped, but I could now hear other sounds—including the familiar sound of gunfire. "Just as a matter of curiosity," I said. "Who would be attacking this place? I'm assuming you know, whether you're going to tell me or not."

"Elements from elsewhen, of course," the serpent replied. "As to their intentions, I cannot say. It is perhaps you they seek, perhaps it is me. Others will be arriving as well, and there will be a decision for you to make. I must make one as well, although I fear mine was made long ago... and all that remains now are consequences."

It was only much later I realized it had been a trap baited for me—but by that time it was apparent what an inadequate trap it had been.

I have no more ever spoken to a 'selenite' than has any other sentient with a mind and a will of its own. They communicate with others by infecting their dreams, and I neither sleep nor dream. They prey upon humans and other creatures for reasons of their own, mutilating or mutating their victims in accordance with plans that play out over scales of time so vast only an angel could appreciate them.

Finding a time when they knew we would be separated, they took Aelia. To have such knowledge required eyes among us I later found... and removed.

The story of how I retrieved my love and what was done to her is a story for another time. Let us simply say that I have had allies from time to time, and that those who thought it might be easy to drag me into the outer abyss were badly mistaken.

They were also mistaken if they thought I would not retaliate.

It was a mistake, one for which I suffer to this day. I let myself be provoked into wrath. In that wrath, I attempted to contravene the will of God. I cannot know what divine plan is served by letting the universe grow thin, I only realize there must be one. I was less sure of this then. What I did know was that I had the power to end it... at least in this one small place.

I sealed this world that day. I told the Fortuned, their adversaries, their allies, and any others that had come here from other universes that this world was *protected*. I told them to go—and that they would not return.

And then I did it.

I cannot really explain to you what I did, any more than I can explain how the force of my mind animates this puppet masquerading as a serpent, or manipulates the objects embedded in you so that you may hear this voice. On that day, I exerted the force of my mind upon the very stuff of the universe. I sealed the flaws God had permitted.

Or so I thought.

In my anger, I convinced myself that if God had granted me the power to do this thing, if it had been God's will that I should learn to love as mortals love, and be moved by that love to act... then that act was equally a part of God's plan.

I now know I was wrong.

I bought but an instance, five hundred years as humans reckon time, and in the process diminished myself more and faster than my previous slow decay. I devised this puppet because it is easier to control than the one I once used to pleasure my sweet Aelia, and so allows me to conserve what power I retain.

What is worse is that the one for whom I did these things is more mortal than I had thought. I had thought she would age as her father's people age, living agelessly for thousands of years, then fall to a rapid and painless end. She may yet have thousands of years to come, but she will not age as the Fortuned age. Already, she fails in small ways. She sleeps much, forgets much. She remembers that she loves me, she remembers that we both swore to defend her mother's people from themselves and any others that might hurt them.

And the true tragedy is that those others are now arriving anyway, and I am diminished past the point of opposing them. And humankind is still far from ready to oppose them on their own. I cannot say it was for 'nothing.' for I have loved someone as mortals love, have done so for the entire time your current civilization has endured.

No other angel or mortal, to my knowledge, has done any such thing. And I always knew that, however long it lasted, I would last longer. Even now, as diminished as I am, my true form will remain within this puppet until the end of time—even if I am so weakened at the end that all I am capable of is endlessly watching as stars burn out and galaxies collapse... and all that I have ever loved or built fails into the void that eventually claims all things.

Unless judgment finds me first.

nine: kayce

It was utterly dark by the time we set out to return to San Antonio. General Bush insisted he was fine to drive back, even though I had my doubts.

So did Admiral Díaz. "Neither of us will be of much assistance to our countries lying dead in a ditch, Jorge. You should permit me to drive."

"Hell, Hiram–you were up all night last night, talking to your fellow brass hats back in Cali. I expect you're a damn site more tired than I am!"

"But I have not been drinking."

General Bush glowered. "Shiner Bock ain't drinking, and I already switched to Dr. Pepper anyhow. We'll be fine."

They finally agreed to take turns, with the admiral to take a nap on the middle seat row while General Bush took the first shift at the wheel. I offered to drive as well, but the admiral waved it off. "Jorge and I both know these roads, you do not–we'll be fine. Just make sure that I am awake in two hours."

"Aye, sir."

Aurora, Texas disappeared into the darkness behind us. General Bush had turned on the radio, found the loudest, most raucous station he could, and jammed the volume as far as he could.

Good, I thought. Maybe we'll get back to San Antonio in one piece.

* * *

Ruhl Skattersmithe was more human than the thing I'd seen in the auditorium in Dayton. Take away the mechanical implants and the tissue damage, and he would've been something very close to human.

And possibly even beautiful.

"Unlike your pickled little green guys," General Bush said, "our guy *talks*."

The table we sat at was apparently Ruhl's work table. It was littered with Sci-Rom magazines and books, what looked like textbooks, and what looked like drawings. In the dim light, I could tell that the rest of the room was similarly littered.

"Thank you for bringing others for me to talk to," Ruhl said. "Particularly Saul Ellsberg."

"I figured it was about time." General Bush turned to the admiral. "So now you know. If you think he looks bad now, you shoulda seen him when we dug him up. That ship of his was busted up even worse than *he* was."

"I'm amazed that you have kept this secret for so long," Admiral Díaz said. "It has been over a century."

"Over a century since he crashed, but Ruhl spent most of that century in an unmarked plot in the Aurora graveyard, after what was left of his ship got shoved down an abandoned mine. It wasn't until after that thing crashed in Corona that the Texas Air Force got interested in this kinda stuff."

"You mean," Saul said, "not until after a 'mystery disk' crashed in Texas and the U.S. Air Force took it off your hands."

Bush glared for a moment, then smirked. "You mean after we *let* them have it, Mr. Ellsberg.

"It's a story for another time, but we got a *good* look at that thing before the Yankees showed up to grab it. The only thing about it that made any sense was the big hole someone had made in it. As far as my predecessors were concerned, having that thing somewhere else if whatever had made that hole came back to finish the job... seemed like a mighty good idea."

"There was a thunderstorm when the crash happened at Corona," Admiral Díaz said. "That 'hole' was caused by lightning."

"A thunderbolt brought me down as well," Ruhl said, turning to face the admiral. "But it was no random thing."

"Then what was it?" the admiral asked.

"There is more to your world than you know," Ruhl said. "My people and the little grey people once traveled here at will... others as well. My people once ruled yours, Díaz–but that ended when we were cast out, banished from your world. The lightning that struck me was punishment for defying the ban."

"We have no history of this," I said. "'Banished' *how*?"

With a faint whir of clockwork, Ruhl turned to me. “I am still learning to think like your people, Commander Cullen–so please correct me if this is not rightly said.”

I nodded.

“If I told you my people were driven from your world by an angel with a fiery sword or cursed by an angry demon,” he said, “would that be ‘history’?”

“No.”

“But the book called ‘Holy Bible’ that Marietta brought me from the Aurora Public Library contains such things. Is it not ‘history’?”

“No.”

“Perhaps it *should* be,” Ruhl said. “What about me? Will I ever be what you call ‘history’?”

“Probably not,” I said. “You are a secret.”

“Just so,” Ruhl said. “And it does not even matter enough to me whether I am part of your ‘history’ that I would try to change it. You are not alone in keeping secrets, Commander Cullen, just naïve enough to think none have been kept from *you*.

“We *were* banished–by something so powerful and so secretive of its own nature that I am unsurprised that it erased itself from your history. But I do not need your kind’s history to tell me that my people were banned from your world–for I was there to see it happen.

“My people were banned–so were the little grey people, so were others. I was later sent back to find out if the ban still held. Later still, while I was dead, a craft of the little grey people came to do the same. The ban still held... and they struck down as well.

"But something happened while I was dead, something I don't understand. The *demiurgos* has either spent its wrath or squandered its power. Or maybe the Greater Cosmos itself has somehow changed. But the ban that struck me down... exists no more.

"With my senses restored, I now know when craft from elsewhen enter the space around this world, and I know where on your world they go. The little grey people are returning, others as well–*too many* others... and I don't know why.

"I also see what look like craft of my own people, but they are *not* doing what I would expect... maybe they are being cautious–or maybe they have a plan I don't understand."

"Are you able to *talk* to them?" Saul asked.

"I am *also* cautious, Ellsberg–and you should be glad that I am. If they *are* my people, and they are returning here to rule, I might easily be seen as an easily removed liability.

"Or they may not even really be *my* people. Passively using my senses draws no attention. Better that I wait until I am sure of what I am seeing."

"Better that you wait, *period*," Bush said. "Let's not forget why you ain't *dead*."

"I do not forget my debts," Ruhl replied. "*Or* my obligations. It is in our aligned interest that I do nothing... at least for now."

"Are *my* people included in that 'aligned interest'?" Admiral Díaz asked.

“The books Marietta is kind enough to bring me explain the differences between Texicans, Californianos, and Yankees, Díaz. I mean no offense, but these distinctions mean almost nothing to me, would mean even less to my people. But, for now, it is my aligned interest with *all* of your kind… that I do nothing.

“The problem is all the *other* things I see that make no sense. I *know* the little grey people are infecting you with dreams, Ellsberg, but you are being used in other ways as well. *Something else* is breaching the walls between worlds… in a way I don’t understand.

“Either *many* things changed while I was dead, or I am not as recovered from being dead as I would like. Reaching out to what *seem* to be my people before I am more sure of things might be a good way to wind up dead again–and this time… I would likely stay that way.”

“I still want to know *why*,” Saul said. “Why did any of this ever happen to *me* in the first place?”

Ruhl smiled a sad smile. “My people have fought with the little grey people since before your people ever were. Despite their shape, they are *nothing* like your people or mine. They don’t think like we do, act like we do, or plan like we do. You could’ve been picked at random, Ellsberg. You could’ve been picked for reasons neither one of us could ever comprehend.”

“Then I’ll never *really* know,” Saul said. “None of this will ever *really* make sense.”

“Perhaps what you think of as ‘making sense’ doesn’t truly make sense, Ellsberg,” Ruhl replied. “The map of the world you hold in your mind is only a map. If the observation of your senses contradicts the map… the map must change.”

"How much did *your* map change," I asked. "When you... woke up?"

"You mean, Commander Cullen, when I stopped being dead? The 'map' I had is worthless. Almost *nothing* I experience now fits that map. Your kind should not have acquired the skill to revive me a mere hundred years after I died. The walls between worlds have thinned to the point of chaos. The little grey people are moving *you* the way they move themselves. None of this makes sense to me."

"Do you have any idea," Saul asked. "Why any of this should have happened?"

"Suspicions," Ruhl said. "But nothing more. There is perhaps a way to find out. But it could be even more dangerous than reaching out to my people."

* * *

I moved as far away from the dashboard radio as I could. General Bush drove pretty much the same way he flew–which should've unnerved me, but didn't. His focus on the road was absolute. Stretched out in the seat in front of us, Admiral Díaz had begun to snore. I felt badly about waking him in two hours, but orders are orders. I rolled up the window and gestured for Saul to join me.

"We need to talk," I said, after he was close enough to hear me over the blaring radio.

"Agreed," he said. "Where do we start?"

"Let's start with 'Ruhl Skattersmythe', but I also want to talk about *you*. I still think there's something you're not sharing–but we'll get to that. For now, I need something to be really, *really*, clear: do you think Ruhl and his ship are *real*–that this isn't just some bamboozle the Texicans cooked up to get information from us?"

"I don't see how it could be," Saul replied. "If Ruhl was a made-up martian, he'd look more like something out of one of those televisor serials Ameryst is so fond of–and the people who produce those things would give their family jewels to pull off special effects as good as Ruhl.

"I don't think we're being 'bamboozled'. I think it's legitimate. It also fits into the dreams I've had since we left Dayton."

"And *that's* the other thing I wanted to talk about," I told him. "When we landed in San Antonio, you were *more* than recovered from what happened in Dayton. I think you've seen something you're not sharing... want to talk about it?"

Saul looked out into the darkness blasting past us, but it didn't seem that he was looking at the scrubby Texas wasteland rolling past in the car's headlights. Whatever he was looking at was much, much further away.

"Ruhl said I was 'infected with dreams'," He finally replied. "That's the first time I've ever heard it put that way... but it's true. He thinks the dreams are being fed into me by what he calls 'the little grey people'... and I think so as well. I think Ruhl is right about there being something physical in my head."

"Ruhl also said 'something else' was reaching out from another world," I said. "That's part of what you're not talking about... isn't it?"

"I think he might be right," Saul said. He ran his fingers through his hair and clasped his hands behind his head. "I've *never* had one of these implanted dreams when I knew I was dreaming, but I do now–things have changed.

"Someone else is reaching into my dreams, someone who talks to me, who at least *seems* to be human. But he knows things a human being shouldn't know. If he's real... I don't think he's from around here."

"What is this... person telling you?"

"He says we're being pulled into a war," he said. "Not the war that idiot U.S. President wants to start, but something bigger... *far* bigger. You teach history–what's the closest the world ever came to a *true* world war?"

"A *world* war? Probably the Alaska Dispute, 1929. The Russian Empire attempted to exercise territorial claims on Alaska, the Yanquis allied with them, then attempted a sneak attack on the Pacific Federation base at Pearl Harbor. The attack failed, the Yanqui presidente was impeached. Had a few key alliances not held... it could have been far, far worse."

"Okay," he said. "Now, just imagine that war had *actually* happened–and imagine living on some island out in the Pacific, far from *everything*, one of those places where they might not have even known there *was* a Pacific Federation–and might not even be able to find Russia on a map. And then, one day–for whatever reason–the war comes to your island.

"*We're* that island, Kayce, *Earth* is that island. But our isolation is ending."

"Why now?" I asked.

"I take it you don't like Ruhl's explanation?"

"Sorry, no–I don't believe in angels or demons."

"Then what do you think 'struck down' Ruhl's ship and the mystery disk the Yanquis are holding?" he asked.

"Until I see evidence to the contrary," I replied, "Lightning is *just* lightning. And history really *is* history. If you think otherwise, maybe you should ask your new informant about it."

"I may have a hard time getting his attention," Saul said. "But that actually might not be a bad idea."

ten: murphy

"And that's *everything*?" I asked.

"Essentially," replied the serpent. "You know now what I need you to know. What I have done since closing this world to ensure my privacy in this part of it is not important... and not entirely your concern. It is the least of my interference in this world's affairs."

"It may matter more than you think. As near as I can tell, the main difference between this Earth and the one I came from... is *you*. Your counterpart considered Earth a place of exile, appreciated humans mostly for their entertainment value. Not that *my* opinion matters–but I kinda like what you did with the place."

"Given that you are here either as my savior or executioner," said the serpent, "your opinion is of no small consequence."

"Are you guessing at why I am here–or do you know?" The gunfire and explosions I had heard in the background as the serpent told its tale had ceased. This did not seem a good thing.

"I knew of your presence upon this world almost from the moment you set foot on it. Although the craft that brought you was stealthed in many ways, it could not conceal itself from *me*. But even had that not been so, I still would have known of the devices you carried, could guess at the intent of such things. It is not truly 'dawn matter' you have fetched to this world, but it is so much like unto it that the possible purposes are few–and almost none that do not concern me."

"I was not aware of *any* purposes not concerning you," I said.

“You were told what you ‘needed to know’... as is always the case. Even a close approximation of the stuff of creation is rather more power than should be in the hands of any less than angels. The ones that sent you have hardly any less arrogance or hubris than did I. They may yet pay for theirs as well.”

“Above my paygrade,” I said. “Nothing I’ve any interest in having on my hands in the first place. I’m happy enough to make delivery and be on my way.” It had been very still once the gunfire ended, but now I could hear what sounded very much like booted feet on paving stones... and not far away.

“That is not so easy as it might have been upon your arrival,” the serpent said. “I know that you have taken precautions to ensure that these devices remain where you intend until you have decided how to use them. Those precautions may be insufficient. Leaving the temple will be difficult for you, if not impossible. Others have detected you as well, they now approach–and I must go. Try not to die, Murphy.”

Several things happened at once then, all very quickly. The door to my cell glowed very brightly for a moment, then became dust. The serpent uncoiled from its position on the end of my cot and disappeared into a hole I had not previously noticed, probably how it had gotten here in the first place. It moved like a ‘real’ serpent, but far more quickly—gone in the blink of an eye.

Lastly, armed and armored men surrounded the space outside my cell’s vanished door, and one of them stepped into the cell. Given more time, I might have followed the serpent’s example—but time had just run out. Instead, I made a point of sitting as still as possible.

The man who entered my cell was wearing black tactical gear hardly any different from the last assault team I'd ever led, and a visored combat helmet that could've been ordered out of the same catalog. Less so the weapon he carried, which was pretty much something out of vintage *Star Trek*.

He raised the visor—human, alright, not that I'd really doubted it. Looking at me with an expression of cold contempt, he raised a wrist-mounted comm device to his face while his weapon remained leveled at mine.

"Found another one, sir," he said. "Yep, another half-breed–high yellow, just like them others. We're detecting heavy traces of wellesium all through here, but no point sources. I don't think it's here."

I couldn't quite hear what he was listening to, but I could tell that a headset of some sort had to be built into his helmet. He was nodding as he listened to the voice I couldn't quite hear. I noticed that his uniform included an armband with an American flag on it—a flag with far more than the 20 or so stars it was supposed to have in this world.

"Will do, sir," the man said. "Over and out." He looked at me and jerked his head. "Get up," he said. "Take it slow, take it easy. And I want your hands on your head."

I did as I was told. I noticed more troops in the corridor as I did. More than I felt like trying to take on, particularly with some sort of fucking raygun pointed at my face.

Once the rest of his squad had me covered as well, the one who'd disintegrated the door bound my hands behind, speaking as he did.

"I don't know if you can understand this," he said, "but I'm required to say it anyway: this temple, compound, or whatever *the hell* it is... has been declared a protected Freedom Zone and is now under the protection of the United States Space Force Barsoom Expeditionary Unit. It has also been declared a protected resource extraction area–with penalties for *any* unauthorized extractions.

"Until such time as your status and compliance with your enforced freedoms has been fully determined, you will remain in protective custody. *Maximum* force has been authorized to ensure your compliance with your protection and enforced freedoms. Please do *not* attempt to leave the Freedom Zone. Do you understand?

"I'm gonna ask one more time, boy–*do ya*???"

About the Author

A.J. Curry is a writer with interests including history, fantasy, science fiction, and the occult-in no particular order, and not excluding other interests as well. Their preferred beverage is a dirty martini with pepper-infused vodka.

About the Publisher

Rose City Digital is a Portland-based boutique digital agency offering a wide range of creative and technical consulting services. RCD Press is their publishing consultancy, providing services and assistance to Pacific Northwest self-published authors.

For more information, visit https://rosecity.digital.

Ordo Seclorum

Published 2026 by

RCD Press, Portland, OR

979-8-9985988-6-9

Paperback

www.ingramcontent.com/pod-product-compliance
Lightning Source LLC
LaVergne TN
LVHW020710110826
845149LV00012B/2187

9798998598869